...ey

Tania Kindersley was b................................y at
Oxford and currently live₅ ... London. *Don't Ask Me Why*
is her sixth novel; her previous novel, *Goodbye, Johnny
Thunders*, is also available from Sceptre.

ſ

SCEPTRE

Praise for *Goodbye, Johnny Thunders:*

'The writing is fluent, snappy and contemporary, but the mood is elegiac and deeply romantic. Death, despair and self-destruction hover in the background and the novel brilliantly catches the insubstantiality of young, doomed love and that moment in life when nothing is so intense or so agonising ever again'
Mail on Sunday

'Tania Kindersley captures the dreamy atmosphere of summer in the city, she knows how to keep the pages turning, and her portrait of the uncertainty of a certain kind of relationship is uncannily accurate'
Irish Tatler

'*Goodbye, Johnny Thunders* lets you feel the rush of love and danger. Thrilling, poetic and sexy – a top class talent'
Cosmopolitan

'Brilliantly captures the pain and desperation of falling in love. Eloquently written and utterly believable, *Goodbye, Johnny Thunders* is a real triumph'
Company

'Has the charm of young love, endless summers and tacky urban glamour'
New Woman

'Eminently readable. Perfect for the beach'
Pulp Fiction

'Irresistible . . . a heart-warming romance'
Elle

Don't Ask Me Why

TANIA KINDERSLEY

SCEPTRE

Copyright © 1997 Tania Kindersley

First published in 1997 by Hodder and Stoughton
First published in paperback in 1997 by Hodder and Stoughton
A division of Hodder Headline PLC
A Sceptre Paperback

The right of Tania Kindersley to be identified as the Author of
the Work has been asserted by her in accordance with the
Copyright, Designs and Patents Act 1988.

10 9 8 7 6 5 4 3 2 1

A CIP catalogue record for this title is available
from the British Library.

ISBN 0 340 66026 0

Typeset by Palimpsest Book Production Limited,
Polmont, Stirlingshire
Printed and bound in Great Britain by
Mackays of Chatham PLC, Chatham, Kent

Hodder and Stoughton
A division of Hodder Headline PLC
338 Euston Road
London NW1 3BH

For Dave, with love.

I was just turned eighteen when I first met Virge. Later, when we looked back, we never could believe that. It always seemed as if we'd known each other from infancy, gone to the same primary schools, lost our front teeth at the same time, been together when they finally told us Santa Claus didn't really exist.

It was the summer of '85, not my all time greatest. There had been a boy, the first love, if you like; the first one I'd slept with, anyway. I wasn't proud of my virginity, and I was relieved to get rid of it, but I hadn't expected him to just take it and walk away.

He stayed around long enough to make sure I'd got the hang of it and then he ran for the hills, fast as his little rat feet could carry him. My mother didn't get it, but then she never did. She told me that I couldn't spend the days moping around like a typical bolshie adolescent. She told me that I was too young to know what love meant. She told me that I was making an entire mountain range out of one small mole hill. I said what did she know. Teenagers hadn't even been invented when she was young.

Six Fridays after he left, Mum came into my bedroom and threw a dress on the bed and told me I was going out. I told her to leave me alone, but she had already had three gins and a handful of whatever it was she was taking that week. In the end, I gave in. I put on the dress, which was at least short and black. There wasn't much I could say for my mother, but at least she never tried to put me in watered blue silk taffeta. At least she never did that.

I brushed my hair, which was platinum blonde and cut short to my head, and I put on some deep purple lipstick, which was the closest I ever dared get to punk, and I put my best purple suede stilettos on, and then I gave her a mulish look and said, 'Now what?'

She'd even got me a taxi, waiting at the door. Dad was away on business, which was one of the best euphemisms in the book, and I suspected that maybe she had a caller on the way. I couldn't believe she was doing it for the good of my soul. She said she thought it was time I got out. She said there was a party, she had arranged everything. And then she put me in the cab and waved me off.

We drove along Park Lane, down to one of those hotels that sit like big old ocean liners just waiting for some grande dame to come along and break a bottle of champagne over them. There was a boy waiting at the door, the kind that mothers call suitable. You knew just by looking at his military haircut and his ruddy outdoor skin that he would always do the right thing. He was never going to be the one who got the girl pregnant, or crashed his father's car, or got busted for possession. There was something sandy and wholesome about him, as if he washed a lot.

He blushed when he saw me, and cleared his throat and blinked his eyes and stuck his hands in his pockets and took them out again, and looked around as if someone might come and save him.

For a moment, I felt more sorry for him than I felt for myself. Broken hearts got mended, in the end, but he would be like this his whole life.

'Are you Hugo?' I said.

He let out a deep breath and shook my hand and nodded his head up and down.

'Hugo,' he said. 'Hugo.'

He pointed to his lapel, and gave an eager smile and something between a laugh and a cough.

'I'm the one wearing the pink carnation.' He laughed a bit more, but you could tell his heart wasn't really in it. 'See?' he said. 'The pink carnation.'

'I'm Ash,' I said.

Hugo looked at me without comprehension.

'Ash,' he said.

'Short for Ashley,' I said.

There was a pause. We stood for a moment, in the bright lit lobby, wondering which of us was more uncomfortable.

'Come on, Hugo,' I said. I took his arm. 'This is too embarrassing. I'm sorry. My mother. I had no say in the matter.'

He smiled faintly.

'I see,' he said.

'We don't have to stay long,' I said.

It was one of those parties they give to save things – rainforests, or the Minke whale, or I don't know what. The moment we reached the entrance to the hotel ballroom, I knew it was all a terrible mistake. It was the noise that really got me. It came at me in a wave, a great collective bray: the sound of the English County at full flood.

There were tables laid for dinner, heavy with silver and crystal and linen napkins made into strange fan shapes and incredibly ugly flower arrangements in seven different shades of orange. At our table, there were six other people already there, waiting for the main action. The girls had fat pink faces and tight pink dresses with fleshy pink shoulders bulging out over the top. The boys had glowing florid complexions and smooth oiled-down hair. Two of them, in an attempt at individuality, wore loud patterned waistcoats under their dinner jackets, one in leopardskin spots and the other in lurid tangerine.

They looked up when we arrived, and smiled in recognition at Hugo, but their eyes skated over me as if I had no meaning.

'Ash,' said Hugo, politely. 'This is Camilla and Lucy and Laura, and Tarquin and Johnny and Harry. Everyone,' he said, 'this is Ash.'

Six blank faces nodded at me. I sat down abruptly. I felt like saying something that would really get them, making a nice conversational gambit about sexual deviancy or hard drugs or satanic ritual. I felt childish and stupid. I wanted to stamp my foot and ask them if they'd ever done it with a goat.

One of those weird old toastmaster men in a red frock coat and breeches stood up on a podium and barked something into a microphone about my lords, ladies and gentlemen.

'Dinner,' said Hugo, nodding.

'Dinner,' I said.

There was bad champagne and bland red wine and chicken in white sauce and a crappy band murdering old Beatles tunes.

Everyone else seemed to be having a lovely time.

'Are you coming up for the Oban Ball?' they yelled at each other. 'Are you shooting on the fifth?'

'Did you go to the Barkers' party?' they bawled. 'Millie got thrown in the lake. Harry threw up all over Henrietta's pug.'

Half way through the first course, a boy with a bored superior look and a blue spangled bow tie started throwing bread rolls. 'Oh, good old Johnny,' said Harry and Tarquin, howling with laughter. 'Trust Johnny.'

The girl sitting next to Johnny, the fattest and pinkest of all, nearly fell off her chair laughing.

'You know,' she said, stuttering with hilarity, 'he bought that tie in Croydon.'

That really killed them.

'No,' said the other girls, in perfect unison. 'No, no, no, don't tell us.'

'Yes,' said Fat Pink, looking vastly pleased with herself.

'*No,*' said the girls, gasping and raising their eyebrows and making pantomime gestures of incredulity. I couldn't tell if they were shocked at the hideousness of the tie, or the fact that someone they knew had actually been to Croydon.

'You're having us on,' said Tarquin.

'You don't mean it,' said Harry.

Johnny smirked, reached right across the table to my sideplate, took my bread roll without so much as a by your leave, and lobbed it across the room.

That slayed them. They were rolling in the aisles. It was several minutes before they could speak for laughing.

Hugo told me he was in the army. I said I'd never have guessed. He looked at me for a minute, something half questioning in his eyes, the beginnings of comprehension, and then he laughed, which made me repentant. It wasn't his fault, after all.

'I'm sorry,' I said. He grimaced at me, making small apologetic peaks with his eyebrows, which made me think maybe he was half human after all.

'It's my father, you see,' he said. He shrugged, and shifted in his seat. 'Thinks the army makes a man of you.'

'Does it?' I said.

'Not sure, really,' said Hugo. He frowned and scratched his ear for a moment and considered. 'Have to do something,' he said. 'I'm not much of a thinker, to tell you the truth. Too thick for university.'

I forgave him everything then. I was having a horrible time, and I was surrounded by the kind of crowd I thought should be sent to the salt mines, but he was only a boy after all, and he was doing his best.

'You shouldn't run yourself down,' I said. 'There are different kinds of cleverness.' I didn't really believe that, not then, but I wanted to make him feel better.

He gave me a grateful look, and I felt like the biggest bitch in the universe.

'What I'd really like to do,' he said, suddenly confidential, 'is breed horses.'

'Is that right?' I said. I didn't know diddley about horses, except that my Dad regularly lost money on them.

'Horses,' said Hugo. His round face lit up, almost reaching animation. 'That's what I really love. Beautiful animals.' His face fell suddenly. 'Dad won't hear of it,' he said, sadly. 'Says it's a mug's game.'

'Well,' I said. 'You never know.'

Hugo brightened up a bit, and nodded his head faster than ever, up and down.

'You do,' he said. 'You never know.'

After the food, there was a general move. People started swopping tables and tripping off into corners and looking for sofas to snog on. The fat girls at my table gathered up their bags and went off in a little gaggle to the ladies.

'That'll be half an hour,' said Johnny, who had given up throwing things and was smoking a great fat Monte Cristo cigar. 'Christ knows what they do in there.'

The band started playing 'Tie a Yellow Ribbon Round the Old Oak Tree'. They surely knew their audience. The minute they struck up the first verse, everyone went nuts. They stormed onto the dance floor and started jerking themselves about.

'You're not having an awfully nice time, are you?' said Hugo, seeing my face. 'I'm sorry.'

'It's not your fault,' I said. 'It's just not my kind of thing, that's all. It's not you.'

'I can see,' he said. 'I expect you're one of those, what's it called? Bohemians,' he said, bringing the word out with pride. He smiled with a forbidden guilt, as if he had said something rather daring. 'Beatnik sort of thing.'

'Sort of thing,' I said, laughing.

'It's the hair, you see,' he said, sagely. 'And my mother told me you got a scholarship. Different league, that.'

'Hugo,' I said, seriously. 'You are a very nice man, and I sincerely hope that one day you marry a very rich woman and let her buy you many horses, and then you can tell your father to stuff the army. I hope that one day you breed the winner of the Grand National.'

He looked astounded, and then a shaft of delight broke through his face, some faint outlaw spirit cutting its way out of his rigorous upbringing.

'I should like that,' he said.

Later, one of the blonde braying girls came up and took Hugo off to dance. Tarquin and Harry were busy telling the table about the sixty birds that they'd gunned down the week before. The girls, who had come back from the loo with layers of pale pink shimmery lipstick all over their mouths, were hanging on their every word. Without Hugo to shield me, I felt more ostentatiously invisible than ever. I tried to look nonchalant and as if I really didn't care. I smoked a cigarette and yawned a bit and looked at my watch.

It was still only ten o'clock. I knew if I got home any earlier than twelve, there would be hell to pay. I wondered what I would do for the next two hours. I wasn't sure that I could talk to Hugo about horses for that long, and anyway, I didn't want to keep him away from the fun. These were his people after all, and he had a right to join in the party.

I left Dead Eye Dick and his friend to it and walked off to see if I could find anything apart from the filthy red wine.

I thought the only thing to do was to get drunk. I had that tight knotted feeling in my stomach of being on the outside looking in. I didn't really get it: it wasn't as if I wanted to be on the inside, not with this lot. I thought it was strange that however much you despise people they can still make you feel inadequate. I had a sudden petulant desire to just keep on walking right out of the door and into the street, but I didn't know where I could walk to.

There was a small bar over in the far corner. When I got there, I found a tall girl who looked even more out of place than I did, haranguing the barman.

I stared at her, my interest caught. She was almost six foot and she had dark pink hair and her skirt was so short it hardly counted.

'What do you mean?' she was saying. 'You must have some brandy somewhere. You must have something above two per cent proof.'

The barman said, very clearly, 'I've told you, we have red or white wines only.'

He was a small man, and I had an impression that he was standing on tiptoes.

'For God's sake,' said the girl.

'Sorry,' said the barman, in the way that people do when they're not sorry at all. 'Wine only,' he said, and he dished out the haughtiest look that you can give to someone who is four inches taller than you, and then he walked away.

'Fuck,' said the girl.

'Brandy,' I said, in a conversational kind of way, 'is all I want.'

She turned and looked straight at me.

'What is all this?' she said.

'I don't know,' I said. 'I was forced into it.'

There was a pause. She kept right on staring at me.

'Listen,' she said. 'Have you got any money?'

'About thirty quid,' I said.

She took this straight on the chin. She didn't say, What did you do, rob a bank? or anything annoying like that.

'Do you want to get out of here?' she said.

I looked back at her.

'More than anything in the world,' I said.

She put her head back and laughed. It was a good proper laugh that came right from her belly.

'I know a place,' she said. 'Let's do it.'

I went to find Hugo and say goodbye. He was on the dance floor with a small round girl, throwing some shapes to an excruciating rendition of Peggy Sue. I tapped him on the shoulder, and he stopped and gave me a questioning look. The girl looked furious and surprised, as if she was trying to figure out how he could know such a non-person.

I put my mouth right up to Hugo's ear and spoke loudly into it so he could hear me over the music.

'I'm going,' I said. 'Do you mind?'

'Not at all,' he said kindly. 'I don't blame you.'

I kissed his cheek. His tiny rotund friend looked as if she was about to spit.

'Bye,' I said.

He gave me a formal little salute, as I turned to go. 'Have a good time,' he said.

2

The tall girl was waiting at the door, smoking.

'Escape,' she said, when she saw me coming. 'Let's get out of here before my godawful date sees me.'

'My name is Virge,' she said, as we clattered down the stairs, through the lobby and out through the swing doors to freedom. 'And I don't even want to tell you what I was doing in a place like this.'

'My name is Ash,' I said. 'And I don't even want to tell you what it's short for.'

Outside, the warm summer air hit us.

'Yes, yes, yes,' said Virge, looking up at the night as if it belonged to her. 'Taxi,' she added, to the doorman.

We drove through the ghostly hushed streets of Mayfair, the houses all shuttered and silent and dark.

'Thank you for not smoking,' said Virge, reading the sign on the glass partition of the cab. She blew out a plume of blue smoke through her nostrils. 'Thank you for nothing. Thank you for not going to stupid bloody charity balls, more like.'

'Where are we going?' I said.

'Soho,' said Virge. 'I know a place. You'll like it.'

'Well,' I said. 'Soho.'

I had lived in London my whole life, but I never went to

Soho. I had some strange fear of it – that it was a place for being older, and artistic, and wild, and too clever for your own good. Hugo had been wrong, I wasn't a Bohemian. I had aspirations, was all, but I had never acted on them.

'What is Ash short for, anyway?' said Virge.

'Ashley,' I said.

My Dad, who had fancied himself as a bit of a bookish type when he was younger, had named me after Lady Brett Ashley in *The Sun Also Rises*. She was one of the coolest heroines in twentieth century literature, but it was a bitch of a name to be saddled with.

'Oh dear,' said Virge, shaking her head. 'Parents really shouldn't be allowed, should they?'

'No,' I said. 'They bloody shouldn't.'

We crossed over the wide curve of Regent Street and into the backstreets beyond, and we took a right and a left and another right, and then, suddenly, we were in Soho, right in the heart of it, and there was light and noise and the traffic all jammed up and men on motorbikes and people everywhere, spilling out of bars and cafés, and sex shops and minicab shacks and amusement arcades and all kinds. It was like some great, gaudy carnival, like something I'd imagined but never seen.

'Just here,' said Virge to the driver.

I paid the cab and followed Virge a little way up the street. A big man stepped out in front of us. He had a broken nose and a low forehead and a widow's peak, and I felt a small lurch of fear, but to my absolute surprise Virge walked straight up to him and held out her arms and hugged him and kissed him on his bashed-up nose and ruffled his hair.

'Here she is,' he said generally, as if she was so known that he didn't have to specify. 'Here she is.'

'Don,' said Virge. 'My dearest dear. This is my friend Ash.'

Don looked over at me, and smiled more broadly than ever and shook my hand.

'Come on,' said Virge to me. 'You'll like this.'

Don led us down a small dank alley to a hidden doorway and knocked three times, and the door opened up and we were in. I had a sudden feeling that I had stepped from the orchestra pit into the screen and found myself in a real life moving picture.

There was a cashier in a booth just inside, but Don waved at him and said it was Virge, she didn't have to pay. Virge kissed him again, and told him he was a perfect dear, the dearest man she knew, and we walked down some rickety narrow steps into a dim basement with a low ceiling and a smell of cigarettes and perfume and last night's red wine. It was filled with people, and they all looked up and seemed somehow relieved – it's odd, but it's the only way I can describe it – as if now that Virge was here everything would be all right.

I wondered who she was. I wondered how it was that I had come to be with her. I felt frightened and excited and as if all the things I had dreamed of might just come true after all. Later, when I knew Virge better, I learnt that that was one of the things about her, one of the things she made you feel, that anything and everything was possible, but just then, it was all new and strange and mysterious, and I had no idea how it worked.

I followed Virge into the room, and stopped for a moment, and looked around, taking it all in. There were three tables and a bar and kitsch decor – candles stuck in Chianti bottles, and fake plastic greenery. There seemed to be some kind of obscure tartan motif running through it, for no obvious reason. There was tartan carpet and tablecloths and banquettes. I thought it looked lovely.

A small crowd gathered round Virge, all talking at once. I watched them, curious. They were maybe the same age as the ones at the party we had left, but they looked as if they came from another world. There was no pink taffeta uniform, instead they wore a kind of fancy dress: one girl was in a sheer fifties flowered frock, another in black and white, like a Pierrot, another in yellow shantung; there was a boy in Teddy gear, and a couple of sharp Blitz kid suits, and one in a Sid Vicious T-shirt and red winkle pickers, and one in head to foot green velvet.

We sat down at one of the tables and a waiter brought us bottles of beer and no glasses.

'This is Honey,' Virge told me.

'The party girl, la di dah,' said Honey, seeing Virge. 'Was it beyond? How did you manage to escape so early?'

'I had help,' said Virge, magnanimously, pointing at me. I felt proud and fraudulent, because I felt it was she who had rescued me, rather than the other way round, but I let it go, all the same. I allowed myself a small undeserved moment in the sun.

'This is Min and Lula and Bluey and Dean and Stretch and Jez and Ange and Little Pete,' said Virge, pointing at the strange faces round the table. 'That's Jack the Hat, who thinks he's a gangster, and Mean Gene, who thinks he's hard, and Backstage Dolly, who wants to get front stage, if they'll take her.'

'Hello,' I said. 'Hello, how do you do, I'm Ash.'

'Don't ask her what it's short for,' said Virge, and she laughed, and the whole table laughed, as if they got the joke, and I looked round at their clever pointed faces and I wondered how anyone ever got to know people like this. I wondered how it was that Virge had found them. I wondered how she knew people with such exotic names and such outré clothes and such panache. It was what I had wanted my whole life.

She sat, centre of the dance, effortless, and I watched her, and I was suddenly reminded of a film I'd seen once, about one of those golden Californian college boys. Everything came too easy to him, that's what they said: it all came too easy to him. I didn't really see how things could come too easy, the easier the better, that's what I thought then, in youth. Things came hard to me. I was used to a struggle, fighting to get what I wanted. It seemed, then, as if things came easy to Virge. I envied her that, although I didn't resent it; watching her, with her strange hair and her tiny clothes and her great height, I could see at once that she deserved it, and I wanted to sit close to it, this easiness, as if some of it might rub off on me.

After midnight, the music was turned up loud and a few couples started to dance. There wasn't really a dance floor, just a space between two tables, but nobody seemed to mind. The music was old Caribbean calypso, and everyone moved fluid through it, as if they had always known how.

Virge went to dance with the boy in the green velvet suit. I talked for a while to the man called Jack the Hat about metaphysics, which surprised me, since I knew nothing of them. I had never read Donne or Marvell, and I was not precisely au fait with the philosophy of first things, but there was something with those people, that night, a quality which I later recognised to be in a way the quintessence of Virge herself, a trick of making you feel you knew more than you did. I found myself speaking with authority on the sexuality of Byron, and the nature of genius, and whether Marilyn Monroe had really been done in by the CIA.

Later, Virge came back and sat down next to me and told me that she had perfect parents.

'Please don't hold it against me,' she said. 'I bet you hate yours.'

'I do,' I said.

'See?' she said. 'See? I bet your mother takes pills and takes lovers and all that.'

'She does,' I said.

'Do you hate her?' said Virge. 'Do you?'

'Yes,' I said. 'I worry that I'm an unnatural child, hating her the way I do.'

'Don't,' said Virge. 'I'm the one that's unnatural. I love mine. I really do. They're bloody perfect, my Mum and Dad. I'm the only one.'

I smiled at her. All at once I felt a hundred years old, steeped in wisdom.

'Sometimes,' I said, 'it's harder to be understood.'

She stopped, like someone doing a double take, and then she laughed, and then she looked hard at me, as if there was some hidden thing she could see in my face, and then she sucked on her cigarette, and then she laughed again.

'You're all right,' she said. 'You can talk, can't you.'

'A little,' I said. 'Not always.'

Virge lifted her glass.

'Here's to always,' she said.

People came and went. There was no rhyme to it, and less reason, which seemed to me the last word in sophistication. There were no hours to be kept or etiquette to be observed. The air was thick with smoke and laughter and insults and jokes and non sequiturs.

I looked at my watch and saw that it was almost two o'clock, which gave me a start. Mum, hypocritical to the last, got shirty if I stayed out after two. I wondered if I should call a cab or think about the night bus in Trafalgar Square. Trafalgar Square suddenly seemed an awful long way away.

Then Virge said, 'Ash, this is Gus, you must meet Gus.' She said it with tremendous conviction, as if this meeting Gus was a real important thing that I had to do, an urgent imperative, and I thought that another half hour wouldn't hurt, and maybe someone would turn out to have a car, and maybe they would be going in my direction.

Gus stood in front of Virge, looking down at her, waiting. He seemed to know that there was something to wait for. He was tall, with long loose limbs, and he held himself with an arcane pride, as if he were really some mysterious foreign potentate who had lost his entourage for the evening.

'Gus likes sailors,' said Virge. 'Don't you, darling?'

I had never heard anyone my age use the word darling before. It sounded right and unaffected, the way Virge said it.

Gus shook his head, and came and sat down next to me.

'Don't pay her any mind,' he told me, as if he was my long lost best friend. 'It's just that I'm undecided about my sexuality. She still thinks all the nice boys like a sailor.'

Virge laughed and leaned over and pulled his ear and kissed him on the mouth.

'I'm just jealous,' she said. 'I want him all to myself. I'm not sure I like all this ambidextrous thing.'

I had to stop myself staring. I had to stop myself letting my mouth hang wide open in mute surprise. I knew about men and men, of course, I had read Oscar Wilde and Noël Coward; but I didn't know about people liking both, or not being able to make up their minds. I felt my youth, suddenly. I liked to think I had some worldly wisdom, but among these people I felt that I had hardly cut my milk teeth.

'Gus, this is Ash,' said Virge. 'Say hello.'

Gus held out his hand, and we shook, seriously.

'It's my pleasure,' said Gus, as if he meant it. He looked closely at me, without embarrassment or apology.

'Strange,' he said. He had one of those low sure voices, which make things sound as if they've never been said before, but as if it's something you've always known, at the same time. I was seduced, just then, by the idea of reincarnation, of many lives and many worlds, and I looked at his dark eyes and red fox hair and I thought he must be an old soul.

'What is?' I said.

'Very nearly symmetrical features,' he said.

'Oh, don't,' said Virge, laughing. 'He'll start telling you about drawing a perfect circle being the sign of genius in a minute.'

'She has,' said Gus. 'Look. Not quite, but almost.'

I didn't know what I looked like. I had coloured my hair to try and make myself look like something, or someone. I had opaque blue eyes, which sometimes looked grey, and sometimes almost green, depending on which mood I was in, and where the light was coming from. I had a mouth which wasn't full enough for voluptuousness, to which I aspired, and a wide face, and not enough cheekbone, and freckles. I wanted to remind myself of someone – Rita Hayworth, or Siouxie from the Banshees, or Jean Seberg, or Audrey Hepburn. It wasn't so much beauty that I desired, it was definition. I felt there was something missing from my face, something nebulous, unformed. I wanted people to say, Oh, you look just like . . . But they never did.

'Is that good or bad?' I said to Gus, sensing that he might be able to help.

'Good,' he said. 'For a painter.'

'Gus is a painter,' said Virge. 'So he says.'

'Oh,' I said. I snuck another look at my watch, and wondered if Gus might have a car or live near Maida Vale and if I would be brave enough to ask him. I didn't want to break up the party. I didn't want to go just when he had arrived. And then I thought it was just too late to even think about it, and maybe it was time to be a real rebel for once, and that I shouldn't start worrying about such boring things as getting home to Mother, not when there was music and dancing and a fine time to be had, and waiters called Honey and girls with pink hair and men in bottle green velvet suits.

3 ∫

I lost Virge after that. We stayed late in that dark hidden bar, and talked as if we had known each other forever, so when I left it had seemed inappropriate and indelicate to ask for such dull usual things as names and addresses and telephone numbers.

I wanted, more than anything, to be her best and most cherished friend for ever and ever. I wanted us to be seventy, right now, to be able to look back over years and years of unbroken intimacy, and remember the old days.

But she didn't say anything, and I didn't say anything, and I had at last gone home, because it was past my bedtime, and I walked away into the night with a terrible sense of loss, a dark intimation of missed chance. There was a humming hopeful inevitability in me, that said of course, of course, we would meet again, but the prosaic half said we wouldn't, not in a city of ten million strangers.

I had never had a real friend before. I had had people I knew, from school, but there was something in them, or in me, which was transient, that sense of compromise, of it doing for the time being, nothing that will last. The moment the common ground was pulled from under our feet I never saw them again. Sometimes, I allowed myself to romanticise this; to say, Oh, well, it's worth waiting for the right one, the right ones, the true soulmates. Sometimes, I thought it was just that I didn't know how to make friends, or how to keep them, anyhow. So I longed and longed for Virge, and I didn't see her, and I felt sad.

And then September came and I went up to Oxford. I bought books and folders and files and ruled paper and pencils and pens and blotting paper and a small record player. I dreamt of *Zuleika Dobson* and *Brideshead Revisited*. I thought of Auden and Isherwood and Shelley and Byron and all the spies and subversives. I thought the moment I walked into those dreaming spires I should find myself surrounded by poets and playwrights and people who were going to change the world.

The place didn't let me down. Oxford is one of those towns, like Venice or New York: however hackneyed the idea of them has become, however much their images have been traded and sold and disseminated and familiarised, the reality is there, solid against its copyists. It took my breath away, the first time I drove into Oriel Square, my little car packed with my worldly goods. There was the aged yellow stone of Oriel, the blackened cobbles of the square, the looming arch of Christ Church, the porter with his bowler hat. The moment I stepped into the college, I felt that nothing bad could happen to me here, that the bomb would never fall, that western civilisation could crumble quickly around, but leave this small corner untouched.

It was the people. They didn't look like anarchists or academics or geniuses. They wore jeans and jumpers and aggressively ordinary anoraks. They didn't speak in Iambic pentameter or prose verse. They paid cursory notice to their august surroundings, not even refusing to be awed by it. They weren't awed by it. It was just another place, it was just the place where they would get their qualifications, the letters lined up nice and neat after their names, and then go on into the world.

The porters made it better. At least they looked the part, in their smart shiny ill-fitting suits. They consulted lists and called me Miss, and held an undefinable air of being put upon. I found my room, which was small and panelled, on the ground floor of Peckwater Quadrangle, which they all referred to, with easy familiarity, as Peck. If I leaned out, and craned my neck, I could see the wide arcs of the library windows.

I got my boxes in, and unpacked. I had stolen things from my mother. A woven rug, which looked as if it might be Afghan, and a pair of heavy silver plate candlesticks, and a curving looking glass, something I think was called a butler's mirror, which had a tarnished gilt frame and reflected me in convex. I had old leather-bound books, and rather bad pictures in good frames. And I arranged everything, until it really looked like a room, my very own room, and then I looked round in satisfaction, and wondered what happened next.

I had a sudden sense of anticlimax. I walked round my room with uncertain steps. Outside, people were going about in little packs, laughing and talking and calling out to each other. They all seemed to have somewhere to go. I sat down abruptly at my desk and started to leaf through the flyers that I had found in my pigeon hole. I was invited by the Christian society to a welcome tea at four-thirty. I shook my head crossly. I didn't want the Christian society, I wanted my life to begin.

Just as I was building up to a real mood, Virge came and knocked on my window. I felt astounded and unsurprised at the same time. I threw up the big sash window and she climbed in, Gus behind her.

'I brought Gus,' she said. 'He's cross because he's in Meadows.'

'How did you know?' I said. I wouldn't have been at

all surprised if she had just told me that she had psychic powers, that some mystical agency had guided her to my room, to find me.

'You told Jack the Hat, don't you remember?' she said. 'About Oxford. And he told me. So I went to ask the porters. They know all about you. Oh, yes, they said, the one with the hair. You've made quite an impression in the porter's lodge.'

'Well,' I said. 'Well. What do you know?'

Virge looked around and walked over to the sofa, which I had covered in a worn bedspread in a William Morris print, and settled herself on it, as if she had been here forever. Gus smiled at me, and wandered along one wall, looking at the pictures.

'Hello Gus,' I said.

'I'm across the way,' said Virge. 'Round the corner in Canterbury.'

Gus made a face. 'Some people,' he said.

'You can visit, darling,' she said. 'You can just scuttle through the cloisters and welcome yourself to the civilised world.'

'Sebastian Flyte lived in the Meadow buildings,' I said. 'Remember the lunch party, where Anthony Blanche recites *The Wasteland* through a megaphone, and all the rowing boys on their way back from the river are so surprised?'

'All those meaty boys,' said Virge, with vague reminiscence. 'It's a book, lovey,' she told Gus. 'Gus only reads Ruskin,' she said to me. 'It's no point going literary on him.'

She smiled up at me, and lit herself a cigarette. She was dressed in a long scarlet coat that went all the way down to her ankles, and her hair was the same dark pink as it had been at the party. I thought she looked splendid. I wanted her to sit in my room for ever.

'They're terrible, these pictures,' said Gus, in a genial way.

'They are,' I said. 'But the frames are pretty.'

'You should get some of Gus's oeuvre,' said Virge. 'To do them justice.'

'I haven't any money,' I said.

'He'll take an IOU,' she said. 'It wouldn't do for him to have to move out of his garret just yet. You know how we all have to starve to be any good.'

Later, we went across to Virge's room, because she said she thought there were some people coming.

'I think my brother might pass by,' she said.

Her room was twice the size of mine, on the first floor. It seemed absolutely typical of Virge that she should get a room in her first year which was normally fought over by people in their third. I thought it must have been something to do with her, that she had had a word in the right ears, but later we discovered that there had been a muddle in the censors' office. Anyway, it was a lovely room, suiting her absolutely, wide and square and crammed with curious things.

'My parents have an attic,' she said.

There was a bust of Voltaire and two fat stone urns with geraniums growing out of them. The floor was covered in a Portuguese tapestry carpet, and she had good pieces of furniture, a couple of chairs which looked like Chippendale and an eighteenth century card table. Two walls were taken up with bookshelves, and the other was covered in architectural prints, which surprised me.

'I would be an architect,' said Virge, seeing my look. 'But you have to do two years of plumbing before you can even think about the main action, and I don't think my nerves are up to it.'

'Tea?' said Gus.

'You can make it,' said Virge. She even had proper china, cups and saucers, and a tea pot. 'We must live graciously,' she said, often, all the years I knew her. 'There is so little left to us.'

'I'm allergic,' I said.

Virge raised her eyebrows, impressed. 'To tea?' she said. 'Just fancy.'

'I like coffee,' I said.

'Did you hear that, Gus?' said Virge. 'Coffee.'

So we had coffee instead, and I never saw Virge ask for tea again.

Her brother didn't arrive, but other people did. They weren't the ones I had seen in the club in Soho, but they seemed to be connected with them. 'Lula said we'd find you here,' they said. 'We haven't met, but Bluey sent us a note.'

They weren't like the undergraduates I had seen on my way in. They restored my faith. They were playing their part the same way Virge was, as if to say, we don't know what to do about this pedestrian world either, but we'll just act up a storm and see if we can't make something of it after all. They wore their hair long, boys as well as girls, and their clothes were eccentric and distinctive, and they used words like epicene and pulchritude and my dear.

In that first night, the room was so full that I couldn't distinguish them, one from another, and some I never saw again after that day, so I just sat back and enjoyed the show. This is Oxford, I thought, this is it, I'm really here. Look at all the bright young things.

They were bright, and Virge the brightest of all. As the sun slid gently behind the Palladian façade outside, she opened bottles of red wine, and we sat and smoked and drank and talked. Virge put some Offenbach on the record player. At least, someone said it was Offenbach. I was not educated in the classical canon. I could just about recognise

Mozart, if it was that galloping symphony that everyone knows, but for the rest, I was all at sea.

I sat on the window seat, so that I could watch the small quad outside. I was happy, just to sit, to let the ebb of talk flow past me, to listen, as the light faded into dusk.

Gus came and sat by me. We didn't say anything for a while.

'Are you still undecided?' I said, after a bit.

He seemed to know exactly what I was talking about. There was something about him, some quality, which made me feel that spelling things out would be insulting.

'Yes,' he said.

'How do you know?' I said. 'How do you know that you are undecided?'

I was curious. I had never even thought about girls in that way.

'Because I want both,' he said. 'I've always wanted both. I've always wanted everything.'

'Does Virge?' I said.

'Yes.' He looked at me closely for a moment, as if he wanted to check something, that my features were still as symmetrical as he remembered, something. 'Not sexually,' he said. 'But everything else.'

'I don't know what I want,' I said. 'In life, you know. I didn't ever think that everything was an option.'

'You need to set your sights high,' said Gus. 'Because you never can have it all, but if you try for the top, then you might reach the middle. If you only go for the middle, you might just get the bottom, and that's a terrible thing.'

I didn't think so much about it at the time, but I remember, many years later, recalling that conversation, and wondering. The sureness Gus had then was common currency. There was something in Oxford that allowed for that, even demanded it, and perhaps it was youth as well, the defined black and white of being very young and very ignorant of life, but with Gus, it never left him. He knew what he believed, and he stuck by it, retaining some quiet sureness which most of us left behind the moment we walked away from the safe certain cloistered world of university.

I liked that in him. I found some comfort in it, something reassuring. I liked it then, and I like it still.

'So we must reach for the moon,' I said. 'The giant leap.'

'But of course,' said Gus. 'Isn't that why we are here?'

I looked back into the room, and I watched the gilded youth, draping themselves over chairs and tables, talking and talking and talking, showing off their verbal skills, their articulate cut and thrust, laying out their cleverness, their classical education, for all to see. I thought at once that what it was, about them, about Virge, was that they were not so much affected, or inimitable, or fey, or careless; what it really was about them, the quality that set them apart, which suprised me and drew me to them at the same time, was that they were old-fashioned. Not in any archaic sense, not as if they were stuck in some fusty obsolescent nostalgia, but there was something about them, some evocative shifting thing, as if they held a vague reminiscence of older days.

It's hard to explain, because there was nothing specific about it. There was no definite age to which they harked hopefully back; it wasn't Woodstock they were thinking of, or the golden age before the first war, or the heady fever of prohibition and the jazz age, it was just some sense that they brought with them of something that had gone before. That was what I thought then, and whatever it was, I liked it, and I looked at Gus, and I said, 'Oh tempora, oh mores,' because now I was a real undergraduate, I felt that was the kind of thing I should say, and I thought it sounded like something out of a book, which was what I wanted to sound like, and he looked at me and smiled, as if he knew just what I meant.

4

Virge and I didn't become inseparable right away. I would have liked that, but she was reading another discipline, and in those early weeks there were so many tutorials to go to, and lectures to hear, and book lists to fill, and libraries to visit, and different ones for both of us.

I was reading history, and there were exams at the end of the first term; papers on Gibbon's *Decline and Fall*, which I found dull, and Bagehot's *Constitution of Britain*, which I liked better, and Macaulay's *History of England*, which I thought was the tops, and de Toqueville, who I wasn't sure of, but it didn't matter because we had such a perfect tutor for it, a fellow of All Souls, with snowy white hair and half-moon spectacles and a measured cadence of speech so literary that we almost missed his jokes, which were sly and plentiful.

It was a lot of work, and we had to pass the exam well before we could start the course proper, so there was not much time for anything else. Everyone else had their exams at the end of the first year, so the small pack of historians, bound every day for the library, watched in envy as they loafed around, and made excuses for missed tutorials, and formed brand new gangs of friends. But we had the last laugh, in June, when we could head for the river with easy consciences, and drink Pimms in the afternoon, while they had a whole year of work to revise.

So I saw Virge, from time to time, passing through the quads, surrounded always by a small crowd, and we waved and smiled and sometimes stopped for some conversation, but we were kept apart by practicalities for the time.

In the first two or three weeks, before the work load grew too heavy, we went to the same parties. There were parties every night: parties at the Union, in the gardens at New College, in the hall at Wadham. There were impromtu parties in people's rooms, those kind when people just turned up with bottles and sat on the floor and put some music on, Bob Dylan or Lou Reed usually. There was a pub behind Christ Church with a courtyard outside, and we gathered there many nights, too.

But at the beginning, there was always such a crowd, and a slight sense of panic, as people hurried around, getting to know each other, trying to make the right friends. Of course, it was as obvious to everyone else as it was to me that Virge was one of the desirables, so often it was impossible to get near her. I have many memories of waving at her over the milling heads of eager acolytes.

There was a habit people had of leaving a sheet of A4 paper pinned to their doors, when they were out, so any visitors could write a note. Most of us made do with one sheet, but I remember once arriving at Virge's door, on my way back from a tutorial above the picture gallery, which was just opposite her room, and staring in astonishment at the trail of paper which led down her door, all the way to the floor, sheets and sheets of it, scrawled with impatient writing. GET MORE PAPER, said one note.

I stood there, laughing to myself, and thinking how typical it was of her. She was the queen, just then, and I went quietly away, without writing anything. Many weeks later, I told her that, and she laughed, and said, 'How clever of you, all the other notes were so boring.' Which was another of the ways she had, always making you feel that you had done the right thing.

I learnt my way about quickly. I rode around on my bicycle, over the cobbled backstreets, filled with a growing proprietorial sense, that this town belonged to me. I remember the first time I was stopped by a tourist, a comfortable fat woman from the mid-west of America, who asked me the way to the Turl, and I told her. I walked away, ten feet tall, feeling that she had given me the key to the city.

I sat my exams, and I passed, and my tutors were pleased with me, and I went down for the Christmas holidays with regret, wanting only to come back again. There were many people who didn't make such a fuss about Oxford, to whom it really was just another place, a little more beautiful than most, a little more bent on ceremony and pomp and circumstance perhaps, but nothing more. But to me, it was magic. It never lost its power to thrill me, right until the day I left it. It was somewhere where I felt anything was possible.

London was crowded and cold when I got back, and my mother asked some inappropriate questions and didn't listen to the answers and said that she had to go out, and I was left in the house, with my suitcase and the reading I had brought with me, and a terrible feeling of anticlimax. There was nothing I wanted to do.

I had a mad old godfather, who had finally gone so insane that they had locked him away, since his nagging conviction that he was, in fact, Aristotle, had got the better of him. But before he was sectioned, which was the charmless euphemism they used for shutting mad people away, he had given me a life membership to the London Library. He said it was the kind of thing that a House man should have. The House was the expression that anyone over thirty-five used for Christ Church, and since in his day there had been no women, anyone who went to the House was automatically known as a House man.

I blessed him, that holiday. I wrote him a long letter, telling him that it was a very good and splendid thing, being a House man. I wanted to tell him that we would be doing Aristotle next term, for the political philosophy paper, but I felt that there was a danger he might take it the wrong way, considering his condition, so I didn't.

I went every day to the library, and I sat in the dark reading room, with its red leather chairs, and its old buffers, snoring gently behind copies of the *Telegraph*, and I pretended that I was a visiting academic, working on some great ground-breaking thesis, and felt, for those short dark winter days, some sense of importance.

I got back to Oxford in the middle of one of the coldest Januarys I could remember. But even under the leaden sky of a mean winter, the spires still looked as stately and promising as they had in a warm September.

I settled back in, feeling happy that I wasn't new any more, that I knew the ropes. I didn't see Virge for the first week. I spent time in the library, and went to see my new tutors, and had coffee with my fellow historians, and I didn't think it was drab until I was at a party in the second week, and I saw Virge in the distance, surrounded with the little band that gathered round her wherever she went, and I suddenly thought that the conversations I was having were dull and pointless, and all I wanted was to be the other side of the room. From where I stood, Virge seemed to be having a good time, the best time you could ever imagine, but then that was another of the things about her.

An hour later, she came up by my side, and said, 'Do you like Chinese?'

'Yes,' I said. 'I do.'

'Let's get out then,' she said. 'This is the worst party I've ever been to.'

We went to a curious Chinese restaurant that she knew above what used to be the *Mitre*, on the corner of the Turl and the High Street. It was odd because it was like a seventies pastiche of what Chinese used to be, before it knew better. It was one of those places that undergraduates never went. I had never been there before, and we never went since, but that was where we went that night. We sat solemnly opposite each other in a booth, and they brought us shark's fin soup and sweet and sour pork and fried rice and glass noodles with shrimp.

I suddenly realised that it was the first time I'd been alone with Virge, and it seemed strange, because she was someone I always associated with a crowd, and I wondered what I had done to deserve it, to have her all to myself. She didn't seem at all self-conscious, but I felt it, and the conversation was a little stilted at first.

There were so many things I wanted to ask her, mostly why she had singled me out, and I didn't know where to start. We talked about boys for a bit, and then I said that there had been a terrible older man who my mother had tried to set me up with that holiday, and she asked his name, and I told her, and she threw back her head, and laughed and laughed, and then she told me that the exact same man had tried to pick her up once at a night club, and that was when we became best friends. It really was as simple as that.

Later, we used to look back, and all the years I knew her we always had a habit of looking back, of talking about the old days, and how we met, and how we became friends, and we always agreed that it was when we found we had that man in common that we knew we would be friends for life. He really was the most dreadful man, but we always blessed him, because he broke any ice there might have been, and bound us together from then on.

'What do you mean by perfect parents?' I said.

Virge paused and blew on her soup, which was too hot. 'Well,' she said, considering. 'They don't do all those awful grown up things. They never use the words Wait and See, or When you get to my age. They are entirely delighted by anything I choose to do, they're never shocked, they understand every word I say to them, and they never ask me why I haven't got myself a nice young man.'

'Goodness,' I said.

We sat and ate our soup for a moment in silence. I almost felt like genuflecting or something, the way you do when you come across the genuine article.

'They don't try and make me wear clothes I don't like, or go to things I don't want to, or even tell me to sit up straight and not put my elbows on the table,' said Virge. She stared across me at the crimson flock wallpaper, almost dreamy. 'They never start sentences with the words In My Day, and they don't go on about how fabulous Jimmy Dorsey was and isn't it a shame that they don't play real music any more. They don't ask me if I'm on drugs if I'm in a bad mood, they never embarrass me in public, and they never make me feel guilty.'

'Blimey,' I said.

'Too right,' said Virge. She brought her eyes back into focus and smiled right at me. 'The real McCoy, no substitutes accepted. It's all that stuff about breaking the mould, once you're done. It's the one and only.'

I shook my head. 'I don't know anyone who even likes their parents,' I said.

'Isn't it something?' said Virge. 'I don't know where they

came from. Sometimes I think my real parents must have been kidnapped by space aliens and replaced by pods, that one day Ma will cut her finger and I'll see just a glimpse of metal instead of flesh, and we'll look at each other, and know we know, but nothing will be said, and then, after, I'll convince myself it was just a trick of the light.' She lifted up her chin and half closed her eyes and looked at me through her eyelashes, and then she gave a sudden laugh in the back of her throat. 'Unless,' she said, 'I get rubbed out by the intergalactic committee.'

'It's a very real danger,' I said.

'So,' said Virge, leaning across the table and hunching up her shoulders like a seasoned conspirator. 'Have you lost your virginity yet? Do you mind me asking?'

'Ha,' I said. 'No, I don't mind.'

It grew colder and colder. Virge felt the cold. She walked around town in a floor-length fake fur and one of those Russian army hats with flaps that came down over her ears. She even wore her coat in the library, although she took her hat off. It's one of my enduring memories of winters in Oxford: Virge, covered in fur, only her bright painted lips visible.

There weren't so many parties that term, it was too cold. There was a club everyone went to on Tuesday nights, to dance and drink too much and get off with each other, but mostly we sat in people's rooms, electric fires turned up high. There was a pub hidden down in a back alley behind New College, near the Bodlean, which had low beamed ceilings and braziers burning outside, and we went there for lunch, most days, and complained about our work load.

The authorities were worried about the Champagne Charlie reputation of the great colleges and their stand against it was to give us so much work so as not to allow time for diversions. Virge had two essays a week, and I had three a fortnight, and we used to brandish our reading lists at each other with a kind of valedictory flourish. 'Ten primary sources alone,' we used to say, in lugubrious resignation. 'And that's just for starters.'

Virge, who had a quick and intuitive mind, and could improvise to beat the band, managed to get her work done on library time, packing up each day at six, but I felt uncomfortable unless I had every fact I could get at my disposal, so I would sit up late, with piles of notes written in green ink spread over my desk, watching the single light which burned on the corner of the quad, scribbling eighteen side essays, finishing at two or three in the morning.

I said I had an empirical brain, which sounded good, but secretly I felt that I was more stupid than Virge. I could never take the risks that she did. But that was all right. She surprised her tutors with her leaps of imagination and lack of pedantry, and I pleased mine with my meticulous research and cogent tightly worked arguments. It was one of the differences between us. I regarded history as a maze that I had to go through, carrying my unravelling ball of twine with me so I wouldn't get lost, and she regarded English like a cocktail party. I remember her doing Byron, and talking about him as if they'd run into each other the week before and gone for lunch.

Out of the milling crowd, we found a tight little group. They all belonged to Virge, really, but since her and I became inseparable, they were mine by proxy.

There was Gus, of course, who spent most of his time in Virge's room on account of him never having got used to the dark gothic warren of the Meadow buildings. There were two boys who shared a set above me in Peck and had parties all day long – Stretch, who was tall and Irish and prone to melancholy and had been one of the ones I'd met in Soho that first night, the boy in the green velvet suit, and

Denny, who was his diametrical opposite, broad and stocky and pragmatic and always smiling. They were both reading philosophy, and they never appeared to do any work. Their shutters were usually closed until six in the evening, and they spent much of the day playing Smiths albums very loud and wandering around in ratty old towelling dressing gowns eating cornflakes and toast with taramasalata. They were friends from childhood and bickered all the time, like two old women. All the girls were in love with Stretch, but they went to bed with Denny.

There was Etta, who was reading ancient history at Magdalen and never knew what day of the week it was. She had a long pale face and she looked like something out of a Burne-Jones picture and she always wore black and she moved with a slow grace, as if she was really thinking of something else. It was rumoured that she was lesbian.

And then there was Stevie, who was at Worcester reading politics, and was a feminist, the first I'd ever met. My mother being what she was, I had been brought up to think of feminists as poor sad unshaven things who could never get a man and made up for it by hating them all as a race. Stevie was small and dark with round green eyes and a smart mouth and had more boyfriends than she knew what to do with.

That was the hard core. Virge gathered us around her and kept us there, and there were always other people coming and going, but the seven of us stayed together, through it all, and we were still best friends when we left.

5

It was in the third week of that term that I first met Virge's brother Michael. He was two years above us, and lived out of college in an old crumbling house looking over the Isis. I knew him well by sight, you would have to be blind not to: he was a flamboyant figure, striding around town in a flowing black cashmere coat and Cuban boots, and, occasionally, when the mood took him, a fedora. He was ostentatiously gay at an age when most people were still making up their minds, like Gus, and his defence was to behave as if he were in a 1930s' drawing-room comedy.

I had noticed him at some of the parties I had gone to the term before, standing in the middle of a group of admirers, dressed in narrow cut suits in peacock colours, puffing on a fat untipped cigarette, and rising high above the disapproving stares of the Vincents mob. (Vincents was a sporting club which was made up of boys who believed that men should be men, with a strong cricketing arm.)

I adored him from afar, because, even more than Virge, he really did seem to me like something out of a book. I had this thing about life at that time, some deep horror of the usual, of normality, of nine-to-five and meat and two veg and bread and butter and please and thank you. Although I was an only child, I had never had those imaginary friends that single children talk about; I didn't make up angels or fairies or naughty elves or ten foot pink rabbits with psychic powers, I just read. Books were just about the best thing that had ever happened to me, because everything was so perfect in them, so much better than life.

I wanted to go to a school like Malory Towers and have midnight feasts and get into scrapes, I wanted to be one of the Famous Five and have adventures in Cornwall and lashings of ginger beer, I wanted to have a wardrobe I could walk through and find a fantastical world peopled with Ice Queens and talking lions and fauns called Mr Tumnus.

My childhood was made up of a succession of humdrum schools and boring tea parties and old people patting me on the head and telling me how pretty my party dress was. There were no adventures or diversions, no mysterious strangers or wicked friends to lead me astray. So I read book after book, and pretended that they were my life, because they were everything I wanted.

This habit never left me. I remember feeling like a failure the first time I read *The Great Gatsby* because I had never been to a party like the ones Gatsby gave and I had never met anyone whose voice was full of money. Hemingway planted in me a deep desire to go and hang around in Spain with bullfighters and drink pastis all day. *Vile Bodies* made me furious because I didn't go about with a little gang of flappers who said things like bogus and too shy-making.

So, if Virge, with her fur coat and her pink hair and her habit of calling people darling seemed half like a fictional character, Michael went all the way. If I had been a writer, Michael was the exact character I would create, right down to the tips of his Cuban boots.

He arrived in my room without invitation and without

knocking one dark day at the end of February. I was struggling with an argument about the Angevin kings which had to be in early the next morning, one of those irritating essay questions where the answer wasn't yes or no, but somewhere in the middle, which annoyed me because I was always sitting on the fence and I wanted to be radical for once and I was in a furious temper anyway because I hated the bloody Angevins and all I wanted to do was go back to Louis XV who was far more interesting.

The early English history paper was compulsory, which really annoyed me. If I had my way, I would have just started with Henry VII and not given a thought to Offa and his boring dyke and dithering old Canute and William the stupid Conqueror. But I had to do it – eight essays on such riveting subjects as Was the Magna Carta the product of social and economic change, or Was England much altered by the Gregorian reform of 1066 to 1135.

So when Michael came up behind me and looked over my shoulder and said, 'Green ink. My dear, don't tell me you're a spy,' I was torn between delight that it was him, and despairing fury that he should have chosen to come that afternoon, and me with my essay not even half done.

'I'm Michael,' he said. 'Virge's brother. And you're Ash.'

I thought it was perfectly charming the way he introduced himself, when he must have known that even the most callow first year knew exactly who he was.

'Hello,' I said wretchedly.

He sat down and crossed his legs in a curiously elegant gesture and lit up a cigarette. He was dressed in a needle-thin corduroy suit the colour of aubergines, and his hair was black and slicked back off his face.

'Have I come at a bad time?' he said. His forehead creased with consternation, as if all that mattered in the world was whether I was in a fit state to receive visitors.

'It's an essay crisis,' I said, feeling terribly jejune and like a horrible student.

'Don't speak,' he said. 'What is it this term? All those brutish Anglo Saxons?'

'The Angevins,' I said.

Michael gave an eloquent shudder.

'You wouldn't wish it on a dog,' he said. 'Once you get Mitchell on the Whigs, you're in clover. Do you know they never went to the country because they hated the colour green? But English I is perfectly fiendish and shouldn't be allowed. When's it due?'

'Tomorrow at ten,' I said, staring dolefully at my pages of notes.

'Oh, dear Ash,' he said, as if we had been meeting at smart parties for the last thirty years. 'Do ring up and say a dog ate it. That's what I always do. Then you can spend the evening with lovely me.'

I was usually immovable about getting my work in on time, but I couldn't resist. I went and called my tutor and told him I had flu and couldn't come to my tutorial, which didn't concern him much since it meant he could sit and listen to Wagner and read Whitelock's seminal work on Archbishop Wulfstan, Homilist and Statesman, which was what he liked doing best anyway, and when I got back to my room, I found Michael lying along my sofa leafing through the collected T.S. Eliot.

'I love T.S. almost more than anyone,' he said. 'Although I know I should love Auden more. Do you know he had his affair with Isherwood in that room over there?' He pointed across the quad. I hadn't known.

'Well,' I said.

'What shall we do?' said Michael. 'It's too cold for the Botanical Gardens, which is normally my favourite thing.

I know, I know,' he said, seeing my face. 'Too much Mr Waugh. I can't help it. At least I didn't tell you I had come to ferret you out of your burrow like an old stoat. At least I didn't do that. It's just very unfortunate in this town that if you are a queen and remotely interesting everyone thinks you are trying to be Anthony Blanche. It would be nice if people could credit one with a little more originality. Don't you think?'

I shook my head and laughed. I thought most of all that it was extraordinary that someone my age could talk like a forty-year-old aesthete from before the war, but then I supposed that was the point.

'You're much more handsome than Anthony Blanche,' I said. 'And far less sinister.'

'Exactly,' said Michael. He seemed pleased. 'I'm not sinister in the least. I've never gone for that Basil Rathbone dark sneering thing. It's not me at all. Shall we go and drink something, then?'

He never did explain why he had come to see me, alone, and I didn't ask. He took my arm and we walked across Radcliffe Square and down St Giles to a bar he knew. It was rather pink and very warm and had visible aspirations to an urban sophistication which you didn't find very much in Oxford. It had a proper bar, with glass shelves behind and serried ranks of spirit bottles, and they made real cocktails, in a silver shaker, and Michael ordered dry martinis, because he said that that was what everyone should drink at six in the evening.

'Stirred,' he told the barman severely. 'Not shaken. Ian Fleming got it all wrong,' he said to me, seriously, as if this was something vital that I should know. 'You must never shake a martini. It bruises the spirit. You must stir, gently, in a jug, with plenty of ice.'

The barman, who was at least twenty years older than

us, looked resigned and chastened and put away his shiny cocktail shaker, and made the drinks in a glass jug, and Michael watched with careful attention.

I was entirely enchanted. I had never drunk a martini before.

'Bottoms up, darling,' said Michael, raising his glass. 'As they say in the officer's mess.'

'Chin chin,' I said, hoping to keep my end up.

'Now,' he said, putting his glass down, and regarding me with steady eyes. 'I want you to tell me everything. Are you having a lovely time? Where did you get that hair cut? Are you in love? Will you come to dinner at my house next week?'

I told him that I was having a lovely time, and I got my hair cut at a man's barber off the Edgware Road, that I wasn't in love, although I very much wanted to be, and that I couldn't think of a single thing I would rather do than come to dinner.

'Aren't you wicked?' said Virge. 'Sneaking off with Michael like that for martinis without telling me.'

We were having scrambled eggs and black coffee in a little place behind the covered market. Around us, disaffected third years from Lincoln were eating alone, struggling with the crossword to take their mind off next term's exams.

'I didn't sneak,' I said calmly. 'He just came and collected me.'

'He will do it,' said Virge. She looked at me slyly. 'Is it another conquest?'

'Of course it is,' I said. 'I'm on the floor with love.'

'Not more than me?' said Virge.

'Of course not more than you,' I said. 'I'm not so fickle.'

Virge ate her eggs. 'You aren't, are you?' she said. 'Not one fickle thing about you.'

I sometimes wanted to ask her how it was she knew the

things she did about people. She had a way of making her mind up quickly about the people she met, and she was always right. I liked that in her. I could trust her judgement. So I knew that if she could see that I wasn't fickle, then I truly wasn't, and I was pleased, because I had been surrounded by it from a young age, and I wanted to do things different.

'We are the chosen,' Virge said. 'Dinner at Michael's is famous. You get proper china and real cooked food and good wine and everything.'

I knew what this meant. Student living was baked beans and paper plates and bring a bottle. Real cooked food and good wine was sophistication of a high degree. But then, with Michael, I wouldn't have expected anything less.

'Will I be frightened?' I said. 'Will there be all those scary third years with their scholarships and their repartee?'

'I'll hold your hand,' said Virge.

Everyone seemed to know about Michael's dinner. I had a tutorial that afternoon, with my favourite of all my tutors, Dr Johnson (which we both thought an inspired joke). He had been at Christ Church since 1945, and he was lined and stooped with fine white hair and sharp rheumy eyes. He had a slight stutter, and some trouble with his r's, and he called me Miss Franklin, or Miss F, if he was in an extra specially good mood. I had fallen helplessly in love with him the moment he told me that Louis XV wasn't safe in taxis, and I spent most of my tutorials trying to draw him away from the point, and get him onto stories about the old days and all those rumours about people's tutors lunching at Downing Street once a week and secretly running the country.

We were on the Italian campaign that week, when Napoleon, still young and idealistic, was moving his army swiftly through the massed ranks of Austria, and I was having a fine time. Napoleon was a big hero of mine just then. I even had a bust of him in my room which I had found for thirty pounds in a crowded junk shop in Jericho. It was for many years my proudest possession.

I read my essay – shamelessly one-sided – and we discussed it, and before I knew it the hour and a half was up, and Dr Johnson started rustling his papers and looking at his watch.

'Well, Miss F,' he said, giving me a look over his spectacles. 'European pacifications next week, I think. Don't you?'

He picked his way skilfully over the piles of books that studded the carpet, and started climbing up a ladder that leant against the bookshelves lining the walls.

'And their failure to survive,' he said, his back to me. 'Why?'

I wrote it down. Why indeed? By next week I should know.

'I've got a book for you here somewhere,' said Dr Johnson, scanning the shelves. 'Here,' he said triumphantly. He turned round, ignoring the precarious shift of his ladder, and looked down at me.

'You're dining with Michael Hudson tonight?' he said.

I loved 'dining with'. I thought it sounded just the thing. I wondered how he knew, but then unlike many of the other dons, he spent a lot of time in college, sauntering around the quads looking deceptively vague. There was very little he didn't know about our lives.

'Yes,' I said. 'I am.'

'I taught him in his first year,' he said. 'I seem to remember we spent an inordinately long time on the flight to Varennes and Marie Antoinette's necessaire.' He laughed gently through his nose. 'A very able mind,' he added. 'One of the best I've had.'

There was a pause. Watching Dr Johnson, balanced high

up on his ladder, holding a book in one hand, I was surprised to see a look of sorrow pass over his face. He was so old school English, so essentially academic, that he never betrayed any personal emotion. An occasional skittish levity was the most he allowed himself.

'He won't use it,' he said, sadly. 'It will go to waste.'

I frowned, curious.

'How can you tell?' I said.

'Oh,' he said, shaking his head, and regarding me with a quite uncharacteristic gravity. 'You can always tell, with those ones.'

You can always tell, with those ones. I thought of that remark, often, afterwards. I wondered what you could tell, and why, and what he meant by those ones. All I knew then was that Michael and Virge were the ones I wanted, and there was dinner on Saturday night, and everyone knew about it and I was pleased and proud, to be the chosen.

6

'Come in,' said Michael. He kissed me on the cheek, and held open the door. 'Aren't you clever and punctual?'

I was always on time, but I wasn't sure yet whether it was clever or not.

'Virge is going to be late,' I said. 'She said to tell you.'

Michael smiled. 'There's no need to tell,' he said. 'She's always late, just now. It's her new thing.'

He took me into a wide room overlooking the river. In the bow window a long table was dressed for supper, just as Virge had promised, with a tablecloth and candlesticks and crystal glasses and proper knives and forks and all sorts. There was a sofa and two chairs gathered around the fireplace, and over against the far wall, a bed covered in green velvet. I looked at it in surprise, and Michael saw the look, and laughed.

'It may be gracious living,' he said, 'but it's still a bedsit. Three single rooms, two doubles, kitchenette, and one communal bath,' he added, counting them off on his fingers. 'I don't think the landlord understands about the need to entertain. We did try to set up a dining table in the hallway once, but there was a draught and everyone got a stiff neck.'

He sat me down and gave me a glass of champagne, because he said that was what he was drinking, and we looked at each other for a moment over the rims of our glasses, with that small pause that comes when you are alone in a dark room with someone you don't know very well.

'There's something romantic about bedsits,' said Michael. 'Don't you think? Doesn't it make you think of Joe Orton and Jimmy Porter? Just a little.'

'Except green velvet,' I said. 'And no sink filled with unwashed dishes and the smell of old cabbage and an ironing board and last weeks' papers.'

Michael looked at me in admiration, as if I had said the exact right thing, the thing he wanted me to say.

'Dear Ash,' he said. 'You have read, haven't you, despite your youth.'

I felt my youth, as I had with Virge that first night, as if my years had somehow been shorter than hers and Michael's, as if they had used theirs better, gone out and filled them with the worldly knowledge and sophistication that they carried so easily with them, while I had just sat about, reading books and wishing for something to happen. I wanted to ask Michael how he did it, but I thought it would sound too forward, so I didn't.

'That's all I do,' I said. 'Read books. It's a substitute for living, isn't that what they say?'

'Almost everything is a substitute for living,' said Michael. I wanted to ask him what he meant by that. I wasn't sure. But the doorbell went, and people arrived, so I never had the chance.

'Guests,' said Michael, going to let them in.

He came back with a group of six. They blew into the room full of talk and laughter and complaints about the cold, taking off their coats and shaking their hair and rubbing their hands together to warm them.

'A fire,' they said, as if they had never seen one before.

'Champagne,' they said, as Michael brought them glasses. 'Just fancy. Aren't we posh?'

'This is Ash,' said Michael. 'You must all be nice to her. Shake hands and say how do you do.' He pointed at the strange faces, who stood still for a moment, to allow themselves to be identified. 'This is Clover and Ruby and Con and Chas and Albert and Dimitri,' he said. 'Don't let them all talk at once.'

They smiled and said Hello-how-are-you and moved and broke up and sat themselves down and lit cigarettes and made conversation.

One of the boys came and sat himself down beside me.

'I'm Albert,' he said. 'I know, I know,' he said, as if I had spoken. 'It's not for now, is it? Albert. You need to be sixty, at least.'

'Sixty,' I said, suddenly thinking of it. I was young enough to think that old age was rather appealing; since it was still one of the things that would never happen to me, I could consider it without fear. 'Ashley and Albert would be good at sixty, wouldn't they?'

'Perfect,' he said gravely. 'We could sit in large hotels and watch the young being foolish and impetuous and remember what it was like and think how lucky we are that we won't have to go through all that again.'

'I could wear a hat,' I said. 'Perhaps with a feather.'

I was surprised for a moment at my boldness. This was not the kind of thing I usually said. But in this darkened room, with these assured people, it seemed as if I could be as careless and fey and unreal as they were. It was one of the things I liked in Virge and Michael, the assumption that flights of fancy were the accepted currency in which they all dealt. I thought then, looking at Albert's clever high-boned face, at his clear dark eyes watching me with interest and absolute attention, that I had always had a fanciful streak in me, it was just that I had never found anywhere that I could bring it out, where questions would not be asked.

'A feather would be wonderful,' said Albert. 'You are lucky, being female. Won't it be lovely, being old?' he said suddenly, a small note of regret in his voice. 'We shall be able to wear what we want, and say what we want, and do what we want, and pretend selective deafness.'

'Don't you say what you want now?' I said, wondering. He seemed like the kind who did. He had the same careless ease that I saw in Virge, the one that I wanted.

'Well, yes, mostly,' he said, seriously, as if it were a weighty question. 'But it's an effort now, swimming against the tide. Because of our youth. When we're old we will have deserved it, do you see? We'll have done all that battling and struggling and paid our dues and we will truly deserve a rest.'

'Yes, I see,' I said, thinking about it. 'It will be lovely. Absolutely lovely.'

'Where is Virge?' said Michael. 'We must eat, or I shall do something foolish.'

As he spoke, Virge walked into the room with one of the most beautiful boys I had ever seen in my life. I sat and stared, I couldn't help it. He had a dead white face and raven black hair and bright blue eyes which slanted a little, something Slav about them, and he held himself with a curious hesitancy as if he had no idea of the effect that he had.

'You shouldn't leave the door open like that, Michael,' said Virge gaily. 'I've told you. You never know who might walk in off the street.'

She laughed, and kissed her brother, and put a hand to his cheek, and smiled closely at him.

'Take your coat off,' he said. 'Shed your fur, and we'll eat something.'

'I've brought Keane,' she said, pointing at the beautiful

boy. 'I found him all sad and alone because he wasn't asked.'

'Oh, really,' said Michael. 'Of course he was asked. You know you were asked, Keane. I told you on Tuesday, did you forget?'

Keane stood square in the middle of the room for a moment, narrowing his eyes in thought. Everyone watched him, as if they were used to giving him a minute.

Finally, he nodded.

'I forgot,' he said.

They all laughed, and Michael gathered us round the table and sat us down, because it was time to eat.

When I look back on my friendship with Virge and Michael, I most often remember them together in that evening. Perhaps it was because it was still so new to me then, and I had a sense of wonder, that these glittering people had come and plucked me out of my ordinary life, conferred something of themselves on me, sprinkling me with stardust. They sat together at the end of the table, their heads bent together, the candles shedding a yellow glow over their fine faces. It is the enduring picture I have of them, so young and sure and gleaming, burning brightly into the night.

The talk, at first of many unrelated things, turned to love, which was a big subject of ours just then. I sometimes felt guilty that we never seemed to talk of the outside world, the whole time we were at Oxford. There were jokes and gossip and occasional late night conversations about life and what it all meant, but I don't remember once talking of politics, or the economy, or the state of the nation.

I think it was to do with the feeling that it was our time out of the world: it was our time to be absolutely free, with no responsibility, no cares, no worries about jobs and mortgages and the quotidian realities that came with being grown up. We knew that we would have to face all that, in time, that there was no way we could avoid it forever, but we didn't want to think about it, just then. That was the greatest indulgence we allowed ourselves. We would think about it tomorrow, because we knew we had a full three years when tomorrow would never come.

So we weren't thinking about tomorrow, that night, we were just talking about love.

'I'm in it all the time,' said Michael. 'Every single day. I can't remember a day when I wasn't in love.'

He looked soulful and comical at the same time, as if he knew how everyone would seize on it.

'There's a difference,' said Virge, 'between love and lust.'

'And infatuation,' said Clover.

'And obsession,' said Ruby, with feeling.

'And being in love with being in love,' said Albert.

'And caprice,' said Con.

'And erotomania,' said Dimitri.

'Is that a word?' said Ruby.

'You can look it up,' said Dimitri, with dignity.

'And like,' said Chas, catching the ball and running with it.

'And hate,' said Keane. Everyone turned and looked at him. He blinked his extraordinary sapphire eyes, and raised his head a little. 'It's a thin line,' he said. 'Scratch a lover and find a foe.'

'Stop,' said Virge. 'Someone tell him to stop.'

'He's so annoying,' said Clover. 'You're so annoying Keane. Is it Mencken?'

Keane shook his head, the faintest smile tugging at the corner of his mouth.

'Older,' said Albert, with definition. 'Doesn't it have that ruthless medieval sound? Chaucer, or someone?'

'Don't be silly,' said Dimitri. 'Woody Allen, more like.'

'I never can tell the difference,' said Michael.

'Dorothy Parker,' said Keane. 'Who always told the truth.'

'Keane has a curious tic about the truth,' Albert told me. 'He would like to tell it, but no one will tell him what it is.'

'Whatever,' said Michael. 'But how do we tell the difference between any of them? Are they different at all? Aren't they just all part of the same thing?'

'Don't say the word indivisible,' said Ruby, as if she minded.

'Of course there's a difference,' said Virge. 'It's just you can't tell until afterwards. That's the difficulty. They all feel the same at the beginning. The terrible old joke.'

She laughed gently, as if the joke were on everyone but her, as if she had some secret way of telling, some hidden knowledge that set her apart.

'Don't you wonder,' said Dimitri, 'how it is that everyone will go on believing in one God, when all the evidence suggests that he must have had the most twisted and fiendish sense of humour.'

'Oh, listen to this,' said Clover. 'Dimitri's been reading one of his philosophy books again. That's why we haven't seen him for a whole afternoon.'

'What I want to know,' said Michael, 'is who Ash is in love with.'

Albert took my hand and held it, seeing I didn't know what to say. 'Ash is in love with me, of course,' he said. 'But it's a secret.'

I smiled at him, grateful. It was true. And it was a secret.

Later, Michael put a Charlie Parker record on, got out a pack of cards, and we played poker. Keane won, bluffing his way through a series of dud hands.

'He may not say much, but he's got it where it counts,' said Virge. 'How I like a man with a poker face.'

I suddenly knew the reason she had been late. She

looked over at me, and saw that I knew, and smiled. Then she folded up her hand and put it down on the table.

'I lose,' she said.

'Well,' I said, later, as Virge and I were walking back along St Aldates. 'Well.'

'Well,' said Virge.

She put her arm through mine, and I leant my head for a moment on her shoulder, and we walked like that for a few steps, keeping time easily, holding onto the small physical reassurance of moving like one person instead of two. Then Virge stopped, and laughed, and watched her breath blow out in white plumes in the freezing night, and turned and looked at me.

'What do you think?' she said.

'Virge,' I said. 'For heaven's sake. He's the most beautiful thing I've ever seen in my life.'

'But can he type?' said Virge.

We looked at each other for a moment, and started to laugh, our steps breaking up, weaving about the road in little loops of hilarity.

'He can fuck, though,' said Virge, when she stopped laughing. 'All afternoon. I missed my tutorial. I was supposed to be telling my tutor about dear old Larry Sterne, and what was I doing? What was I doing?'

'What were you doing?' I said. I was impressed, I couldn't help it. It wasn't as if I hadn't done sex, but I knew I could never call it fucking.

'Oh, dear,' said Virge. She put her head back and stretched her neck. 'Three times in one afternoon. It was really dirty.'

'And which one is it?' I said.

She smiled to herself. The night was dark and still and we were the only people up. The lights were all out. The

great arched dome of Tom Tower stood high against the
indigo sky, dwarfing us. Virge looked me very straight in
the eye.

'I don't know,' she said. She paused for a moment, and
then that wide free smile stretched across her face again.
'But I can find out,' she said.

It was the talk of the moment, Virge and Keane. No one
seemed to know very much about him. His full name was
Maurice Horatio Keane, and there was never any reason
given about him being called by his surname. It suited him,
anyway, and that was enough.

'It's almost too much, isn't it?' said Michael. 'I mean the
both of them, and the beauty?'

I knew what he meant. We were walking through the
meadows behind Christ Church, down the wide gravel walk
that led to the river. Since that dinner, Michael seemed to
have decided that I belonged to him as much as Virge, and
he took to passing by my window and taking me away
with him.

'I know what you mean,' I said.

'I'm jealous, of course,' he said. I wasn't sure then if he
meant that he was jealous because someone else had first
call on Virge, or whether he wanted Keane for himself,
and was envious that such a beautiful boy should be out of
bounds. I didn't ask. It seemed inopportune and daunting,
to ask such a question. I felt too young. To cover it, I put
on the special staccato voice that I was learning to affect
whenever I was with Michael.

'Come along,' I said, tugging his hand. 'Let's go down
to the river and look at all those butch boys. That'll cheer
you up.'

Michael smiled at me. 'Darling Ash,' he said. 'I wish I
could just be in love with you.'

'I wish you could too,' I said.

We were always wishing for things in those days, it was one of the things we did. Michael never stopped. It was one of the habits he never grew out of.

7

For the first couple of weeks of Virge's new affair, she disappeared. The rest of us, Gus, Stretch, Denny, Etta and Stevie and me, drew closer together in her absence, and waited for her to come back. We took to sitting in the cramped back room of a pub we liked, with low ceilings and sloping floors and six different kinds of real ale on tap, and talking about Keane.

'No one knows anything about him,' said Stevie crossly. Stevie, who prided herself on having her finger on everyone's pulse, took it as a personal affront when she found someone she didn't know anything about.

'You've asked, have you?' said Stretch.

Stevie looked surprised that he should wonder.

'Of course I have,' she said. 'It's all I've done for the last two weeks. All I know is that he's reading Classics.'

That took us back for a moment. Four years of Aristophanes and Plato and Plutarch was not for dilettantes. It said a lot about a person, what they studied, in our book. Geography was for the dim, obviously, hardly worth mentioning. PPE, which used to court disdain, now indicated ambition, a fast track to a first and the outside world. English and history were honourable and to be expected. Maths and the sciences were in another world, and still bore too-close-for-comfort associations with anoraks and acne. Philosophy was considered endearing, and faintly old-fashioned. Languages were for the sharp and worldly. But classics, that was still for the purists, the real academics. Anyone who could even pretend to read Aeschylus in the original was something else entirely.

'Our Virge,' said Denny, thoughtfully. 'With a classicist. Who would ever have thought it?'

'She's over the age of consent,' said Gus. 'It's her life.' He was touchy on the subject, and I thought that perhaps he was jealous in the same way that Michael was. There was something strange and unguessable in his friendship with Virge, something secret and complicated. I thought for a time that it was simply that he had known her the longest, that in a way he had more claims on her than we did, but later I thought it was more than that.

'Of course, it is her life,' said Etta, in her vague way. 'But it is curious, all the same.'

'I'm not sure I trust him,' said Denny.

'But you don't trust anyone,' said Stretch.

'There is that,' said Denny.

'I don't like him,' I said.

They all turned and looked at me. They were surprised, I could see. They were used to me being charitable about everyone, it was one of the things I did.

'I don't,' I said. I had startled myself, to tell the truth, but I thought I should run with it. I quite liked being unexpected for once.

'Ash,' said Stretch.

'This is perfect,' said Stevie, with relish. What Stevie liked best was confrontation and controversy. She said she'd do anything rather than have a quiet life. She said a quiet life was for the chickens.

'Tell us why,' she said.

I thought for a moment. I wasn't entirely sure.

'It was that poker game,' I said, finally. 'The way he won

all that money, just bluffing. As if he liked making fools of us all. Something.'

'The fine art of bluffing,' said Denny. 'It's not against the law. I'm quite a hand at it myself.'

'And,' I said, not to be denied, not now, not now I'd started. 'And, he just sits there, watching. He doesn't say much.'

'Etta doesn't say very much,' said Stevie. 'Do you, precious?'

Etta blinked her eyes.

'I don't say very much,' she said. 'I never did.'

'It's different,' I said. 'It's not pointed, like it is with Keane. As if he's judging and refining, waiting for other people to say something wrong or foolish, so then he can feel superior. He doesn't give anything of himself. That's what it is.'

'Now look at this student of human nature,' said Denny. 'Listen to this. I'm going to bring all my girlies to you for vetting, Ash, in the future.'

'Don't say girlie,' said Stevie, frowning at him. She had heavy black eyebrows and she liked to draw them down over her eyes and intimidate people. Denny pretended he was intimidated.

'Sorry, my duck,' he said. 'Deep apologies, my old china.'

Denny never did accents, but he had a habit of using outmoded vernacular, straight out, in his nice enunciated educated voice, which sounded strange, until you got used to it.

'Perhaps he's just too handsome for his own good,' said Stevie. 'Perhaps we're all jealous, because we'd all like to be in bed with him. Except Etta, of course.'

There was a measured pause. Stevie sat back and looked pleased with herself. This was what she liked doing best, and she had it to a fine art. We had all heard the rumours about Etta, but none of us had ever dared mention it.

Etta smiled to herself, not at all put out.

'I'm not lesbian,' she said. 'Actually.'

There was another pause. Then Stevie started to laugh.

'Oh bugger,' she said. 'Why not? I did so hope it was true.'

Stevie always said she longed to be a lesbian, it was her party piece. She said it was very difficult knowing just how dreadful men could be and still wanting to go to bed with them. She said that it would be so much easier to fall in love with your own sex, because then there wouldn't be all the complications of the language barrier. She said it annoyed her beyond endurance that she didn't fancy girls. She was way ahead of the rest of us, in some ways, Stevie. When we got to our mid-twenties, it was to become a staple conversation every time two or more women were gathered together, and we would discuss the mysteries of men, and why it was that they never called when they said they would, and how it seemed that they would act so keen one moment and the next tell you that they couldn't deal with commitment and they weren't ready for a relationship, and how we didn't understand any of it, and wouldn't it be so much easier if we just liked girls. But that was far ahead, and so in those days, when we were still in our teens, however sophisticated we liked to think we were, there was something shocking and new in what Stevie said so easily.

'I'm so sorry,' said Etta, 'to disappoint you.'

'Who starts these rumours in the first place?' said Stevie.

'You do, half the time,' said Stretch.

'Don't say what I said about Keane,' I said. I had a sudden access of fear that it would get back to Virge, and she and Keane would get married and I wouldn't be asked to the wedding.

'Of course not,' said Gus, patting my hand. 'You know we won't.' But he gave Stevie a hard look as he said it, just to make sure.

'I expect I'm just cross because he's taken her away,' I said.

'It's all right,' said Stretch. He put his arm round me. He was very protective of what he called his girls. He said he had never had a female friend before university, having no sisters and an education at one of those cloistered boys' schools, and he took pride in it. He had once had to be restrained from punching a cocky second year who had goosed Stevie in the Union, which made Stevie laugh a lot, because she said she was quite able to do her own punching. Even so, she liked that in Stretch, same as I did. There was something comforting in knowing that you had someone there to defend your honour, if it ever should need defending.

'She'll come back,' he said. 'You'll see.'

She did come back, the very next week.

It was before nine one morning, and Denny and Stretch had climbed in my window in their pyjamas, which they did most days. Denny was lying beside me on my bed, and teasing me about Albert, whom I'd been seen with the night before.

'Where is he, then?' he said, peering about under the covers. 'You can come out of the closet, Albert, old chum,' he shouted.

I was laughing and confused, because I did quite hope that something might come of it, and I wasn't sure if I wanted to let on just yet, in case it didn't. Stretch brought us cups of coffee and sat down on the end of the bed, and noticed, and told Denny to shut up and leave me be, and they started bickering, just like they did every morning, and I wasn't even thinking of Virge, when she suddenly walked in, in her fur coat and her hat, just as if she had never been away.

'Look at this,' she said. 'What would your mother say, three in a bed?'

'I know what your mother would say,' said Denny to Stretch.

'I know what *your* mother would say, thank you,' said Stretch to Denny.

'Where's my coffee then?' said Virge, managing to find some space on the bed, and sitting herself down.

'She's back,' said Stretch, throwing his arms round her.

'She's back,' said Denny, kissing her.

'You're back,' I said, smiling all over my face.

'Who is?' said Gus, coming in through the window.

'Does no one ever use the door?' said Virge.

'Virge,' said Gus. 'You're back.' And he got onto the bed as well, and we all started laughing because there wasn't enough room.

'I've emptied your bin,' said my scout, walking into the room without knocking. She stopped when she saw us all there in bed together, her eyes opening wide in shock.

'Oh, thank you, Mrs Grace,' I said, trying to look serious.

'Thank you very much, Mrs,' said Stretch.

'No, thank *you*, Mrs G,' said Denny.

'Don't take any notice, Mrs Grace,' said Gus. 'Don't mind them.'

'Isn't it a lovely morning?' said Virge.

Mrs Grace, outgunned, made a rattling noise in the back of her throat to signal her absolute outrage, put the bin down in the corner, and fled.

'Oh, dear,' said Gus. 'Does that mean we'll all be up before the Dean?'

It was a beautiful day, cold and clear and sunny, and we

went for a walk down to the river, where all the rowing boys were out on the water, and then we went up to the botanical gardens, and wandered round the hothouse, and then we went to a stuffy smelly café in the covered market and had sausage sandwiches with ketchup and cups of thick coffee and cigarettes and Virge told us about Keane.

'He's very strange,' she said. 'I get a shock when I look up and see those eyes looking at me. I never saw anyone so beautiful.' But she said it in a curious, detached way, not adoring or bowled over, just as if it were an odd phenomenon that she had noticed about him.

We all felt it, and no one asked the normal questions, about if she was in love, or anything like that.

'Stevie says he's a classicist,' said Gus.

'I know,' said Virge. 'Isn't that a thing?' And then we changed the subject.

Later Virge and I went back to her room, since the others had tutorials that afternoon. I had done my work for the week and had a day off, so we just sat around for the rest of the day, watching the dark come in, and talking. We talked about other things for a while, and then Virge told me some more.

'It is strange,' she said. 'He has a kind of otherness. Is that what I mean?'

I shook my head. I didn't know.

'As if there is something else there, you know,' said Virge. 'Many hidden parts, and a kind of . . .' She paused, looking about the room. I was surprised. Virge usually had a word for everything.

'I don't know. A mystery,' she said. 'I like it.'

I watched her, patiently. She looked back at me.

'You're good at this,' she said. 'Waiting, for the next part, listening. I wish I was. I'm always talking. I wish I could just sit and wait, like you can.'

I smiled. I had never thought there was a single thing that I could do which she might wish for. It was the finest compliment I'd ever had.

'It's interesting,' I said. 'It is. I like to listen. But then,' I said. 'I wish I could talk like you can. I wish I was brave enough to make more of a noise.'

'We're like Jack and Mrs Sprat,' said Virge, laughing. 'That's why it's so perfect that we're friends.' She stopped, and suddenly looked very closely at me, and leaned over and took my hand.

'We will be friends always,' she said. There was a strange urgency in her voice, as if she really minded, as if it might be in doubt. 'Won't we? We won't drift apart, or marry men that one of us doesn't like, or go and live abroad and forget to write?'

'Of course we won't,' I said. I was surprised that she might think that, that it might worry her. Forever was such an easy thing to think about then, when we were so young. Forever seemed attainable, something that could belong to us. I knew that we would be friends forever. I didn't wonder why I knew, or how. It seemed so obvious to me, something that didn't even need stating. I couldn't imagine us not being together.

'Of course we won't,' I said. 'We'll be friends always.'

'We'll be such grand old ladies,' said Virge, leaning back again. She lay along the sofa, gazing up at the ceiling. 'We'll be seventy, and we'll have protégés, lots of eager young men who come and sit at our feet and adore us, and we'll have lunch every day, and take sherry in the Palm Court at the Ritz, and everyone will wonder at it, that we'll have been best friends for more than fifty years. Think of it,' she said. 'Fifty whole years. Can you imagine how long that will be? Can you think of it? Won't that be something? They'll write books about us.'

I did think of it. I liked the idea of fifty years. Whatever happened, there would always be me and Virge, together.

'Fifty years,' I said. 'Won't that be something?'

8

Term ended, and we all went off in different directions. Keane went to New York, where his father lived, and Virge said she didn't mind, and went home to her perfect parents in the West Country. I, unwilling, got into my car and drove up to London.

My father was home when I arrived, which gave me a start. He was travelling, usually, and it was better that way, because when he was there all that happened was that he and my mother fought all day and drank all night and the house was filled with tension and fury.

'Hello, Dad,' I said, trying to sound friendly.

My father looked up from his paper and gave me a big smile.

'Here she is,' he said, genially. He had this attitude he struck with me, a jocular bantering type of posturing, which he thought made him seem like a big old sweet old Dad figure. He thought if he made enough bluff paternal jokes he might pass himself off as a good father. It had worked quite well until I was eleven.

'The undergraduate,' he said. 'The fledgling scholar. Just look at you. Just look.'

'Just do,' I said. He didn't even know what I was reading. He quite liked the fact that I'd got into Oxford, because he could boast to his cronies about his clever daughter. Dad took any glory that would reflect on him, without shame. But beyond that, the details didn't interest him. My father was far too interested in his own life to have much time to think about anyone else's.

'Your mother's out,' he said. 'Shopping.' We both knew what shopping meant, on a Saturday afternoon.

'Shopping,' I said. 'Figures.'

Dad gave me a sharp look.

'Mid-season sales,' I said blandly.

'I'm going to watch the racing,' Dad said, turning back to his paper. 'Look at the ponies. Have a bit of a flutter.'

'Yes,' I said. 'Good luck.'

I went up to my room, and wondered what to do next. I unpacked for a while, in a desultory way, but I got bored half way through, and left my suitcase open on the floor, and lay on my bed and stared out of the window at the London roofs and the skylights and the chimney pots. I wondered what Virge would be doing. Then I wondered what Albert might be doing.

I had seen Albert quite often, since Michael's dinner. Every time I saw him he was charming and friendly and flirtatious, and each time I hoped it might mean something, and I read a hundred different meanings into everything he said, but nothing happened. He always singled me out, if we ran into each other, and devoted his absolute attention to me, and I thought that must mean that he liked me, that he had what they used to call intentions, in the old days.

I longed for him to have intentions. I went a bit weak every time I saw his tall graceful figure across a crowded room. But then I thought: perhaps he's like that with everyone, because he's so nice, and it doesn't mean so much after all. I thought maybe I wasn't pretty enough, or confident enough, or sophisticated enough, that he was just taking pity on me. But sometimes, he would put his face very close to mine, and look right at me, straight in my eyes, and I was so sure that he was going to kiss me, but he never did.

I hadn't told anyone about it, not even Virge, because I didn't want to be one of those sad people who have unrequited crushes which never amount to anything. It was my secret.

My mother came back later, smelling of toothpaste and too much scent, and made a big fuss of me. Guilt, I thought, letting her.

She insisted that my father stay in, and she cooked, ('I'm going to roast a bird,' she said, peering into the freezer) and we had dinner together, the three of us. It was a terrible awkward evening. It was so obvious that we were going through the motions, pretending to be a family. We never ate together. I couldn't remember the last time we had all sat round a table, and it was so strange and unfamiliar that none of us knew what to do.

At first, Dad did his jolly expansive patter, and Mum had a stab at a bit of a concerned Mumsy number, and asked me if I had made some nice friends at college. I told her that my best friends were a homosexual, a bisexual, and a girl with pink hair, because I wanted to shock her, but she wasn't listening properly, and she just nodded and said How nice.

By the time she and Dad were onto the second bottle, the façade was slipping nicely, and they were back to their usual thing, which was needling each other. I watched in horrified fascination as one of my mother's false eyelashes came loose and started crawling up her eyelid like an insect making for home. I watched as Dad's face grew red and shiny, and his eyes went all glassy and beady and determined, as he cast cleverly disguised insults across the table. It always started off like this, genteel sniping, both of them playing the game. Later, it would degenerate into overt aggression, and things would be thrown and broken, and there would be shouting, and there wouldn't be any pretence any more.

I always wondered why they stayed together, they seemed to hate each other so much. It wasn't for my sake, that was for sure. But watching them now, I suddenly understood. They really enjoyed it, this internecine warfare. They got some kind of charged kick out of it. I wondered suddenly if it was an erotic thing, if they would go to bed after. I had always assumed that they didn't sleep with each other any more, since they both had so much on the side to keep them occupied. But now, I wondered. I thought it made it worse, if they did, even more sordid and degrading. I wondered if they played horrible furious drunken sex games, when they were alone, after all that fighting.

It was only ten o'clock, and I was feeling sick. I made an excuse and left the table. They hardly noticed. I went upstairs, entirely demoralised, and wondered what to do. I wanted, more than anything, to get out of that house and far away. I remembered that I had Gus's number in London. I didn't think for a moment that he would be in on a Saturday night, but I rang it anyway. He answered on the first ring.

'Oh, Ash,' he said. 'I'm having such a horrible time. Are you having a horrible time?'

'Horrible,' I said.

'I am glad,' he said, 'that I'm not the only one. Can we go somewhere and drink something and forget?'

We met in the bar in Soho where I'd gone with Virge that first night. The minute I reached Old Compton Street, I felt reassured. The lights were shining and the crowds were out in the street, defying the weather. The biking boys were parked up outside the Bar Italia, and the hawkers were lurking in doorways, offering girls and exotic substances and cut price cab rides, and the punters were out, looking for the unexpected. It still had all the exotic sheen I remembered from last time, but it was familiar to me now. I didn't feel that I needed a passport to cross the border. I knew where to go.

Don was waiting on the door, looking more like the heavyweight champion of the world than ever.

'Hey Ash,' he said, grinning at me. He had lost a tooth since the last time I met him. 'Gus is downstairs.' He looked quickly over my shoulder, a furtive darting look, as if he knew he shouldn't. 'No Virge?' he said.

I shook my head.

'No Virge,' I said. 'Not tonight.'

I walked down the narrow steps into the club. It was as crowded as before, but the faces had changed. It made me think of the theatre, one of those long-running pro-ductions, like *The Mousetrap* – the same show, but with a whole new cast.

Gus was sitting alone at a corner table, waiting for me.

'Where did they go?' I said, looking round at the crowd. 'Mean Gene and Backstage Dolly and all?'

'They move on quickly, those ones,' said Gus. 'They'll have found somewhere new to go by now.'

I looked at him curiously. I had thought that they were all inseparable.

'I thought they were your best friends,' I said.

Gus leaned his elbows on the table and smiled at me. I smiled back at him. I felt better already.

'We were, then,' he said. 'But just for the time. Virge and I were very good at finding ourselves in a gang, you know. We always had one. But it changed, with the season. We were forever finding new best friends. We just went to the same places, that was all. We didn't call each other on the telephone, or anything like that. It wasn't intimate.'

I thought this over for a moment. Gus let me. A waiter came and brought us green bottles of beer.

'Where's Honey?' said Gus. 'Is he working tonight?'

'Immigration,' said the waiter, darkly. He put the bottles down on the table and hurried away.

'Do you think,' I said to Gus, 'that it's different with us?'

'Yes, I do,' he said, with the instant conviction that he did so well.

'Virge says we'll be friends forever,' I said.

'We will,' said Gus. He nodded slowly. 'For ever and ever.'

'But how do you know?' I said. I knew that I knew, but I didn't know how. There wasn't a reason. It was hope, more than anything.

'It's our age,' said Gus. 'We'll all go on changing, now, but it's not fads, not like it used to be, when we were little teen angels. Remember how you could be best friends with someone just because you both liked the Clash, or had been to see *Christianne F.*, or hated the New Romantics?'

I nodded. I remembered.

'It's different now, isn't it?' I said.

'It's different,' said Gus, nodding slowly. 'It's more than that. It's because our horizons are widening. Look at you and Virge. It seems so unlikely from the outside – she so theatrical and ostentatious and impulsive, and you so quiet and thoughtful and unsure.'

I had thought about it. There were many people, later, who found it strange that Virge and I should be such friends, being as different as we were. We were different, but for all that, we were the same too. It was just that that was the part that wasn't so obvious, to the naked eye.

'What about opposites attracting?' I said.

'No one believes that,' said Gus. 'Besides, you and Virge aren't opposites, that's the point. You just have different styles, is all. But it's more than that. That's what happens, when we grow up a little.'

I nodded. I knew exactly what he meant. We were growing up, a little. At least, that was what it felt like.

'Quiet and thoughtful and unsure,' I said. 'Is that what I am?'

I wasn't sure yet what I was. I wanted to find out. I wanted people to tell me.

'Yes,' said Gus. 'Not unsure in the way you think I mean.' He looked at me closely, in examination, in that direct way he had. 'I mean,' he said, 'that you are still looking about for all the things you want to know, and you want to believe in, and you don't know yet what you want to be, and you don't pretend that you do. You're brave like that.'

'Brave?' I said. I didn't think of myself as brave. I spent far too much time not daring to do all the things I wanted. Virge was the brave one, the way I saw it.

'Of course,' said Gus. 'Because you don't play a part.'

'Do you?' I said.

He paused for a moment. Around us, there were crowded tables of people talking and laughing and striking sparks off each other. I felt suddenly very adult and secret, in our dark little corner. I thought of the awful scene I had left behind in my parents' house, and how I had known them all my life, where I had only known Gus for a few months, and how strange it was that if they were listening to this conversation they wouldn't understand one word of it, when Gus understood every single thing I said, and I didn't have to explain anything to him.

'Yes,' he said. 'Sometimes, when I need to. I think sometimes that I'm more conventional than I give myself credit for. But it's easier to play the outsider. That's a good safe part. People have been doing it for years.'

'And you're so good at it,' I said. I thought perhaps that his definition of conventional and mine might not agree, but I saw what he meant, all the same. It can be a good defence, to decide not to belong.

Gus nodded.

'It's good practice,' he said. 'For life.'

Spring came suddenly, overnight, the next week. The cherry trees along my street blossomed, and the sun came out, and everyone looked surprised, just as they did every year, as if they had expected the winter to go on for ever and ever.

I had hoped that my father might leave, on a business trip, but he didn't. The atmosphere in the house grew and thickened.

There were points of farce. Even though there was no one to see or judge, both my parents hid their bottles all over the house. I think they liked the drama of it, the mystery of the furtive drinker. So there were times when they would both creep around the house, heading slyly for their secret caches, and one time they found that they had both hidden the gin in the same place, and bumped into each other, and for a moment even they saw the funny side, and started to laugh, but then my mother decided tears were a better option and there was another scene.

'For God's sake, Ashley,' she screamed, turning to find me in the doorway, watching. 'Couldn't you behave like a normal teenager, and go to parties, and stay out all night, and have boyfriends, instead of lurking around the house all the time like a ghost?'

'It's not her fault,' said my father. He wasn't defending me, he just liked disagreeing with my mother.

'It's not *my* fault,' my mother shouted, because it never was, not in her book. Nothing was ever her fault. Her face was puffy and swollen and smeared with mascara and self-pity. She was well on the way to becoming a parody of herself, my mother, and she was not even fifty yet.

* * *

I was tired of being brave and stoical. I was tired of living in a real-life Bette Davis picture. I felt hollow and worn out and empty, so I called Virge and asked if I could come and stay, for a couple of days.

'Please, please, please,' she said, her voice carrying strongly down the telephone line, as if she was in the next room. 'I long for you here. I would have asked, but I wasn't sure.'

'Sure of what?' I said.

'You know,' said Virge. 'I didn't know if you had plans.'

'Oh, Virge,' I said. I couldn't believe that she, of all people, might have felt shy to ask me to stay with her in case I had something better to do. 'Can I come this minute? You wouldn't believe what it's like here.'

9

There was a train at lunchtime, and I arrived in the afternoon. Virge and Michael came to meet me at the station. They looked so exotic and lovely, standing on that station platform, in the middle of all the ordinary people with their ordinary clothes and their ordinary lives. Everyone looked and stared as Virge and Michael fell on me and hugged and kissed me, and made exclamations of delight and greeting. I was glad. I wanted them to look.

Michael drove, and Virge and I squashed together in the front, and she kept her arm round me the whole way, and I told them a little about what I had left behind.

'You poor poor darling,' said Virge. 'You poor poor thing. The monsters,' she said, furiously. 'I could kill them.'

I looked at her and saw that she was really angry, shocked and affronted, as if it had happened to her. I felt weak and grateful and strange. No one had ever been angry on my behalf before.

'It's all right,' said Michael. 'You're with us now. We won't let you go back. Will we, Virge?'

'No,' said Virge, shaking her head quickly. 'You'll just stay here till term starts again. I can't even bear to think of you in that house. You're with us now.'

The light was just starting to fade when we reached the

house. We had driven through rolling open land into the hills and woods that made up the Isle of Purbeck, that mysterious ancient part of Dorset that is surrounded on three sides by sea. All I knew about Dorset was that Hardy had lived there, although Virge told me that was in quite another part, further north, near Dorchester. Later, when I looked it up on the map, I was even more surprised to find that we were so close to the sprawling seaside towns of Poole and Bournemouth. It felt miles from anywhere, a little world apart.

We drove down a rutted twisting drive, covered with an arcade of sycamore and oak, so that the light came through in random shafts, making strange patterns on the ground. I felt a curious mixture of excitement and calm. I felt as if there was something magical here. Virge's father told me later that there were many barrows nearby, ancient burial mounds, so perhaps I wasn't being so fanciful after all.

We turned a corner, dropped down into a little valley, and the house came into view.

'Oh, Virge,' I said.

She smiled, and took my hand.

'See?' she said. 'See why you had to come?'

I saw, exactly. It was the most beautiful house. Not in terms of architectural merit, or gracious lines, or pure aesthetics. It was not a Palladian folly or a baroque mansion. It was a curious sprawling mixture of parts, rickety barns and outhouses with sagging tiled roofs gathered around a little courtyard, where wild flowers grew through the flagstones, and a family of ducks sat serenely on a small pond, and then an incongruous archway with Ionian columns and classical pretensions leading to another collection of buildings which made up the house itself. There was a very ancient sloping part in dark stone, which looked as if it might be Tudor, leading onto a square upright section with battlements running round the top. This fell down to a wing in pale

Georgian stone, with french windows giving onto a terrace, which stretched out into a small lawn, bounded by a stone wall. Beyond the wall the country took over again, as if barely held back, the hills and fields and woods, and in the distance, just the faintest glimpse of the sea.

Virge and Michael, walking either side of me, their arms around my shoulders, took me into the house, through a low dim hall with dark panelling and a heavy stone fireplace and diamond pane windows, along a passage and into a high, wide room, the heart of the house, the part where I learned that they all lived. It was a storey and a half high, with a minstrel's gallery running round the top, and high curving windows, and a flagged stone floor, most of it covered in a jumble of rugs.

I looked around in wonder.

'Goodness,' I said.

'Goodness,' said Michael, 'had nothing to do with it.'

'It's eccentric, but it's home,' said Virge. 'Do you love it?'

'I love it,' I said truthfully. It was as extraordinary as the rest of the house, that room. It was a kitchen and sitting room and study all rolled into one. To the left, between two small stairways leading up to the gallery, there was a long sofa, at least twelve foot long, with a tapestry hanging behind it. Further along the far wall, which was covered with pictures, seemingly arranged without thought or artifice, there was a fireplace, with chairs and more sofas gathered round it, and tables covered in papers and books and magazines. Under the two great windows, there were long window seats, and a little further in, to our right, there was a kitchen, with an old coke-fired cooker, and pots and pans hanging from hooks, and a scrubbed kitchen table, covered in early spring bulbs just coming into flower.

'You see,' said Virge, sitting me down at the kitchen table, 'before my Pa had any money, him and Ma took in lodgers so they could keep the house, and so they lived in this part. And then, when he became rich and the lodgers left, we liked it so much, we thought we'd keep it like this. What do you think?'

'I think it's perfect,' I said. 'I wouldn't change a thing.'

'The only difficulty,' said Michael, sitting down next to me, 'is cooking. No frying allowed, because of the smell. Pa had a rush of blood to the head once and made some chips, and we all had to walk around waving incense for three days after.'

I laughed. I had a vision of them all walking around this great hall, solemn as altar boys, wafting joss sticks in the air.

'Look,' said Virge. 'She's laughing. Look, Michael.'

'She's definitely laughing,' said Michael.

'You must promise,' said Virge, very serious, 'that you will come here every holiday. You mustn't ever go back to horrible awful dreadful Maida Vale and those horrible awful parents. I never saw a face like yours when you got off the train, all white and pinched up and miserable. Please promise.'

'I promise,' I said. Virge sat back, reassured.

'Good,' she said. 'That's settled then.'

'Was it very dreadful?' said Michael.

'Yes,' I said. 'But it's all right now. Now I'm here.' And I changed the subject, because I felt uncomfortable being the focus of so much generous sympathy. I felt as if I didn't deserve it, not really. Many people had worse things to deal with, beatings and poverty and fatal diseases. Anyway, everyone got on badly with their parents, it wasn't just me. Everyone, except for Michael and Virge.

'What did your father do, to get rich?' I said. I suddenly realised that Virge had never spoken of him, not as an individual, only as one half of her perfect parents.

Virge and Michael looked at each other, a funny secret look, and laughed.

'He writes plays,' said Virge. 'And films, and things.'

I stared at her.

'Your father is Jonathan Hudson?' I said. 'Why didn't you tell me?'

'Well,' said Virge. 'We're a bit shy about it, to tell the truth.'

'Famous is a funny thing,' said Michael. They both looked at me, and then at each other, and then they laughed.

'You won't think differently of us,' said Virge. 'Now you know?'

'Of course I won't,' I said. It was exactly right, that Jonathan Hudson was their father. They deserved a father like that. It would have seemed strange and disappointing if he had been an accountant or a stockbroker, something usual and everyday.

'Except,' I said, 'won't I be intimidated?'

'Not at all,' said Virge. 'He's the least frightening man you'll ever meet, our Pa.'

'Ma is the one you have to watch, these days,' said Michael. 'She's been sculpting in obscurity for the past twenty years, quite happily, and now she is being made fashionable. Everyone wants one, all of a sudden. We're watching very carefully to see if it goes to her head.'

A door slammed, and Virge's mother walked into the room.

'Is this Ash?' she said. 'I'm Diana. You poor thing,' she added, coming over to me and kissing my cheek. 'We're so glad you came. Have you had some tea?'

'Ma,' said Virge reproachfully, 'Ash can't drink tea. She's allergic.'

'Coffee, then,' said Diana, 'and there's cake. Your father made it this morning.'

Virge gave me a look.

'Pa loves to bake,' she said.

We ate tea on the terrace. It was a clear still afternoon, the only sound the faint call of the pigeons in the woods. I watched Diana Hudson, curious to see which parts of her she had given to her children. She held herself like they did, graceful and upright, and she had the same fine open face. She wore her age easily, as if she saw no reason to fear or fight it. Her face was lined, and her hair was turning grey, but she had the same beauty that they did, that kind of beauty which is less to do with perfect features and high bone structure than expression and movement.

Watching her, sitting in front of her strange and lovely house, as the sun moved lower in the sky, casting a gentle diffused light over the distant trees and hills, I thought that there was something reassuring about her. She had the look of someone who is in the right place, who has found what they wanted, where they belong, and is clever enough to realise their own luck.

'Come and look at the roses,' she said to me, after tea was finished. Virge and Michael took the plates and cups away to the kitchen, and I followed Diana round to the other side of the house, where there was a sheltered south-facing walled garden, filled with rose bushes. Most of them were not in flower yet, but there were a few early blooms, defying the season.

'Aren't they brave?' Diana said. 'I love these early flowering ones.' She looked round her garden for a moment, smiling. 'Originally I wanted to make a formal rose garden,' she said. 'When I was younger. I had a grand plan, box hedges, and topiary, but in the end I just planted them anyhow. I think it's better this way.'

'It's lovely,' I said. 'It's all lovely. It's the nicest house I've ever seen.'

'I'm glad you think so,' said Diana.

'It's very kind of you to have me,' I said. 'I hope it's no trouble.'

'Dear Ash,' said Diana, 'of course it isn't. It's a pleasure for us. See how big the house is, what a waste, all those bedrooms, empty. Jonathan and I don't care much for what people call entertaining. It's much more fun for us having Virge and Michael's friends than our own. The young,' she said, with delicate irony, 'don't need so much looking after. When people are fifty they are so faddish and set in their ways. You have to get in special kinds of tea and make sure that dinner is at a reasonable hour. You know how it is.'

I didn't, but I nodded anyway. We sat on a bench, set to catch the last of the sun. Diana lit herself a cigarette. I liked the way she smoked it, as if she was savouring the taste, not just puffing at another gasper.

'You mustn't feel guilty,' she said. 'About your parents. You mustn't blame yourself. Families are strange and mysterious things.'

I wondered how she knew. I wondered if it was her, or whether it was part of the wisdom that age was supposed to bring.

'I do though,' I said. 'As if it's my fault. How did you know that?'

Diana smiled gently. 'It's the way of the world,' she said. 'People who don't know say that Jonathan and I have become reclusive, because we don't go out in society. I was very much part of what people call the world, when I was younger, and I saw enough of it. It doesn't mean that all I think about is roses and greenfly.'

'My parents are in the world,' I said, thinking about this. 'And they don't know anything. They don't understand anything. I wish I could love them, but I can't find anything to love.'

'There's nothing to feel guilty about in that,' said Diana. 'It's entirely natural.'

'But it doesn't feel natural,' I said. 'It feels as if there's something I'm doing wrong. That I should try harder, or not make such a fuss, or something.'

Diana finished smoking her cigarette. She sat beside me, listening, calm and still. I liked that. I liked it that she didn't make a big reaction, gasp or stretch her eyes or seem horrified. It made it easier. I wondered that I was telling her this, as if I had known her for years, as if she was a trusted confidante, but then it wasn't so very strange, because she had the same trick that Virge did, of making you feel that you had known her for ever, and that whatever you said, it wouldn't be the wrong thing.

'I wish terrible things sometimes,' I said. 'That they would die in a car crash or something, so I could be a proper orphan, something that deserves some sympathy. But all it is is that they're not very good at being parents, and it's not such a very bad thing, millions of people have much worse.'

'Plenty of people have much better,' said Diana. 'Sometimes it's the small things that are hardest to bear. Unhappiness is not a relative thing. Saying to yourself, at least I haven't suffered something really bad, something big, like death or destitution, doesn't make it any better.'

'I do that,' I said. 'All the time. I think because I'm not living in a cardboard box, or as a political prisoner, being tortured or something, it can't be so bad.'

'It can,' said Diana. 'Because it's happening to you.'

'I want to punish them,' I said. 'For being so mad and drunk and awful. I want to hurt them, but I never dare say anything. I just turn silent, or I run away.'

Diana turned to look at me. She took my hand and held it in both of hers.

'This isn't running away,' she said. 'You know what they say, about living well being the best revenge? Well, you can just stay here and live well.'

I thought about what Diana said that day often, afterwards. She hadn't said a word about forgiveness or acceptance, because she knew it was too early for that. It was many years before I could forgive my mother and father, before I could understand why they were the way they were, and learn to have compassion for them. Sitting then, in that garden, I couldn't begin to think about forgiveness. I blamed them terribly, because I couldn't understand why they couldn't be like other parents, like parents are supposed to be. I couldn't understand why they couldn't change.

But what got me through was that idea, of living well. I clung to it, like a solid plank of wood in a stormy sea, in the times that came after. It became my mission, to live well. It raised me up, stopped me falling into the dark pit of self-pity and victimhood. I didn't have to suffer with all the impotent resentments and furies that I had carried with me for so long. I had an alternative. I could live well, and have my revenge.

10

By the end of the first week, I felt completely at home. I had been put in a little turret room above the main hall. It was old-fashioned, with wallpaper covered in cottage roses and a brass bed with a blue silk eiderdown, and a small square window looking out over the country, and a bookcase filled with interesting books – Molly Keane's early novels, and Muriel Spark, and Doris Lessing, and Djuna Barnes.

'We thought you'd like it best,' said Virge. 'Instead of the grand rooms.'

She showed me the rest of the house. There were grand bedrooms, with huge carved beds and heavy wall hangings and French pieces of furniture, and she was right, they would have been too much for me, just then. I felt safe and secure and happy in my little turret, and after that it became my room. They even said that, Ash's room, they called it, and every time I heard that it gave me a good warm feeling inside, a sense of belonging.

Although I loved Diana, it was Virge's father that I adored most. She was right, he wasn't frightening at all. He carried his cleverness lightly, and his success lighter still. He was one of those ones that if you hadn't been told you would never have guessed. I had half expected that he might sit around talking about Marlowe and Racine, but he didn't.

He woke very early, and worked from six until eleven

every morning, and then he came out of his study and spent the day wandering around the house, smoking and drinking black coffee. He liked cooking, unlikely things like bread, and fruit cake, and strange new recipes of his own design. He spent much time in the greenhouse, growing plants and flowers from seed, and he had a passion for trees. Saplings were always arriving from the strangest places, like Korea, new hybrid breeds, which he planted with great ceremony and watched over tenderly, seeing if they would take so far from their native soil. He had a mania for country and western music: he had catalogues delivered by post, and he would pore over them and select new albums which were sent down from London. Every time one arrived, we would all gather round the record player and listen to it, as solemn as if it were Mahler or Rimsky Korsakoff.

At three, he would go back into his study, and review his morning's work, and at seven-thirty he would turn on the television and watch *Coronation Street*, which was his favourite programme. I was really amazed by that. I would have expected him to be a strict BBC2 man, *The Late Show*, and obscure documentaries about Russian dissidents, that kind of thing. The idea of the venerable playwright sitting down to watch life on the street surprised me.

'I'm a populist, Ash,' he told me, many times over the years I knew him. It was one of his big themes. 'I hate the idea that great art must be the province of the small educated elite,' he said, over and over. It was a subject on which he was passionate. It was one of the things I liked in him, that passion, which he carried into all areas of his life, whether it was his country and western records or his trees or his work.

'Think of it,' he told me. 'In his day, Shakespeare was for the ordinary people. Now the educated middle class have erected a barrier of mystery around him, as if he is something that only the highbrow can appreciate. But that's the whole point, the reason we still go and see him is that he writes about all the universal human themes, not just the great elevated ones, the everyday ones, petty jealousies, greed, envy, foolishness, misunderstandings. Just because it's written as poetry doesn't mean that everyone can't understand it.'

And on other occasions, over dinner, or lunch, warming to his theme, 'Think of the classic novels – Dickens was serialised in magazines, an episode a week, making it up as he went along, hurrying to fill the next instalment. There's an idea now that a literary novel must somehow be difficult, inaccessible, that obfuscation indicates cleverness. Now think, Ash.' He always said that – now think – not just as a manner of speech, but something he really meant. That was what he wanted, was for us all to think, not just sit at the feet of received ideas. 'The classic novels are not difficult, they're good stories. They last because we still want to turn the page, to see what happens next. That's what a story should be, at its simplest, an invitation to see what happens next, not a form of oneupmanship. Do you see?'

He always said that too – Do you see, Ash, do you see? – as if he really minded what I might think, what I might see. He was a tall man, and ill-coordinated in his movements, and his way of dressing made his family laugh. He had no thought for clothes and wore strange clashing colours and often odd socks, sometimes with a trouser leg tucked into one, because he had forgotten to take it out. When he talked, he shook his head and moved his hands quickly to mark a point, and many times we had to rescue a glass or a bottle in danger of being sent flying across the room.

'Do you see, Ash,' he would say. 'That intellectual snobbism is the worst of all? Why should a writer spend his time producing something only for people who live in

Islington?' Islington was his word for the self-consciously intellectual urban middle class, the kind who do sit around talking about Marlowe and Racine and would die rather than watch *Coronation Street*.

'But,' I said to him one time, 'all those Islington people love and worship you.'

'Ah, yes,' he said, giving me a sharp and mischievous look from under his eyebrows, 'but that's because I have somehow managed to find the art of playing to the stalls and the gallery at the same time. If they want to read many deep and hidden meanings and subtexts into my simple plays, who am I to tell them different?'

'But excuse me,' I said. 'What about your principles?' I had quickly fallen into the same teasing way of talking to him that Virge and Michael used, although sometimes I wondered at my daring.

'But don't you see, Ash?' he said. 'Infiltrating the enemy ranks. Revolution can only come from within. Look at the French.'

'No,' said Virge, coming in from the garden. 'Will you two just stop for a minute? We can't possibly look at the French, because we'll have another three hours of Napoleon, and Gus is coming and he doesn't know anything about history.'

'Gus,' said Jonathan, getting up and putting the kettle on. 'Now there is a purist. Can Ash and I have another cup of coffee and a cigarette and a quick diversion on the return from Elba before he arrives, or is that not allowed?'

Virge smiled at us and looked at her watch.

'Not,' she said. 'Ma went to get him from the station. They'll be here any moment. Get out the Crown Derby, Pa, and some of that cake. You know how Gus likes eating his cake.'

'Don't we all?' said Jonathan.

He put his arm about Virge's shoulders and gave her a

little squeeze. She smiled up at him, her face very close to his, and rubbed the back of her hand against his cheek, and they stood like that for a moment. I had to look away. I wasn't jealous, not really, but sometimes it gave me a turn, seeing them together. I had no memory of being touched by either of my parents. Even looking back right into my early childhood, I had no memories at all of being held.

The spring weather stayed sweet. Gus, Michael, Virge and I spent many afternoons sitting on the beach at Studland Bay, or Lulworth Cove, getting the sun on our face and watching the sea, and talking. The seaside out of season still gives me a sharp pull of nostalgia for those times.

We liked Lulworth best, because it had such a history, of smugglers and invasion scares and Rupert Brooke, and Bertrand Russell bringing all his friends there to swim naked and shock the locals.

The beach was made of heavy dusty white stones, smoothed and polished by the sea, and the cliffs curved round it in a tender embrace, so that the water in the cove lay flat and still, protected from the rough sea beyond. The fishing boats were those old-fashioned wooden ones, painted in bright colours, very Italian, we thought, entirely continental, and most times we were the only people there, except for a man who sometimes sat on the jetty mending nets, and sending burning glances over at Virge. He looked very strong and brown and weatherbeaten and handsome, and sometimes he took his shirt off, and Virge shot him naughty little looks of admiration and Gus told her to stop leading him on.

'Why can't I lead him on?' she said. 'He's leading me on.'

'Because,' said Michael, 'you are in love with Keane and it's not fair.'

'I love the way you talk about fair, with your proclivities,' said Virge, pretending indignance.

Michael talked a great deal about going down the Dilly and committing unspeakable acts, but in fact he was a true romantic, his vaunted promiscuity all talk. What he really wanted was to fall in love and live happily ever after.

'Anyway,' said Virge. 'Who says I'm in love with Keane?'

'Aren't you?' I said. Virge hovered close to the telephone every night at six o'clock, impatient, and when it rang she picked it up and sounded surprised when it was Keane, calling from New York, and then took it in the other room. Taking it in the other room sounded like love to me, but then what did I know?

'I might be,' said Virge. 'And then again, I might not.'

'See,' said Gus. 'She wants to be all mysterious and languorous and Bloomsburyite and Otteline Morrell and keep us guessing.'

'Excuse me,' said Virge merrily. She loved it when the joke was on her. 'It's not me that's keeping anyone guessing, thank you very much, Gus. What was the sex of the last person you had sex with?'

Gus lay back on the beach, stretching his legs out and putting an arm across his forehead as if to shield his eyes from the sun.

'I haven't had sex,' he said, 'actually.'

'Ever?' I said. I was surprised. He spoke of his indecision with such authority that I had presumed that he must have experimented, that he must be talking from experience.

'Gus,' said Virge, laughing with incredulity. 'You mean you've been a virgin all this time and you never told me?'

'It's such a dull thing to be,' said Gus. 'I didn't know how to put it.'

'So you've never done it at all, with anyone?' said Virge. 'Not even fiddling?'

'Virge,' I said. 'Please.'

'Sorry,' said Virge. 'I was trying not to be vulgar.'

'I'd give it up as a bad job,' said Michael.

'Well,' said Gus. 'I haven't and that's all. It's all in my mind. In my mind, I'm the biggest slut on the planet.'

'You *are* a purist,' I said, remembering what Jonathan had said.

'All mouth and trousers, more like,' said Virge. 'All that talk. You should take the plunge soon,' she said seriously, 'otherwise you'll just go on thinking about it and thinking about it and then you'll become paralysed by thought and you'll never do it at all and one day you'll wake up and you'll be seventy and you'll never know what it's like.'

'What is it like?' said Gus.

'Shall we tell him?' said Michael to Virge and I. 'Or shall we keep him in suspense?'

'I don't know if I could say, anyway,' I said. My only affair had been not at all what I'd expected. I had hoped for something smooth and swoony and instinctive, but really it had been more awkward and embarrassing and not knowing what to do with your hands. I didn't want to admit that, in case it was different for others, and it was just my pitiful lack of experience.

'I think we should keep him guessing,' said Virge. 'Anyway, if we tell him it's dreamy and ecstatic and an out of body experience he's bound to pick someone dreadful and it will be sad and hopeless and then he'll ask for his money back.'

'You can do it without being in love, Gus,' said Michael. 'You don't have to save it for the one and only. You can just go ahead and do it and then you'll know.'

Gus sat up again, and stared out over the sea, which was stirring a little in the wind. Virge leaned against him, and put her arm round his neck.

'Darling Gus,' she said. 'It doesn't matter. We're not even twenty yet. And we won't tell anyone.'

*   *   *

Not even twenty yet. Looking back, it seems unimaginably young. It seemed to me that we never felt as young as we were. Even though I felt a lack of sophistication and worldly wisdom compared to Virge, I didn't feel like a child. I regarded all of us as adult, it was just some were more grown up than others. It was only later, when I did grow up and understand a little more about the way things worked that I started to feel young. It's funny – when you are nineteen you feel as if you are thirty and you want everyone to know, and when you are heading towards thirty, you feel like you are seventeen and you hope no one will notice.

The summer term was the best of everything. Virge and I went around wearing our matching summer wardrobe of flirty little printed dresses and impenetrable black Jackie O sunglasses, which we thought the last word in sophistication.

There were parties all day and every day: picnics by the river, and punting parties, and those lazy summer parties which start in someone's room for no particular reason and just go on until bedtime. On Sundays we would drive out to a pub outside of town and sit in the garden and drink Pimms. We ate strawberries and drank champagne, and did all those things that undergraduates aren't supposed to do any more, and we knew it was clichéd, but we didn't care, because we were having such a fine time.

And the other really good thing about that term was that I fell in love.

Virge and Gus came to collect me one Saturday morning.

'What are you doing, still in bed at this hour?' said Virge, climbing in the window.

'Sleeping,' I said, with dignity. Stretch and Denny had given a party the night before, which meant getting in a lot of rum and putting Tommy McCook and the Supersonics very loud on the stereo and letting everyone get on with it.

The porters had tried to close it down three times, and then given it up as a bad job. They couldn't resist Denny and Stretch any more than anyone else, and they couldn't bear getting strict when it made Stretch look so sad and crushed. There was a rule that more than eight people in a room constituted a party, and to do that you had to go and get permission from the senior censor, which was a bit of a business, so we usually didn't bother, just played it on the wing and hoped for the best.

So when the head porter arrived and saw at least twenty people in the room, he had started to count, but when he got to eight, Stretch started to look so melancholy and pitiful that he had stopped.

'Eight,' he said, staring hard at the twenty of us. 'Well, I suppose that's all right. As long as it's only eight. And you could turn the music down, a bit.'

So we had carried on until late, and I was tired, this morning.

Virge, who had a trick of catching three hours sleep and getting up looking as if she had just come back from a long restorative sea cruise, wasn't having any of it.

'Come on,' she said. 'The grass is high and the sap is rising. It's June, June, it's come too soon. We're going punting. Look at Gus's hat.'

Gus was wearing a panama hat, which really wasn't him at all.

'Isn't it unexpected?' said Virge, laughing.

We drove down to the boathouse. It was deserted, still too early for the crowds, all the punts lined up in neat rows, rocking gently on the water.

'Come on,' said Virge. She was excited and impatient,

looking at her watch, as if there was some deadline for her to meet. 'Come on.'

Gus took the pole, and guided us out into the water.

'Isn't he good?' said Virge. 'Watch his wrist action.'

'I'm a natural,' said Gus, giving her a look. 'Don't let anyone tell you different.'

We slid slowly up the backwaters. It was cool and dark there, the trees shading the river from the sun. I had never been in a punt before. It was so smooth and silent, only the faintest splash of water from the pole. Gus moved rhythmically, a practised hand, and Virge and I lay back and sent him admiring glances and watched the heavy green of the trees drift by over our heads.

'Here,' said Virge, suddenly. She pointed, and Gus and she gave each other a secret look. Gus turned the punt across to the far bank, and as we reached it, a boy I had never seen before came through the bushes and slid down the bank and got into the punt, which rocked a little. He sat himself down on the bench opposite Virge and I, and Gus cast off again, and pushed us out into the deep water.

'Timing,' said Virge.

She turned to me and gave a wicked smile. I was so surprised by the whole thing that I was still a step behind.

'Say hello,' she told me. 'This is Hem. Hem, say hello to Ash.'

'Hello, Ash,' the boy said.

Then Virge made everything clear.

'His real name is Peter Hemingway,' she said. She started laughing so much she almost fell out of the boat.

'Careful,' said Gus, above us, steadying himself.

'But everyone calls him Hem,' said Virge, stuttering with laughter.

Hem smiled quietly to himself, unmoved. I wasn't sure if he knew the joke, if Virge had told him, or whether he had that kind of self-containment that doesn't mind unexplained laughter.

'No relation,' he said. He had a low steady voice, with a faint smoker's rasp. I liked it. 'Which is just as well,' he added. 'Bad blood.'

'I long for bad blood,' said Virge, with an inconsequential air she took sometimes. 'Don't you?' she said to me. She was laughing again. She was enjoying herself vastly, I could see.

'No,' I said, truthfully. 'I have plenty to be going on with, thank you so much.'

'Ash has psychotic parents,' Virge told Hem, in a conversational way. 'What can you do? Luckily we think it skipped a generation, with her.'

Hem looked straight at me for a while, as if considering. He had muddy green eyes, the same colour as the river, and sallow skin, and very black hair. I thought he looked like a bandit. Then he smiled, and suddenly I forgot all about Albert, and smiled back, without quite meaning to, and Virge saw it and started laughing again, and I looked away.

We stopped for lunch in a hidden corner of the river, behind a curtain of weeping willow which fell right down to the water. Virge had brought a basket with cheese and salami and tomatoes and bread, and we ate and drank red wine, and smoked cigarettes. Hem smoked Gitanes, which I thought beyond perfect. I aspired to French cigarettes, with all their intimations of sex and Rive Gauche and Jean Paul Belmondo, but I couldn't pull it off – they caught at the back of my throat and made me cough, which ruined the effect. Hem seemed to have the trick perfectly, puffing away like a native.

Virge, having had her little joke, was behaving perfectly, making polite conversation and acting as if nothing were out of the ordinary. I didn't care anyway. I was having one of those moments of revelation, the kind that you watch in films, when it seems as if everything has gone into slow motion, when the world goes out of focus, and the only thing sharp and defined is the face in front of you.

After a while, Virge and Gus packed up the lunch basket and we set off again. Hem sat himself next to me, so that his leg touched mine. I stared at it for a while. I was vaguely aware that we were moving, the trees and water and sky drifting past. I could hear Gus saying something, and Virge laughing. Then we came out onto the Isis itself, the main river. It gave me a shock – it was so wide and light, and there were other boats, and the rowers out practising, and I shook my head a little and sat up and looked about.

'There's Ed,' said Virge, pointing at a boy we knew. 'Rowing. Watch those muscles ripple. Look at those pecs, would you please?'

She stood up in the punt, balancing precariously, and waved. 'Ed,' she shouted. 'It's us. Look, Gus,' she added. 'It's Steady Eddy.'

Gus started to laugh, and he and Virge started chanting 'Steady, Eddy,' over and over, and Ed, who was known to take his rowing very seriously, tried to ignore them, and they shouted louder and louder, and laughed more and more, and then, quite without warning, they both overbalanced and fell into the river.

'Well,' said Hem, looking at me.

The punt drifted serenely on, rudderless. Behind us, Virge and Gus surfaced, spluttering and laughing. Gus was still holding onto the pole.

'You brutes,' called Virge, after us. 'You might have stopped.'

'What should we do?' I said, concerned. Hem gave a tugging smile.

'There's nothing we can do,' he said. 'We'll have to

follow the river until it stops.' He seemed pleased by the idea.

'Where does it go to?' I said.

'I don't know,' he said. 'Stratford, maybe?'

I started to laugh, and suddenly I didn't mind at all, because I was with him, and we could just sit back and see what might happen.

After a while, the punt drifted into shore, not very far from Christ Church.

'Perfect,' said Hem, getting out and tying it up.

'What shall we do?' I said again. 'We should take it back to the boathouse.'

'Tomorrow,' said Hem. 'Gus can collect it. He has the pole.'

I almost started to protest. I almost said that we couldn't just leave it here, that it might be stolen, that we would have to pay extra, but then he took my hand, and I stopped worrying about boring practical things, and thought that if he could just let it go, so could I.

We walked for a while, not saying much. The sun was starting to go down, and the light took on that thick blue aspect that it sometimes did on summer evenings. I looked down and realised that Hem was still holding my hand.

'Where do you live?' he said.

I looked across at him. 'Peck,' I said. 'On the ground floor.'

'Can I come back with you?' he said.

So when Gus and Virge climbed in my window the next morning, they found the two of us there, lying in my bed, the sheets all twisted about us.

Virge didn't miss a beat.

'Where did you leave the punt?' she said.

'I've got the pole,' said Gus, pulling it in the window behind him.

'Hello, Hem,' said Virge.

'It's by the bridge,' I said.

'Hello, Virge,' said Hem. 'Gus.'

'I'll make coffee then,' said Gus.

Virge settled herself on the end of the bed, and regarded Hem and me with her clear eyes.

'We got terribly wet,' she said. 'But it was worth it just to annoy that serious rowing boy. Gus thinks he's coming down with diphtheria, but I told him nobody has that any more. Not these days. Not in this day and age. I told him that all that went out with empire waistlines and cupping and the workhouse.'

Gus brought us some coffee, and we drank it, and Denny and Stretch came and poked their heads in the window, and took a good long look at Hem, and said they were going to the covered market to shop for coffee beans and taramasalata because they were out.

Hem seemed to take it all in his stride. I thought about offering an explanation, telling him that this happened most mornings, that it wasn't that he was the floor show, but he didn't seem to mind, so I just let it ride.

After a while, Virge and Gus left to get the punt.

'The poor man at the boathouse,' said Virge. 'Do you think he's sat up all night, like a father whose teen angel has gone out on her first date?'

'No,' said Gus. 'I don't.'

After they had gone, Hem looked at me, and started to laugh.

'Is it always going to be like this?' he said.

I wondered about always. He hadn't said anything, about what all this was. I hadn't either. And now he said, Will it always be like this, so I thought perhaps I could suppose that it was something, that it might be something.

'I don't know,' I said. 'Yes,' I said. 'Maybe,' I said.

Hem nodded, and looked at me, and I felt my heart turn over, and I blessed Virge, for making her secret plan.

This is what I learnt from Hem: that there are some things which don't have to be spoken and some questions which don't have to be answered. I didn't learn this at the time, the time we were together, it was only in retrospect, when I looked back, that I remembered and understood, but they were valuable lessons, all the same.

He was a curious boy. He had a habit of taking each moment as it came, which at first I found strange and disconcerting. I thought of the future, and the past, but he just thought of the present, which was a trick that not many people had. He was a gypsy too: my first impression, that he looked like a bandit, wasn't so far off the mark. He had an appetite for danger and the unexpected, and he wanted things, but he didn't know what they were, he was searching for some unnamed goal. He said he wouldn't know what it was until he got there. He became a photographer, later, and he went all around the world, taking pictures, for which he acquired a small fame, and he sent me postcards, and they all said, NOT HERE, written in heavy black capitals, and I knew that he was still looking.

But that was later. Just then, he was only in search of knowledge, his restlessness still cerebral rather than physical, so he was happy to stay where he was, in Oxford, which he liked, and with me, which he liked as well.

That first day we went for a walk, wandering round the meadows, through the high grass, and along the wide path which ran beside the river, and he told me some things about himself, and asked me some things about myself, and kissed me, and I was perfectly happy, because I knew I was in love, for the first time.

'Isn't that lovely?' said Virge. 'We can double date.'

We were sitting in her room, later that afternoon. Hem had gone back to Oriel, where he lived, because he had an essay to write. I missed him already.

'How did you know?' I said.

Virge gave me a wise old look, and shook her head.

'Easy,' she said. 'It was the name that got me thinking. I met him with The Poet, you know. They're friends, sort of.'

Virge had started calling Keane The Poet the week before. She said that he had written a poem for her. She said it was very mysterious and oblique and strange, and she didn't know if it was good or bad, but it showed some curious undertones, or overtones, she wasn't sure about that either. Whatever it was, he was The Poet from then on.

'Hem's a romantic,' she said. 'Like you. And I got to thinking. So I told him to meet us by the river.'

'It was a bold plan,' I said. 'What if it didn't work? What if he didn't like me?'

'I knew he would,' said Virge, placidly. 'The Poet says he makes up his mind quickly. He's not a philosopher, not like Stretch.'

She paused for a moment, and smiled at me. 'It's your birthday next week,' she said. 'I wanted to make sure you had a nice present.'

'Thank you,' I said. I looked at her, and smiled right back. 'He's the best present I ever had,' I said.

12

Sometimes, I look back and think that summer in Oxford was the most perfect time of my life. To be in love, in the summer, in that beautiful city, was like living in a dream. I had two loves, just to make it better – I had Hem, and Virge. I couldn't have asked for anything more.

The weather held, sunshine day after day, glancing down on the yellow stones, so that they gleamed and glowed. Oxford was made for fine weather. In the winter, when it rained, it could seem dark and oppressive. It was built on a bog, like London, and it had the same damp quality, that way of hugging the wet weather to it, so the chill grows into your bones, never quite leaving you, however many clothes you wear. But in the summer, in the sun, it came alive, its beauty sleepy and benign and reassuring, this wide golden city.

On Sunday mornings, Hem, Virge and I would get up early and walk down the deserted high street to a bakery we knew which opened at eight, and made bread just like the kind you got in Paris. It was a time when we felt the city really did belong to us, too early for the tourists in their coaches, with their cameras and their thirst for genuine antiquity. As the sun came up over Magdalen tower, the pavements blue with shadow, the air still and cool, we would walk gaily past the cupola of

Queen's, and the stern battlements of University College, and buy our bread, still warm from the oven, and take it back to my room, and sit in the sun that came in through the windows and eat it with jam and coffee. I loved those Sunday mornings, when it was just us, walking through the empty streets, arm in arm, leaning into one another like drunken sailors, wandering through the beginnings of the day.

Virge never brought Keane for those breakfasts. She had a strange thing about Keane; she kept him in another part of her life. She always visited him in his rooms at New College, rather than letting him come to her.

He lived in the most ancient part of the college, in a tower room where the walls were four foot thick, built to repel invaders. Sometimes, Virge and I would go and walk in the gardens on Sunday evenings, where it was very quiet and still, and we could hear the faint lilt of the choir singing evensong, and the distant tolling of church bells from across the city, that city of a hundred spires. Afterwards, we would go up and pay Keane a visit. He was always lying on his bed, reading, when we arrived. He read such strange books – Anaïs Nin, and De Quincy, and Shelley, and Keith Thomas on witchcraft and the medieval world.

I never felt quite comfortable with him, those times. He had a way of looking at you and not saying much, as if he was thinking one thing and telling another. He just lay there, raised up on his elbows, watching us with his startling eyes. I found him difficult and enigmatic; I never knew what to say to him, or how to act. He made me feel my shyness, which was something I despised in myself. With Virge, I was learning to overcome it, to leave it behind me, but with Keane, it came back as if it had never gone away, and I remembered all those helpless hopeless feelings, and I slid back into the shallow pit of my own inadequacy, and didn't have the energy to pull myself out.

Virge basked in it, this strangeness.

'He has dark secrets,' she told me, often. 'He has a strange and sinister life.' She liked that, revelled in it, although she never told me what the dark secrets were, and I didn't ask.

I asked Hem, once. I remembered what Virge had said, that he and Keane were friends, sort of.

'What does sort of mean?' I said. It was a Sunday, and Virge wasn't with us, for once. She had gone away with Keane, to London, for a party.

Hem looked at me. He didn't ask what I meant. One of the things I loved in him was that he always knew what I meant.

'We've known each other for a long time,' he said. 'We were in school together. We did lessons together, and the same sports. I did archery and fencing, because I didn't like cricket or rugby, but I think Keane did them because he wanted people to notice that he was different.'

He paused, and lit one of his French cigarettes. The Sunday papers were scattered all over the floor, surrounding him. I watched him, thinking how lovely and young and Bohemian he looked, in his white T-shirt and his black trousers and his tatty old gym shoes, sitting in a little pool of black and white print. I thought he looked like a photograph.

'So, you see,' he said, 'we've had a lot of years together, but I can't say that we're friends, not really. I don't know him, at all.'

'No one does,' I said, thinking of Stevie, who was still on the case, investigating. She regarded it as some kind of quest now, a matter of honour, but despite it all she still came up with nothing. No one knew anything about him, and his secrets, except for Virge, and she wasn't telling.

'I think he's a phoney,' said Hem, with sudden conviction. 'Do you remember that part in *Breakfast at Tiffany's*?

When the little fat man says to George Peppard, "So what do you think of the kid, is she or isn't she?" And George says, "Is she what?" and the fat man says, "A phoney." And then he says, "Well, I'll tell you, she is and she isn't: she is a phoney, but she's a real phoney, because she really believes all this cockamamy shit that she believes." Or something like that.'

I nodded, smiling. I liked it when Hem did this. He went to the pictures often, and when he liked a film he would watch it over and over, until he knew half the scenes off by heart. He said that films were a guide for life, that the good true ones reflected little slivers of universal truth, that we could learn from. Hem was a modernist, and a populist, a little like Virge's father. He was studying English, and he had enough respect for all those venerable old poets and playwrights he read, but he said that it wasn't set in stone. Nothing is set in stone, he said, often.

'Do you think Virge is a phoney?' I said.

Hem shook his head.

'Oh, no,' he said. 'She just doesn't have much to do with the real world. She likes making up her own version. But she's not a phoney.'

'Perhaps that's why I love her so much,' I said. 'Because of that world that she makes up.'

'I expect,' said Hem. He looked at me strangely for a moment, as if considering. 'But you, you are a creature of the real world, even if you think you don't like it very much.'

'How do you know?' I said, curious. I didn't know what I was, yet. I hoped one day I might find out. I was still casting about, wondering who I was going to be.

'I know,' said Hem.

'Is that why I love you so much?' I said.

Hem laughed. 'You love me because I smoke French cigarettes and I'm good at sex,' he said.

'Ha,' I said. 'So that's what it is. And why do you love me?' I said. There was a way he had, of making me brave.

Hem smiled at me, and threw open his arms. 'I don't know why I love you but I do,' he said. Then he looked at me very seriously. 'You are my first great love,' he said. 'Whatever happens, you will always remember that, won't you?'

I looked back at him, into his long green eyes.

'Yes,' I said. 'I will remember.'

My little band adopted Hem quickly. I wondered sometimes what it was that made them decide, but whatever it was, they gave him the once over and decided he would do. In his turn, he liked them. He said they made him laugh. So we went everywhere together, for those long lazy summer days, through those golden sunlit days – Gus, and Stretch and Denny, and Stevie and Etta, and Virge, and me and Hem, always together.

We found strange libraries to do our work in; Duke Humphrey's, which was an ancient part of the Bodleian, with dark panelling and diamond pane windows and strange hidden corners, and the Codrington, which belonged to All Souls, and was high and long and had a paved black and white floor and a serious hushed air and high arched windows and a huge stone statue just stuck in the middle for no particular reason that anyone could see.

We went on punting expeditions, and walked through the botanical gardens, and spent a lot of time idling in the meadows, laughing at the rowers.

Virge never brought Keane, and in the end we stopped asking. Michael joined us sometimes, but he was busy with finals, and even he, for all his eccentricity and je ne sais quoi, held that strained look of three years of work to memorise.

We went to meet him from his final exam, and he came out, still managing to look better than everyone else in his long gown, and we sprayed him with bottles of cheap champagne – 'Nothing more potent than cheap champagne,' he said, managing to get a bottle by the neck and tip some of it down his throat – and then we all went to celebrate.

In the last days of term we went to the May balls. We dolled ourselves up in long dresses and the boys wore white tie and everyone looked lovely, and we wandered through the quads of the great colleges, usually so stately and hushed, now all lit up and full of people and music and hurdy gurdys and carousels and rock bands. After the last one, Hem and Virge and I walked back to Christ Church through the dawn. We had lost Gus.

'Let's go and find him and have breakfast,' said Virge, who never wanted to go to bed, in those days.

So we crossed Peck, and went through the arch into Tom, the main quad, the biggest in Oxford, where long yellow stone pavements ran around the sunken quarters of the quadrangle itself, centred on a fountain, with a small statue of Mercury poised over it. It was empty, the sun just starting to touch the crenellated tops of the thick old walls. Then, over in the far corner, we saw another reveller, a tall straight boy in his white tie and tails, shoes in hand, walking silently towards us in his stockinged feet.

'Ah,' said Virge, stopping for a moment. 'Now that's a sight for you. A mysterious stranger, sharing our dawn.'

We nodded to each other as he passed by, and then we carried on walking towards the Meadows buildings to find Gus, and breakfast.

'Do you think,' said Virge, 'that we'll run into that boy again when we're all old and bent and grey, and we still won't know who he is or what his name is, but we'll remember his face, and it will remind us of this early morning, when we were young?'

'Oh, Virge,' said Hem, putting his arm around her shoulders. 'You will always be young, however old you get.'

A week later, Virge and I gave a farewell party, to mark the end of term. We held it in the cathedral gardens, the long smooth stretch of lawn which ran beside the high dark walls of Christ Church cathedral. It was to say goodbye: to Michael, who was going down for good, and the other third years we knew slightly, and also to each other.

Stevie and Etta were going to spend the summer on a tour of the Greek islands, ('It is a pity that Etta isn't really a lesbian,' said Stevie. 'It would be so appropriate.') Stretch and Denny were going across America on a Harley Davidson, going to get their kicks on Route 66. They were much taken with all things American at that time, especially the new brat pack novelists, although they had found reading *Less than Zero* such a traumatic experience that they had kept their shutters closed for a full three days afterwards, unable to face the light of day.

Virge and Hem and Gus and I were going on a driving tour of France and Italy, all the way down to the south, where Hem's parents had a house. (Hem's father had made a ton of money in the mail-order business, and the one thing he believed in spending it on was property.) We were to meet Keane in Rome. Virge had thought up the plan. She said she liked it because it sounded like the old days, and anyway she liked telling people that we were off to the south.

'The deep south,' she said, over and over. 'Just listen to how it sounds. Bandit country. It must be right.'

Virge and I had been to a rerun of *Funny Face* at the picture house in Jericho the week before, and she had been so inspired by the Think Pink episode, the part where the fashion editor based, we supposed, on Diana Vreeland, but without the nose, had decided that everything was to be pink – bury the beige, burn the black, bury the blue – Think Pink.

'We'll have a pink party,' said Virge, as we walked back along St Giles. 'Pink, why not?'

'Why not?' I said.

The trees were full in the sun, and the streets were crowded, everyone out and about, freed from libraries and essays and tutorials, since it was the end of term, and time to have fun, the last giddy whirl before everyone went down and left the town ghostly and empty for the long vacation.

We stopped off at the Ashmolean, and went to have a look at the classical statues. It was one of Virge's favourite places: she never regarded it as the august museum that it was, more a kind of corner shop that she would drop into any time she was passing. Right at the front, there was a long high white room filled with monumental pieces of antiquity, old pillars and plinths and vast heroic statues. Virge liked to walk through it, and have a good look, as if to check that they were all still in the right place.

'Pink,' she said, looking up at a thoughtful Artemis. 'Won't it be just the thing? And it goes with my hair.'

So we made pink drinks, out of vodka and cochineal, and wore pink dresses and pink lipstick, and I put a pink rinse in my hair so it went a kind of sheeny strawberry blonde, very fetching, I thought, although it made Hem laugh, he wouldn't say why.

Everyone joined in the spirit of the thing. Stevie came in fuchsia satin, 'Second hand,' she said, with some nonchalance, swirling her skirt. 'It's the old look new look.' Stretch and Denny came mixing and matching, Stretch in a pink shirt, and Denny in pink trousers, and walked around all evening side by side, to achieve maximum effect. Michael wore red, because he said that he felt like making a statement, although he wouldn't say which statement it was.

'One must preserve a little mystery, Ash,' he said. 'If I can't keep people guessing from time to time, I shall give it all up.'

Etta came in green.

'I'm colour blind,' she said, when pressed. 'Didn't you know? My yellow receptors are fucked.'

As the evening drew to a close, Virge and I went and sat at the end of the garden, on a sloping bank of grass, and watched everybody. 'Don't we all look fine?' said Virge. 'Isn't it perfect?'

I looked around the garden, the shadows lengthening, the light settling into a heavy blue haze, and everyone wandering about, talking and laughing and drinking and smoking, the myriad shades of strawberry and rose and fuchsia and scarlet mingling and glimmering against the venerable stones of the cathedral, and I thought I'd never seen anything so perfect in my whole life.

'It was the best idea,' I said.

Virge smiled, one of her secret smiles, and let out a long sigh.

'It was,' she said. 'Wasn't it?'

13

A week later, Virge, Hem, Gus and I set off for the continent, as Virge insisted on calling it.

'We're off to the continent,' she said, to whoever asked. 'We're very hot on the continentals.'

It made Gus laugh. He said that she sounded just like an Eastbourne landlady, the way she carried on.

'All those continentals,' he said, with a disapproving sniff, 'with their greasy food and foreign ways.'

Virge said what did he know about bed and breakfasts in Eastbourne anyway, giving him a suspicious look, as if he had been sneaking off for illicit meetings with young boys.

We stayed the week before we left at Virge's house. It was a fine week, with the sun out, and all of us gathered together in that lovely house. Michael came down on the third day, looking pale and tired after a weekend on the tiles in London.

'Have you been cottaging again, you awful bugger?' said Virge, gaily. 'Have you been retracing the steps of Joe Orton? I suppose you had better tell Gus all about it.'

Michael smiled and refused to be drawn, but later he took me for a walk around the garden, and said that Virge wasn't far wrong.

'I think I may be starting a promiscuous phase,' he told me seriously. 'All I want is to fall in love, and I just end up having sex, which isn't the same thing at all.' He looked at me for a moment, as if wondering what I would make of it all.

'I don't know why I always tell you all this, Ash,' he said.

'Because I'm good at listening,' I said. 'That's what Virge says. I like it.'

'And you're never shocked,' he said. 'Why aren't you shocked?'

'Michael,' I said, suddenly feeling intensely worldly and sophisticated, almost his equal in knowledge. 'If you had seen what my parents have been doing for the last twenty years you wouldn't think that sex with a few pretty boys was such a very shocking thing. It's more aesthetically pleasing, anyway.'

Michael started to laugh.

'Oh, Ash,' he said, shaking his head. 'So it's all right as long as it looks nice?'

'Well,' I said. 'You must admit I have a point.'

Michael smiled and took my hand.

'You do,' he said. 'I shall remember. And they were very pretty,' he said, reflectively. 'Every man Jack of them.'

The four of us, little band of travellers, packed up my car and left at six o'clock the next Sunday morning. Diana and Jonathan and Michael stood outside the house in their dressing gowns, waving us off.

'My dearest dears,' said Virge. 'How like Noël Coward you all look.'

And then we drove away down the long winding drive and took the road to Dover. We caught the ferry at lunchtime and headed across to Paris for the night.

'Drive on the right, drive on the right,' sang Virge. 'Oh, the perfection of the continent.'

We had the strangest night in Paris. Jonathan had given us the address of a man he knew who lived in Montmartre and was an anthropologist and a biologist and had been studying the social habits of monkeys for the last thirty years.

'The monkey man,' said Virge thoughtfully. 'Strange place to choose for it. You'd have thought he'd have gone to Africa or somewhere.'

The monkey man lived in a minute apartment in a twisting back street, and we all sat in a room stuffed with books and monkey skulls and strange embalmed things in bottles, while he gave us small revolting glasses of thick cooking sherry and told us about his work. There was a very strong smell of formaldehyde, which made Virge laugh.

He took us through the darkened climbing streets of Montmartre to a tiny restaurant he knew, which had three tables and lace curtains and stuffed animals everywhere ('Must make him feel at home,' said Virge to me), and we ate strange foreign things like knuckle of veal and pigs' trotters and brains. After the food was finished, the professor became rather excited and ordered us a thick yellow liqueur called Strega.

'The witch,' he kept saying. 'It means witch in Italian.'

'Delicious,' said Virge. 'The witch, what could be better? Let's have more.'

The next day we drove south, through the wide spaces beyond Lyon, and then up into the mountains, and down the high twisting Route Napoleon, the road the exiled Bonaparte had taken on his triumphant return from Elba.

'How did they manage,' said Virge, staring at the treacherous precipices and hairpin bends. 'They should have taken the autoroute like everyone else.'

We stayed the night in the hills behind Villefranche, and then took the coast road over the Italian border and down the riviera through San Remo and Santa Margherita, where we admired the palm trees and the boulevards and the grand hotels and reminisced about the man who broke the bank at Monte Carlo.

And then, the next night, we got to Rome. We fell in love with Rome the minute we entered the city, just like you're supposed to. The moment we drove down the wide curving road that passes the Coliseum and found ourselves in front of the ridiculous wedding cake palace built for Victor Emmanuel and saw the policeman standing on his raised bollard, directing the cars with his white gloves, and heard the hooting and the shouting and the revving engines which characterises Roman traffic, we knew we were in love.

'Oh,' said Virge, smiling all over her face. 'Rome. The eternal city, just see how lovely and eternal it is. I am glad we came.'

Keane was staying in a dark airless apartment in the Campo dei Fiori, and we spent a week sleeping on his sofas, while he wandered around looking moody and mysterious and taciturn.

'When in Rome,' said Virge. 'Don't you love that Byronesque thing he does?'

'Virge,' I said. 'It's sinister.'

'I know,' she said, in rapture. 'Isn't it sexy?'

'What's he doing in Rome anyway?' I said. 'All by himself, in this big old doomy apartment? What's all that about?'

'I don't know,' said Virge. 'You know Keane. I didn't like to ask.'

We spent the days wandering about the city, with our guide books and our cameras, to the Forum and the Vatican and the Piazza Navona and the Villa Borgese and the Trastavere and the Spanish Steps, and the little house where Keane had spent his final months. Virge almost started crying when she saw the cramped room where he died, with his single iron bed and his death mask in a glass case.

'Just think,' she said furiously, 'of him sitting here and eating his poor consumptive heart out for bloody Fanny Brawne.'

In the evenings, Keane took us to strange back-street bars that he knew, where the lights were so low that you had to walk carefully through the gloom, for fear of bumping into the furniture, and everyone dressed in black and drank green chartreuse and wore purple lipstick, even the boys.

'Typical Keane,' said Hem, to me. 'How phoney can you get.'

When the week was over, Keane flew off to New York, no one knew why.

'Things,' said Virge, darkly. 'To do. Is it a double life, do you think? I do hope so.'

With Keane gone, we continued our tour. We drove down to Naples, along the thin twisting road that ran along the coast. We visited Positano and Amalfi and took the ferry across to Capri for the day, where we sat in the tiny Piazza Umberto and drank Negronis and Virge recited all the words to *The Bar on the Piccola Marina*. 'Life came to Mrs Wentworth Brewster, great flushes of delight suffused her,' she sang, ignoring the scandalised looks of the chic Italians with their Hermès bags and Gucci shoes. 'They don't write them like that any more.'

'Just as well,' said Gus.

The next day we went further south, through the strange dusty villages they have down there, ancient houses clinging to the hillside, where old women dressed all in black sat outside in the sun and children played in the streets, and no one spoke English. It was like going back in time.

At the end of the week we arrived at Hem's parents' house. It was built on top of a hill, miles from anywhere, a great sprawling villa, arranged about a courtyard, with vines growing round it and a garden running wild. From the third floor windows, you could just catch sight of the sea.

'Oh, Hem,' said Virge, when we arrived. 'This is perfect.'

We had planned to stay for ten days and then continue with our tour, but every morning we woke up in that great old house, with its high ceilings and flagged floors and crumbling pillars, and we couldn't bear to leave. It seemed so strange and right, just the four of us, rattling round those vast rooms. It was an absolute fantasy world, something from a story book.

'It's another life,' said Virge. 'It's nothing to do with anything we know.'

Our days fell quickly into a routine. We met for breakfast on the terrace at ten, in our dressing gowns, and drank strong Italian coffee and smoked our first cigarettes. Then we would get dressed, and Virge and I would lie in the sun and talk. Hem, who didn't like the heat, sat in the library, which was the size of a tennis court, with all the shutters closed against the blinding sunshine, and read his way through bookshelves filled with dusty old volumes of Tolstoy and Turgenev and Dostoevsky, which he said was perfect because he had always felt he should go through a Russian stage.

'A Russian stage,' said Virge, in rapture. 'How absolutely right and perfect and proper and correct. You must do it now, Hem,' she said, very seriously, 'because when we're older and out in the world we won't be allowed, people will just say it's sad and pretentious and then where will we be?'

Hem listened to this with grave attention, and nodded, and said he was glad she approved.

And Gus, who liked doing nothing at all, would settle himself in a hammock which was slung between two gnarled old olive trees at the side of the house, and swing gently all morning, thinking his own private thoughts, until it was time for lunch.

After lunch, we walked down to a wide shallow river not far from the house, and swam. Tea was taken solemnly, with just the barest hint of irony, at four punctually each afternoon. Virge had found a proper tea service, with bone china cups and a silver pot and a spirit lamp to keep the water hot, and she brought it out every day with great ceremony, (but made coffee to drink of course, not actual tea, on account of my allergy), and we would sit round like dowager duchesses in the eighteenth century and drink our coffee and eat little delicate pastries dusted with fine sugar which we bought every day from a bakery in the village.

After tea, we played cards or backgammon for high stakes, ten thousand lire a point. Virge always won, which delighted her, although she pretended it meant nothing. At six, all bets were off, and we would go down to the village and sit outside a bar in the square and drink Negronis for an hour and listen to the church bells ringing for early evening mass, calling the faithful to prayer.

'What heathens we are,' said Virge, watching as the square emptied, leaving only us and the barman, who was a communist and didn't believe in God, and spent the holy hour defiantly polishing glasses and reading the sports page of the local paper and smoking small pungent cigars, while the rest of the village went to pray for their immortal souls.

'What pagans,' she said, 'living for pleasure as we are. Lucky we don't believe in hellfire, or I expect we should burn in it for eternity. Isn't it lucky we don't believe in hell and damnation? Isn't it just our luck that we never read Dante at an impressionable age?'

At seven we went back to the house and changed for dinner, which we ate in state, gathered around one end of the long dining room table, which we set with silver and candles. And then we would talk until late, that kind of rambling searching talk that you can have when you know that you have nowhere to go and nothing to prove, the kind of talk that you have when you are young and brave and careless, when you have all the time in the world. If the night was clear and the moon bright, we would walk through the wild garden and lie on our backs and look at the stars which were scattered all over the sky, everywhere you looked, we never could believe that there were so many.

That was what we did all summer. And one day it was September, and we suddenly realised that we had to go back, to our other lives, to our real lives. We felt sad to go, but there was impatience too, as if this doing nothing, this long lazy halcyon time, had made us ready again for action and people – except for Virge. Virge was inconsolable.

'I can't bear it,' she said over and over again, as we closed up the house, locked away the silver, folded up the bed linen, drew the shutters. 'I can't bear to go,' she said, as we packed up our suitcases, and went along the washing line, taking down the last of our clothes which were drying in the sun.

'We'll come again,' I said, as we loaded the luggage into the car and hid the key under a flowerpot. 'We'll have other holidays.'

Virge got into the back seat and closed the door behind her.

'But it will never be so perfect again,' she said.

It was Hem's turn to drive, and as we bumped away over the rutted drive, Virge twisted and turned and craned her neck, to catch a last glimpse of the house, until finally it was lost from sight.

'Never ever ever,' she said sadly. 'It will never be so perfect again.'

14

Perhaps she was right. But then Virge had a different idea from me – I always had a hope for better things, that happiness could be repeated, that perfect moments would come again, that there were things always to look forward to. But for Virge, such times as that summer, that perfect still time, as if all the clocks had stopped and there was nothing to disturb us from our little private world, were almost painful, because she had a conviction that they never would come again, that she had stumbled over a pot of gold and then left it behind, something she would never find again. She had a nostalgia, even in the present, for times that would never be so good again.

We didn't repeat that summer. I had hoped we would. The second year went quickly past, different from the first, but also the same. We missed Michael, who had gone to study at the Sorbonne and wrote us long, picaresque and frankly unbelievable letters from his apartment in the Marais, but there was our little gang, still together. And of course, I had Hem, and Virge had Keane, and there was a whole influx of first year students, whom we fraternised with and allowed ourselves small secret feelings of superiority towards – 'Let's have those lovely young first year boys to tea,' Virge said often, in what she called her old-fashioned voice.

She and I moved into a new set of rooms in Peck, and we had Stretch and Denny next door, and we kept open house and generally felt ourselves to be very much the thing.

The winter was even colder than the one before, and we spent much of it driving up to London, where at least it seemed warmer, and then the summer came again, and the parties and the river and all. I had just assumed that we would go back to Italy for our holidays, but one day Virge said that she was going to Mexico with Keane.

'Mexico,' I said stupidly. I was shocked. I was hurt, too. It was the first time she had ever hurt me, but I was too young and proud to show it, so I just said, Fine, and that was that.

So when the term ended, we said goodbye for three whole months, and off she went with Keane, and said she would send a card, and I felt absolutely eaten with jealousy. I tried not to make a big thing about it, but I couldn't help it. I felt as if I had lost her, as if this great friendship which we were going to have forever had crumbled to dust, because she had chosen Keane over me. I felt absolutely betrayed, but I didn't say anything.

I think that Hem knew, for all my bravado. He was clever like that, observant and intuitive, although he didn't show off about it. Seeing that I was all at a loss, he made arrangements for the summer, and took me away with him. He just packed me up and put me in his car and drove me off to Italy.

We didn't go to his house in the south. I think he knew that that would have been too much, to go back there without Virge, that there would have been something sad and melancholy in it, just the two of us trying to recreate something which had passed. So he took me to Venice, where his aunt had a small apartment beyond the Rialto, and we lived there for the three months of the long holiday.

Hem had an idea about places abroad, he liked to settle in, get to know them as if he lived there, rather than just visiting, passing through. He always said he would rather go to one place for a good long time, not rush through many different towns, ticking them off in the guide book.

After a while, I forgot my hurt about Virge, and started to realise that I was having a lovely time. We avoided the main drag where the tourists thronged and jostled, and kept to the dark back streets and the secret places. We visited the outlying islands, Murano and Burano and the cathedral on Torcello, and we went to the cemetery, and Hem said he would buy me a plot there, if I wanted, which I did, very much. We took the traghetto across to the fish and vegetable market most days, and took to haggling as if we had been born to it. We wandered round the Ca D'Oro, that great perfectly preserved palazzo with its eighteenth century ghosts, and took pride in finding forgotten Titians in tiny hidden churches, and went to Harry's Bar every evening at six for prosecco, and quite soon the barmen got to know us, and kept our own special table, reserved until we arrived.

Michael came down from Paris one weekend, and we went out on the town – sitting outside Florian's café on Mark's square, listening to the orchestra play, and drinking Peroni beer on the terrace of the Monaco Hotel, looking out over the grand canal, and sitting up late in Haig's bar, which was always filled with disreputable men and fast women, and never seemed to close. Michael had had a special Italian wardrobe made for the trip, by a canny old tailor he had found in the sixième, long cut suits and many silk shirts in peacock colours, which we admired very much.

On Michael's last night, sitting in a little restaurant overlooking a narrow canal in the San Martino district, where they had the best fish in the city, he told us that he was in love.

'Michael,' I said. 'All this time and you never told us.'

'Well,' he said, taking my hand. 'I'm rather shy about it, to tell you the truth. And there's tempting fate and all those dangerous things. But it is love, for all that.'

'Who is he?' I said.

'He's Italian,' said Michael. 'He's called Giovanni. He's a critic, and a writer. He's older.'

I looked at his happy face, and I knew suddenly why he hadn't told, why he felt strange about it, why he had always made so many jokes about his state, all those lines about the Dilly and lovely young boys.

'You never thought it would happen to you, did you?' I said.

Michael smiled, and shook his head.

'That's what I love about you, Ash,' he said. 'No, I didn't.'

Hem smiled, and lifted his glass, and said, 'Well, here's to love,' and he looked at me as he said it, and I thought that for all Virge's defection, here I was, in Venice, in love, and I was having another almost perfect summer, and I wondered what I had done to deserve it.

But for such happiness, it seems that there is always a price to be paid, and in our last week the bailiffs came to collect. I was too young then to know they would – I just thought that because I loved Hem so much, and he loved me, and it was so simple and straightforward and lovely that it would go on and on, that there was no reason for any change. Perhaps I didn't know Hem as well as he knew me, or perhaps I just didn't want to see.

We were sitting on the balcony of our apartment, drinking our morning coffee, and watching as the real Venetians came back to the city after the summer away, when they had abandoned it to the hordes of visitors. I felt warm and brown and entirely content, as if I had lived in the city forever. I didn't have any intimations or suspicions. I wasn't thinking at all: there was something about Venice that did that to me, as if being surrounded for such a long time by so much beauty had made my brain a little soft, sunk into some aesthetic reverie. Or perhaps it was just the sun, and letting the days slide past without wondering about them so very much.

Hem opened a letter which had come for him that morning, and a strange expression came into his face. I wondered suddenly if it was bad news, but it was only a vague thought. I still didn't think that anything was going to go wrong.

'What?' I said. 'What is it?'

He blinked and hesitated and folded the piece of paper over and over with his long fingers.

'It's a job,' he said.

My face cleared.

'That's marvellous,' I said. 'Isn't it? Isn't that what you wanted?'

Hem was in the year above, and we hadn't really talked about what we would do now he had gone down and I still had a year to go. I had just assumed that he would go to London and work, because that was what everyone did, and I would see him on weekends. I didn't think anything would change very much. I couldn't imagine anything changing, not when everything was so easy between us.

'It's good,' he said, but there was something unwilling in him, uncomfortable, unlike himself; there was a strange constrained note in his voice which I didn't recognise, and I had a sudden idea that my sureness was misplaced, that something was about to go terribly wrong with my unspoken plans.

'It's in Los Angeles,' he said.

So that was it. That was the end of it. I wanted to scream

and shout and ask him why he couldn't take his bloody pictures in London, but I didn't. I knew there was no point. He said there was a possibility of going to Sydney after that, and then perhaps Peking. He was starting his great searching voyage, as if he had stayed still too long, and now he had to start moving, like one of those animals, sharks I think it is, the kind who have to keep moving or they die. I knew he was sad, to leave me, that he would miss me, but I wasn't enough to hold him. Just me wasn't enough, the pulling impulse of his wanderlust was too much. And it was a great job, a great opportunity, one he would be crazy to pass up.

So that was that, and there was nothing to say.

The last days in Venice were unbearable, for me. We went through the motions, not saying much; pretending, like those sad married couples you see in restaurants, the ones who make polite stilted small talk because they have run out of things to say to each other. I felt that I was being pulled apart, into small pointless pieces, but I didn't want to tell him that, so I put my nice brave face on, because it wasn't really his fault, and when he was asleep, I would go and sit on the balcony and look out over the darkened square, and cry long racking tears, stuffing my fist against my mouth so as not to wake him with the noise.

At the end of those four endless days, we got in his car, and drove silently back to England. We drove and drove until we reached Oxford, and then we stopped. I couldn't really believe that we were here, back at the beginning, where it all started.

I was living in Michael's old house, and Hem took me there and helped me in with my bags, and then we stood, out in the street, staring at each other, and then he kissed me on the cheek, and looked sadly at me for a moment, as if he knew that he was breaking my heart, but he didn't know what else to do.

'You will remember,' he said suddenly, 'what I told you that Sunday in your room?'

I knew what he meant; what he had told me about me being his first great love. I knew he meant it, but now, standing there, saying goodbye, I wondered what it counted for. It was words, was all. Words weren't enough.

'Yes,' I said.

He nodded, and then he turned and walked away.

No one ever tells you about the first time it happens. It's not as if it gets any easier, with age, but at least then you know what to expect, it's a familiar feeling, something remembered, known. But the first time, the shock of it is overwhelming. Watching Hem walk away, realising finally that I might not see him again for who knew how many years, I felt as if my insides were being pulled out. I just stood, paralysed, on the steps, astonished that such a small physical action could produce such a shocking pain. Just someone walking away, someone getting into their car and driving down a perfectly normal street.

It didn't make any sense. I had heard about hearts aching, but no one had told me that it doesn't hurt in the heart at all, not in the chest, that it feels like someone has punched you and slapped you and then kicked you in the stomach. I really hadn't known that was what it would be like. Maybe they don't tell you, like people don't tell you about childbirth, because if people knew no one would ever do it in the first place. Maybe there just isn't any point in telling, because it wouldn't make much difference. Maybe they just think everyone has to go through it, so we all might as well find out in our own time.

'What's happened?' said Virge. 'What?'

I brought my eyes into focus and saw her standing at

the bottom of the steps with her suitcases. She was very brown and thin and tall and her hair was grown longer, and jet black now, and cut into a faintly Aztec shape, I thought, inconsequently.

'Hem's gone,' I said.

She dropped her suitcases and ran up the steps and put her arms round me and held me tight to her.

'Poor Ash,' she said. 'Poor, poor Ash.'

She stepped back after a moment and looked at me.

'I left Keane,' she said. 'So it's just you and me now.'

She went back and got her cases, and took my arm and drew me into the house.

'Come on,' she said. 'Let's have a cup of tea.' Then, seeing my face, she started to laugh. 'Just joking,' she said.

'Why did you run off with Keane?' I said. 'I thought we were going to Italy again. I thought you didn't love me any more.'

Virge looked shocked.

'Did you think that?' she said. 'I can't bear that you thought that. Why didn't you say anything?'

'Because,' I said. I shrugged. I felt helpless and stupid and empty. 'Because I couldn't.'

'Well,' said Virge. 'It's all right now, because there is no more Keane, and I'm sorry, I am, I truly am, because I shouldn't have gone and left you, just like that, and it was a dreadful thoughtless thing to do, and I won't do it again, ever ever, I promise. I promise.'

'What happened?' I said. I wanted to talk about her, because I couldn't yet talk about me, because it was just too much. I think she knew that, and she didn't ask me any questions, just answered mine. I think she knew that I would tell her what I needed to when I was ready.

'A dreadful thing happened in Mexico,' she said. She stopped for a moment, as if she were about to tell me what it was. 'A terrible thing.'

'What?' I said. 'What did he do?'

I could imagine him doing something terrible, taking her halfway across the world and then doing something cruel and shocking. I had always thought he looked like he would.

'It was awful,' said Virge. Then she looked at me. 'I don't want to say, just now,' she said. 'Do you mind? I can't say. But it was the end. I knew that at once. And I was trying to get flights back and I didn't have enough money and I was too proud to ring home and ask them to send me a banker's draft or whatever it is, and so I went off by myself until it was time to come home and it was lonely and awful and I stayed in a dreadful little flea pit hotel run by a toothless señora, the kind of place which looks as if it's just a front for a global money laundering operation, and I got bed bugs and I didn't know anyone and there was this sinister American car dealer who followed me round everywhere and I thought I was going to end up with a knife in my ribs. I thought I was going to end up in a laundry basket, shipped off to Morocco by white slavers. I thought that I'd never see dear old Blighty again. I thought that I would be one of those women, the kind when everyone says Oh, yes, we knew she was heading for a bad end. I thought I was going to have a bad end. Isn't it strange? I had thought I would have a good end, I'd always wanted a good end.'

She laughed suddenly, a faint edge of hysteria to it.

'What a summer we've had,' she said. 'Oh, Ash, dear dear Ash, what a summer we've had, we must never go away without each other ever again.'

Then the door slammed open, and Gus came in and flung all his worldy belongings down on the floor, and threw his arms round both of us at once.

'Where's my room?' he said. 'Have you taken the best rooms already?'

'Yes,' said Virge. 'Of course we have.'

'Guess what I did this summer?' said Gus.

'What?' I said.

'I lost my virginity,' he said, grinning all over his face. 'It's lost and buried and gone forever and hallelujah for that.'

'Which one with?' said Virge.

Gus looked at us, and smiled and smiled and smiled and started to laugh.

'Both,' he said. 'But not at the same time.'

So, there we were, together again. It was a big house, and there was room for all of us, Stretch and Denny and Etta and Stevie as well. The year went quickly by, very different from the first two, somehow: we were out of college, for one thing, and there was always the shadow of finals looming in the distance, and now we had things like kitchens and telephones the tenor of our life shifted a little, as if unconsciously mimicking what it might be like out in the real world (having people round for supper, calling to make plans – things that had never impinged on us before). And when the end of the year came, and we sat our exams, and finally packed up and left Oxford for good, we just moved from one house to another.

My poor dear mad old godfather died and left me his house in London. I had visited him a great deal in the last weeks of his illness. I had never seen a real mad person before, it was a word so overused as to lose its meaning (disc jockeys, game show hosts, comic actors and almost everyone who ever called a radio phone-in *panting* to confess: 'Oh yes, I'm mad, me.') Confronted for the first time with the real thing, I found it frightening and shocking to witness.

He had no memory, asking the same question over and over, and within the same five minutes he would know me and call me by name, and then ask me who I was, and then talk to me as if I were someone else, his dead aunt, or a complete stranger. He had sudden terrifying moments of absolute clarity, which came without warning, and that was the worst, because in those moments we both knew that he was aware of his madness, of the slow sure rotting of his brain. I could have borne it better if he just didn't know, lost happily in the haze of complete lunacy, but he did know, in those blinding seconds of sanity, and that was the cruellest blow of all.

The only thing that cheered me a little was that the day before he died I went to see him, to tell him that I had got my exam results. Virge was with me. She came often, something in her allowing her to deal absolutely with the gibberish and ramblings of the dying man. It made me feel frightened and impotent, but Virge somehow went with it, talked her own nonsense back, as if she saw nothing strange in it. It made it easier for me, having her there. So we sat opposite my poor old friend, propped up in his bed, with his mottled bald head and his wasted hands, and I told him we'd got our degrees.

'Virge got a first,' I said. 'Of course. And I got a two:one.'

He had been ranting only moments before, but suddenly his sunken old eyes came into sharp focus and he looked right at me, and he said, very clearly,

'Just as well.'

Virge and I looked at each other.

'Upper second,' he said, his shaky old voice suddenly firm and filled with authority and conviction. 'A respectable kind of degree. Never forget that men are frightened of first-class women.'

There was a blaze of pleasure in his face, and then he sank back into his private world, and we left soon after, and the next day the lawyers rang me up to tell me that he had died in his sleep and the house was mine.

15

Virge and I moved in straight away. Gus and Stevie were coming to lodge with us, but they were both travelling that summer. Stevie went to visit some relations in the South Seas ('What a place to have relations,' said Virge, 'How like Stevie,') and Gus went to the west coast of Ireland, to look at the mountains. So for the first two months it was just Virge and I, rattling around the five floors.

Having no family, my godparent had left me not only the house, but also all its contents, and we spent days and days sifting through all his stuff, finding strange objects and old letters. The kitchen made us sad, because it was bare and drab and dark and neglected and we found a cupboard filled with tins and tins of Heinz soup and dry biscuits.

'Oh,' said Virge, the exact same dying fall in her voice that there had been when we went to the Spanish Steps in Rome to see the room where Keats died. 'Please please promise that we won't end up sad and alone and mad with only soup to eat.'

'I promise we won't,' I said, but I felt some chill of fear as I said it, that there were people who did, that sometimes life just happened like that. I had never thought about it before: I had a vision of old age as a nice comfortable golden twilight, filled with old friends and relatives and children and grandchildren and all those other things, like the Waltons. I had never pictured it as something lonely, living in a huge old house with cupboards full of soup and not even a cat for company.

'We won't,' I said. 'We'll always have each other, for one thing.'

'Yes,' said Virge. 'Yes. We will.'

We had to go to see the lawyers quite often, to sort out the details of my bequest and sign pieces of paper. Virge enjoyed these visits tremendously, dressing up for them in little black suits and a hat which she had bought specially in a theatrical shop in Islington.

'Do you think I look just like Margaret Leighton, or someone?' she said.

'Just like,' I said. 'Almost exactly.'

She liked sitting in the dusty panelled legal offices, in her preposterous hat, flirting gently with my godfather's solicitor, who was approaching eighty himself, and holding onto all his faculties with a crabbed and faintly desperate grip.

'Well,' she said to me. 'Isn't it nice, you being an heiress and all?'

I wasn't an heiress exactly, but there was a yearly income left me for keeping up the house, and it did feel then like untold riches. I couldn't quite believe that this huge old house with all its strange furniture and heavy oil paintings and shelves of rare books was actually mine. It felt like the kind of thing that happened in Dickens or Trollope, something out of a book.

Virge was delighted by the whole thing. We spent a lot of time that summer sitting in the long drawing room on the first floor, planning what we should do with the house. We did a great deal of furniture moving, seeing where things looked best. Virge loved moving furniture.

'Come on,' she would say, lugging yet another vast day

bed across the floor. 'Let's see what it looks like in the window.'

In the end, we put everything in the least likely places, so we moved bookcases and busts and tallboys and grand old paintings into the kitchen and the bathrooms, and kept only the lightest pieces of gilt furniture in the drawing room. From being a dark gloomy room it became light and spacious, and we took down the heavy green curtains and put up Venetian blinds and painted the walls an esoteric shade of pale violet and took away the dark Persian rugs and left the floorboards bare.

'It's perfect,' said Virge. 'Now the downstairs loo looks like the Wallace collection and this room looks like something out of a Mediterranean villa. I think that's quite as it should be, don't you?'

I had no clue when it came to interior design, so I just agreed with all her suggestions, and by the time we had finished the whole place looked like a stage set, which pleased Virge's keen sense of the theatrical. It was crazy, in a way, but it was lovely too. It was sort of perfect.

The night before Gus and Stevie came back, Virge and I made a special dinner, and put on dresses, and sat round the kitchen table, and lit candles and ate. Virge had found a cellar filled with venerable bottles of wine, so we had chosen a nice Lafitte from the seventies to go with our boeuf en croute.

'Well,' said Virge, raising her glass. 'Here's to the house.'

'Here's to it,' I said. I looked around the kitchen, and thought how grand it looked, with all the walls covered in pictures in carved gilded frames, and the two Venetian mirrors above the fireplace, and all the huge bits of furniture we had filled it with.

'What a curious thing,' I said. 'That here we are, living in this great old grown up place. It's like being seventy.'

'So much better to have it like this now,' said Virge. 'We can go in reverse, so when we really are old we can live in two rooms with posters of Jimi Hendrix on the walls.'

'Thank God for it though,' I said. 'What would we have done without?'

'Oh, you know,' said Virge. 'We would have got a lovely little rented place and had that flat share thing, you know, spaghetti bolognese for supper and underwear drying over the bath and fusing the electricity from our hairdryers.'

I thought about it for a moment.

'I'm quite glad that we're not,' I said. 'I quite like the grand life.' There was a note of doubt in my voice, as if all this shouldn't really be mine.

'Come along,' said Virge, firmly. 'Think of living well and your revenge. It's the least you deserve, after being brought up by the Addams family.'

'I suppose there is that,' I said. I looked around again, still amazed that all this belonged to me. 'But what will we do with it all?'

Virge looked at me, with a daredevil light in her eye.

'We'll have parties,' she said.

There were a lot of parties, in those first two years after university. It was a strange time. Gus, Stevie, Virge and I quickly settled into the house. Gus had the whole top floor, for his studio, and painted all day, and when he was extra broke went out and painted people's houses. Stevie got a job with a theatrical agency, and became very urban and professional and ambitious, and spent a lot of time bringing astonishingly handsome young actors home for supper.

I had vague ambitions to go into publishing, but none of the job offers seemed quite what I wanted, so I took work in a local bookshop in the meantime, and I never left. It was always supposed to be an interim measure, just to make ends meet, but I found I liked it, pottering around the cluttered dusty shop, finding out-of-print novels and getting authors in for signings.

I felt faint guilt about not getting on the fast track, because it was the eighties after all, and the yuppie boom was still booming, and a lot of people we knew had gone into the fashionable new jobs like management consultancy and the futures exchange, and worked eighty hours a week and were already earning thirty thousand pounds a year, but the thought of all that made me feel rather ill and not myself, so I just said that I wasn't cut out for the high life. I stayed in my bookshop, and decided that I might turn into one of those bookish Bloomsbury type women, an idea which I was rather taken with, although Virge said it took a bit of getting used to, especially since she had never heard of a Bloomsburyite with platinum hair and purple nail varnish.

She, of course, had managed to get herself the dream job to end them all, seemingly without trying. She always said she never quite knew how she did it, and I sometimes wondered if there was something she wasn't telling me, but whatever it was, she had been given work by a film company, in development.

'Imagine,' she said. 'I get paid a fortune to read books all day and decide whether they should be made into films.'

'Do the words money, old, and rope, ring any bells,' said Stevie. 'At all?'

'Oh, the eighties,' said Virge. 'I suppose they are good for something after all.'

But for all her talk, she loved her job, and quite soon afterwards, she got poached by one of the big Hollywood giants, who set her up in a smart office in Soho, and paid her to scout for new young British talent – novelists and playwrights and anyone who had ever put pen to paper, in case they might be able to write a perfect screenplay in three acts with a good meaty part for Meryl Streep in it.

'Oh, the hardness of my life,' said Virge, gaily. 'Now not only do I have to read books, but I also have to go to the theatre and take a lot of starving young talent out to slap up lunches on my expense account.'

Because it was Virge, none of us grudged her her luck, and anyway, it was lovely for us as well, since she was always taking us off to screenings and parties where we had the chance of glimpsing Harrison Ford across a crowded room.

Etta had gone to Harvard, to do an MA in Women's Studies, which was something they had in America, much to Stevie's chagrin. 'I love dear old Blighty,' she said, 'but we are so backward.'

Denny and Stretch had moved into a small flat, two rooms, kitchenette and bath, three streets away, and were working for an advertising agency, which they loathed and hated and despised, while they wrote a satirical revue in the evenings.

'Oh, Gus,' they said, when they came to visit, 'how lucky you are not to have to bother with a day job.'

'But I'm broke,' said Gus, logically.

'At least your artistic integrity is intact,' said Stretch gloomily, 'which is more than I can say for mine.'

And we did have parties, just as Virge had said we would. There was something about those years, of our early twenties, which demanded a crowd. I'm not sure now what it was, whether for all our professed delight in being out in the world, with our own front door keys and our jobs and our salaries, all those badges of independence and supposed adulthood, we were still afraid to go all the way; that this need to always surround ourselves with people, of carrying on the university life even though we no longer had tutorials to go to, was a kind of insulation against the real real world. Perhaps I'm reading too much into it. Perhaps it was just that we were still young, however sophisticated we felt, and we wanted to have fun.

Whatever it was, we still hunted in a pack, felt strange if we ever sat down to eat with less than eight people, or if a week went by without a party to go to. There were so many excuses, not just the obvious ones, like birthdays or promotions or new jobs. We celebrated everything we could lay our hands on. We had parties for the fourth of July, as well as the fourteenth, for the anniversary of the I have a dream speech, for Rosh Hashana, and the Chinese new year, which was one of our best – Virge and I went to Chinatown and bought piles of that old delicate painted paper money, which we burned for luck, just as they do in Peking. We had parties for any excuse we could find. Once, when there was a week when it seemed that nothing had happened in the entire history of the world, no revolutions or epoch-making events, no dead presidents or wars ending, Gus decided to give a party to mark the fact that nothing had happened that week.

The parties we got asked to varied from the exotic (cross dressing in a disused slaughterhouse in Smithfield) to the mundane (bring a bottle in a basement flat in Peckham), but the only ones we ever refused were those which smacked of the County. I think Virge and I still carried with us an enduring memory of that terrible party where we first met, so when occasionally we received an invitation printed on stiff white card requesting the pleasure of our company at a sit down dinner for three hundred, with dancing after, we took great delight in refusing. Virge especially liked stooping to unplumbed depths of silliness on these occasions, and spent time writing elaborate refusals in what used to be called flowing copperplate. She once wrote to the wife of a prominent military man, known for his excessive right-wing views (hanging's too good for them, bring back the birch, ten years' compulsory national service for the underprivileged, etc, etc), saying that she was unable to attend her party due to a chronic attack of Marxism. Gus said that she should have gone with the old French gag about je suis Marxiste, tendance Groucho, but Virge said that because of the County's firm and enduring belief that foreigners were fiends and abroad unutterably bloody and that speaking French involved shouting in English, they wouldn't have got the joke. One thing about Virge, she couldn't bear to see a joke go to waste.

The other thing about those early London years, aside from the parties, was sex. Virge and I had always had a small secret belief in our ability never to follow the crowd, although we would do it sometimes, if it suited us. But for those first years after Oxford, we allowed ourselves a small break from what we considered our utter originality, and went with it. Everyone was doing it, after all, and we decided that we would too. Not that it was a clinical decision, it wasn't as if we sat down and worked out a game plan: we've had our first romantic love, our first heart rending affair, so now we'll just do sex for a while, play the field, break a few hearts ourselves. We just fell into it, if you will excuse the expression.

We had both agreed, when we were younger, that we thought one night stands somehow sordid and demeaning, that it was the kind of thing that only desperate women did, those kind who put on a tough exterior to cover up their own deep inadequacy. Although we considered ourselves fantastically open minded and liberal, in fact in those days we had the absolute judgemental attitude of great youth, an almost mathematical moral idea that $x + y$ ALWAYS $= Z$. Therefore, then, in our eyes, sex + one night − emotional involvement = SLUT.

We were so romantic and ignorant then that we truly believed in the idealised concept that the only real course was to make love rather than have sex, that there was no validity in sleeping with someone unless there was deep love in the equation. We considered ourselves modern enough to realise that certain notions were outdated, the idea that love always led to marriage for example; we felt ourselves radical enough to consign Cinderella to the pre-fifties hinterland of obsolescence. But for all that, it was still love with a nice big capital L that counted, was the only thing that counted.

Now, battle-scarred as we were, our hopeful romantic sensibilities bruised and blunted by the new knowledge that love, while very nice and exciting and enjoyable and all, was also the path to absolute utter agony, we decided that perhaps there was a place for sex alone, without strings.

Stevie encouraged us in this. She was in the vanguard, having discovered the delight of carnal knowledge for its own sake in the third year of Oxford. She said it was the only thing that got her through finals.

Being Stevie, she spun a nice political angle on it. 'Think about it,' she said, over and over. 'Think. If men sleep around they're studs, if women do it, they're sluts. I mean, for God's sake, until Masters and Johnson and the sixties and the acknowledgement of the clitoral orgasm, women weren't even supposed to *enjoy* sex. Let's face it, it was never the men who were supposed to lie back and think of England.'

'Why is the missionary position called the missionary position?' said Virge. 'I didn't think missionaries really did it at all, or am I missing something?'

'SUBmission,' said Stevie darkly. 'Men on top. Think about it. So, now we have the pill, we have sexual liberation, we have *Cosmopolitan*, and it's time that we asserted our right to go out and show that we are modern assured women who can take sexual pleasure without the need for emotional ties and binds of matrimony and procreation. Recreation not procreation.'

'I agree,' said Virge. 'That's why I think it must be so depressing, being Catholic.'

And again, quite apart from any philosophical considerations, there was the fact that everyone was doing it. There was some fin de siecle aspect to it, a feeling that soon the party would be over. The AIDS panic which had peaked in the mid-eighties had settled into familiar news, and as long as you chose your partner and used a condom, there was the thought that today we should take our pleasures where we could, for it was only tomorrow that we might die, and tomorrow, still, was something that we were just managing to stave off, just barely.

It took more effort now. At Oxford it had been easy, and now we had to work at it. I sometimes think that was what all the parties were about; it was our last fling at pretending that tomorrow really would never come, although for the first time we were aware that it would, one day, that we could not ignore it forever. It was as if we were giving ourselves permission to keep our heads in the sand just a little longer, just for one more dance, letting the orchestra play one last waltz after another, so that we could pretend that we would never have to take off our dancing shoes and go home to bed.

It was easy then, because of our age, and because of the mood of the country, to ignore the warning signs. It was so easy just to have another party, another brief encounter, another lunch, another shopping trip to buy that little black dress which we couldn't really afford – everything was on credit. The credit boom still had not gone bust, not quite, and if we were being encouraged to live on borrowed money, it seemed only logical to live on borrowed time.

So, as we sat round our breakfast table on Saturday mornings, and Gus tried not to laugh as a different boy issued from our bedrooms, it seemed that as we still secretly believed we would live forever, so we could play forever as well.

16

There wasn't any single event which came to change all this, but it did change, all the same. It might have been that it happens to everyone, when they reach a point in their mid-twenties, just the simple thing of growing up, nothing unique about it. But then, there are some people who never grow up, perennial Peter Pans, fey little front line soldiers in the battle against age and responsibility. So although there may be something in the idea that every generation thinks they are different from the one before, that their case is always somehow original and individual, there were also many specific things that happened to us which forced our shift in perception.

There was a general change in the mood of the country: the mighty eighties consumer bubble finally burst with the dramatic downfall of Mrs Thatcher and the onset of the recession. Out in the wider world, walls were coming down, entrenched regimes falling, the cold war reaching its bitter end. And there was the planet, too, that needed saving: the sky was truly no longer the limit, because there was a hole in it.

On the streets, we watched the change express itself in the new rave culture, the nostalgic return to hippiedom and the summer of love. The hard synthesiser sound of the eighties gave way to Indie pop and real guitars; power suiting and designer labels gave in to grunge. Suddenly dressing up seemed vulgar and indecent, the dramatic nature of the switch to the furthest end of the scale was as if in apology and shame for the rampant years of conspicuous consumption.

And then, there was the particular, the specific things that came to us, to make us suddenly realise that we were vulnerable after all, that for all our clever defences, we couldn't hide ourselves from the more difficult realities of life, we were not immortal or omnipotent, that we had got away with it for long enough.

They all came, one after another, events piling up, forcing us to see things differently.

It started with a death, in the summer of 1991.

Virge had given a party for her birthday, in the middle of September. The parties were not so frequent now, but we were still giving them, still trying to carry on with the illusion. There had been a lot of the old Oxford people there, almost like a reunion, and the next day, when Gus, Stevie, Virge and I were clearing up and trying to eat breakfast at the same time, Denny and Stretch came by and told us that one of the boys, a quiet, studious boy called Billy, whom we hadn't seen for ages and missed, and Virge had specially tracked down for her party, had had an asthma attack and died before the ambulance arrived.

There was a terrible shocked silence after they told us. No one knew what to say, not even Virge, who always knew what to say. It was the first time any of us had come near death in someone of our own age, someone we knew. People don't just go and die, good nice clever people don't just go to parties and then go home and have asthma attacks and die. They do, of course, all the time. People go and die every day, but we didn't know that then. We still thought that death was something that happened to old people, or people with diseases, or people who pursued dangerous careers like motor racing or mountain climbing, or, mostly, *other* people.

The absolute arbitrary nature of life and death and fate or whatever you want to call it had not impinged on us before, that random lack of logic. It seemed impossible that someone who had been living and breathing and laughing and making jokes in our own garden only twelve hours before now no longer existed.

It's frightening how the first death in your own generation takes you, when you are so young, how complicated and unexpected all the attendant feelings are. I think we all thought that it was just a simple matter of sorrow and regret. After that initial crashing shock, we felt that, we cried tears for poor Billy. We went to the funeral and took flowers and spoke stuttering inadequate words of sympathy to his family.

But that was not an end to it, it affected all of us in strange ways which we would never have expected. I felt a terrible guilt, that there should have been something we could have done, that we should have made him stay the night, that one of us would have been there, could have saved him. I also felt a terrible guilt that it was him and not me, and conversely, that I was so grateful that it wasn't me.

Stevie developed a morbid death fear. For a long time afterwards she refused to go in lifts or aeroplanes or on motorways. She took the stairs or the train or the little b roads, where she was less likely to suffer a fatal accident.

Gus, who had always veered towards agnosticism, took it as an absolute sign that there could be nothing to believe in. He went through a long stage of a kind of desperate nihilism, and painted a series of furious dark paintings which, ironically, became the work which really launched his career, won him critical acclaim and shows in London, Glasgow and Berlin.

Stretch and Denny, who for all their varying temperaments, always seemed to reach the same conclusion, became convinced that each day should be lived as if it were their last, threw up their jobs in advertising and took to writing in earnest. As Stretch always said, with his nicely ironic melancholy, it sounded all very quixotic, but they probably would have been made redundant anyway.

And for Virge, it gave her something else again. She developed a hurried intensity, an impatience, a desperate desire not to stay still. Everything about her seemed to speed up. She talked faster, worker harder, went out more often, met more and more people, took more and more business trips, stayed up later, drank more.

When she was at home, she spent evenings planning her funeral and her memorial service. She drew up lists and plans and wrote out the invitations and a strict page of closely written instructions.

'I don't want it to be sad,' she said. 'I want everyone to have a lovely time.'

She said she didn't want to end up in a box. 'I want my ashes scattered in the meadow at Christ Church,' she said, 'because that was where I was most happy.' She was insistent on it.

'You will promise, Ash, won't you?' she said. 'You promise you won't forget?'

After Billy, there was a series of other things – I can't remember who it was who said that we only learned through suffering, but it seemed that this was our time for learning.

Gus got done over by a journalist, who came round to do a piece on him, acted friendly and charming and stayed for tea, said that he was doing a piece on coming young artists, and then when the article came out it was all bitchy and sarcastic about how Gus lived in a mansion in Chelsea playing at being a starving artist, and two gallery owners read it and rang up and cancelled the shows they had offered.

Stretch and Denny were ripped off by a man posing as a producer, who said he would put their show on, listenened to all their ideas, took money off them, and then disappeared. Stevie discovered that the man she had been seeing was married with three children. We were burgled twice, Virge got mugged on the tube, and I started receiving a series of obscene telephone calls. Even the excitement of Gus's first show was spoiled when he received anonymous hate mail and one of his canvasses was slashed.

And then, just to give us the final cherry on the cake, my mother, her timing impeccable as always, decided that it was high time for her nineteenth nervous breakdown and went into a psychiatric clinic.

It was as if reality, which we had managed to keep at bay for so long, had finally risen to the flood, burst all our carefully positioned sandbags, and was overwhelming us.

Into all this, Hem came back to London. He called up and said he was in town for a couple of days, passing through, and would I have dinner. I said yes. What else was I going to say?

We went to eat in one of those steamy little Chinese places in Gerrard Street. It seemed appropriate, I wasn't sure for what.

Hem arrived before me, and I walked in to see him sitting at a corner table, different but totally unchanged. And as I saw him, I knew that my feelings for him were different, but also totally unchanged, and my heart turned over and I wanted to leave. I didn't, of course I didn't. I walked over, and sat down opposite him, and we both looked at each other in a small still moment of quiet, and then he gave a smile and took my hand, and said,

'Hello, Ash,'

'Hello,' I said.

Hem nodded a little, and smiled again, and ordered me a beer. I lit a cigarette, and played with it a bit, giving myself time.

'So,' said Hem. 'What's been happening with you?'

I told him. It made it easier, having news to tell him, like book at bedtime, just recounting. I told him about the house and all the jobs we had and all the parties. I told him a little about some of the boys who had come and gone. I didn't want to sound as though I was boasting, but I had enough pride not to want him to think I had sat around pining for him after he left me so abruptly.

And all the time I was telling him this, all the time I was talking and laughing and eating dim sum and acting normal, I really wanted to tell him that I still loved him, that my heart still belonged entirely to him, that for all my bravado and my brave new world where I had learnt how to go out and take sexual pleasure and regard one night stands as common currency, I was still the same old romantic at heart, that no one had come along and replaced him, that it was still him I dreamed of at night.

I wanted to ask him how he could have left so suddenly, I wanted to ask if he still thought of me, and remembered all those times we had had together. I wanted, more than anything, for him to say that he had made a terrible mistake, and that he had come to his senses and come back, that he wanted me back.

He didn't say that. He listened to the stories I told him, and he told me a few of his own, but we didn't say anything that mattered. We just went through the niceties, the kind of conversation you would expect two old friends to have after a long absence, as if we were in a play or a film, as if someone else had written the script.

At the end of dinner, we paid the bill and gathered up our things and walked out into the street. Chinatown was bright and bustling and hurried, filled with colour and light, as it always was at night, and we stood for a moment, in the midst of all the people walking and talking about us, and Hem looked at me and said that he was going to Russia, and then on to Burma, if he could get a visa, and after that who knew. Who knew?

And then he said goodbye and kissed me on the cheek and walked away and I stood watching him go, and I despised myself for feeling just as bad as I had the last time.

I found Virge in the kitchen when I got back, watching television and painting her toe nails and eating toast with fried cod's roe on it. She had the most curious eating habits, not that she saw anything strange in it, cod's roe to her was as natural as bread and butter, but it always made me laugh.

'Oh, Ash,' she said, taking one look at my face. 'What is it? Was it awful? Will you tell?'

I shook my head.

'It's okay,' I said. 'What's on TV?'

I didn't want to bore her with it. I didn't want to sit and drone about my sad aching heart and act like a moaning Minnie.

Virge stood up and snapped off the television and looked at me, a fierce look in her face.

'What?' I said. 'I'm fine.'

'Well, you're just not,' said Virge sharply. 'It won't do, this, this thing you do. This pretending you're always fine when you're not.'

I looked at her curiously. If I didn't know that we never

got angry with each other, I would have said she was cross with me.

She sat down opposite me, and faced me squarely.

'You see,' she said. 'That's the thing about friends. It's not proper friends if you only tell me the good stuff. You must tell me the bad things as well. Otherwise what's the point?'

'Oh, Virge,' I said. 'But it's all so sad and dull and I don't want to bore you and burden you.'

'No, no,' she said. 'That's the whole point. It's not a bore and a burden, because it's me you're talking to. That's why we're best friends. When I see you walk in looking like the world just ended, I want to know why. If you can't tell me, who can you tell?'

She was right. She taught me one of the best lessons I ever learnt about life, and friendship; that just giving the good parts isn't enough.

17

The next year, Virge got moved to America for her job. The British film industry, such as it was, was going through one of its periodic slumps, which it always seemed to do just as it had produced a couple of critically acclaimed and even commercially viable films – as if it was approaching that acme of vulgarity, success, and had to take a step backwards in shock and apology. So her company moved Virge out to Los Angeles, with a fat new salary and a big new office looking out over the palm trees and the boulevards and the smog.

Taking her to the airport and seeing her off was as bad as saying goodbye to Hem, although I tried not to show it. I didn't want to make her feel guilty about her great new career move, and after all it was only me – how could I count myself as more important than a whole film studio?

'Oh Ash,' said Virge helplessly, as we stood outside Terminal Four with the bitter English wind whipping at us. 'Why can't you come with me? Why can't you come and get a nice job at Book Soup or somewhere? What will I do without you?'

'We'll write,' I said bravely. 'It won't be forever. There's the fax now, and everything. The world is shrinking all the time.'

Neither of us believed me. Six thousand miles was a long way, however much technology we had at our disposal.

But for all that, I knew that Virge wanted to go. She hid it from me as best she could, but although I knew that she would miss me, she had some wandering desire which I lacked, some impatience to get out and get moving and get on.

Virge put her arms around me and hugged me to her.

'Ash,' she said. 'You will promise that you won't forget me and find someone else who you love more.'

I laughed in surprise. It was such a ridiculous idea, that anyone could ever replace her.

'Don't be silly,' I said. 'Always together, forever and ever, remember? It's not just talk. We've got all our plans for when we're seventy, for heaven's sake.'

Virge let me go, and gave me a good old stiff upper lip smile, best of British.

'Yes,' she said. 'Of course. Of course we have.'

And she picked up her bags and walked away into the airport building, calling over her shoulder,

'I'm not saying goodbye, it's too morbid.'

And I watched her go, and then I got into the car and drove back to London, and when I got to the roundabout at Hammersmith, I had to pull over because I was crying too much to see where I was going.

I adjusted to life without Virge, but there was a great big space left where she used to be. That's the best way I can describe it. It wasn't as if anything changed that much, my life went on, pretty much as before, it was just that there was a gap, a missing part.

Etta was back from Boston, and she moved into the house, so I had her and Stevie, and they were very conscious of Virge being away, and made a special effort to look after me. I loved them, they were equally wonderful in their different ways, and we had that comforting thing of going back a long way, but for all that, it wasn't the same.

I thought about it a lot, those years that Virge was away. It's a curious thing, friendship, because it isn't celebrated in the way that other things are. True love, that old chestnut, gets all the press; poems written about it, and novels, and plays, and pop songs, whole anthologies and books of quotations. Friendship is seen as a poor relation, a quiet mouse of a first cousin, not worth the print.

I wondered why. For a while, I thought that it was me, that there was something in me that was getting the whole thing out of proportion, that perhaps other things in life really were more important, that family, and great love, and work and ambition should be given more gravity, more weight, that perhaps I was making up a whole song and dance about nothing, that this lost dark feeling I had without Virge was due to some terrible inadequacy in me, that it was I who was wrong.

As usual, Virge knew all this without being told, and perhaps, lonely herself in a new city, felt it as well. She wrote to me every week, nice long rambling letters, full of references to our mutual past. 'Do you remember,' they always started, 'Do you remember the time . . . ?' And I would sit and read them, and remember, like it was yesterday, and miss her more than I thought was possible.

Virge liked her job, but she didn't care much for Los Angeles. 'It is,' she wrote to me, soon after she left, 'the most blasted Godforsaken place I ever visited, how I long and long for rain, and lovely English things like greasy spoons and bacon and eggs and oh, I don't know – Radio Four and the Sunday papers and BBC2. Also, apart from the fact that this is a strange spaghetti junction masquerading as a city, and has absolutely no architectural merit whatsoever and no pedestrians, people don't seem to have friends here. They have people with whom they do lunch, or they have meetings, or there are people they hang out with because they are in the same business and they can each show off about how much further up the ladder they are, which makes for a rather edgy and uncomfortable atmosphere, you can imagine. And the very idea of telling the *truth* – I shrivel up when I hear woman A tell woman B how lovely her new hairstyle is, what an inspired cut, etc etc, all but begging for the number of her hairdresser – then woman B leaves the room, and within seconds woman A is full into a diatribe about the absolute dreadfulness of the hair, what was B *thinking* of, and wasn't it time that she had something done about her teeth. Viciousness unconfined. I shudder to think what they are saying about me.'

Writing back, I felt like a mother whose first child has gone away to boarding school. I wrote long reassuring letters about London, about the rain and the traffic and the Northern Line, and how nothing ever changed.

I told her about what the others were doing, about Gus and Stevie and Denny and Stretch and Etta. I told her about what we were doing without her, going out and seeing people. I told her about the old places, still going, and the new ones opening up, that hemlines had gone back up again, just to keep people on their toes, and the seventies revival was surprising everyone by really catching on.

I wondered if she was happy, so far away. I couldn't tell. Her letters were full of jokes and anecdotes and stories, but they didn't tell me very much about her. 'I found this the other day,' she wrote, sending me an excerpt from a book called *The Love and Language of Schoolchildren*. 'This is from a little girl aged nine: 'I have two friends called Carol and Brenda. I like Brenda because she is very funny and very small. I also like Carol because when she has any sweets she always gives me some, and she has lovely curly hair, and she is very nice.' Someone asked me about England the other day, and I said, 'I have two friends called Ash and Gus. I like Gus because he is very funny and very tall. I also like Ash because when she has any sensemilla she always gives me some, and she has lovely platinum blonde hair, and she is very nice.' They looked at me for a moment in absolute astonishment, and started laughing, and said, 'Oh, this is the famous English sense of humour, I see. Is this wet or dry humour? This is irony, isn't it?' And I looked very serious indeed, and said, 'Not at all, it's all absolutely true.' Oh dear, shall I ever learn to get along in America?'

But for all that, she did seem to get along in America, however rude she was about it. 'All we have to read here is the *Los Angeles Times*,' she wrote in one letter, 'which is, as someone once said about another equally august publication, written by those who can't write for those who can't read,' or, 'I was talking to one of my production buddies the other day, buddy here being employed as a loose term for someone who can conduct a comprehensible conversation for more than three minutes without imploding or calling 911.' And while I enjoyed these letters, these barbs, these jokes, they made me sad too, because they reminded me too much of what I was missing.

Virge wasn't entirely lost to me in those years she spent in America. We called each other up and made plans, careful detailed itineraries involving meetings in foreign airports and distant hotels.

The first May after she left, we went to stay with Michael, in Italy, where he was living with Giovanni, still happy. We flew into Pisa, from our different cities, rather astonishing all the other travellers in that little airport by falling on each other's necks with voluble and most un-English exclamations of joy.

'Oh Virge,' I said, circling round and round her, unable to believe that finally here she was, in real life, rather than just her distinctive blue italics on a piece of paper. 'Just look at you.'

She stood still, letting me have a look. The thing about Virge, one of the things I loved most in her, was her absolute inimitable style. She had never been a dedicated follower of fashion; what she did was make it up as she went along, depending on her frame of mind at the time. She would take a character or a period, anything from Audrey Hepburn to Lara in Dr Zhivago, the fifties in Paris or the thirties in Berlin, and then reinterpret it for her own use. It was a gift she had, something I envied in her: I was still, after all these years, hankering after looking like someone or something, and I still hadn't quite got there, although perhaps I was starting to look like myself, but that didn't count, not yet.

Now, she was impeccably groomed, not something I'd ever seen her do before. Until now she had kept a kind of carelessness in her dress, managing to give the clever impression that she had just crawled out of bed and flung on whatever was nearest to hand and made it into something by the sheer force of her own personality. But this was something else entirely. Her hair, now dyed so black that it had a bluebottle sheen on it, was cut into a severe Louise Brooks bob, but she had none of the tragic doomed victim aspect that had infused all those famous pictures of poor Lulu, with her sad eyes and her pearls and that dark air of lost chance that hung about her. On Virge, the hair sat like a valedictory flourish, modern and nostalgic at the same time, and entirely her own.

To go with it, she was wearing a narrow cut mod suit, with a long black jacket and stovepipe trousers, and pointed boots with stacked heels, a modern joke on the early Beatles uniform, unadorned except for a big black patent bag slung over one arm.

'Virge,' I said, in admiration. 'Well. Who would have guessed? The brave new look. The brave new world.'

'Not too butch?' she said.

'Not a bit of it,' I said. 'Just perfect. Chic and minimal, and kind of witty and faintly self referential, and clever and polished.'

Virge smiled broadly. She had never believed that old line about clothes making man, but she always said that they could help, if you knew how to do it right.

'I'm having such fun,' she said. 'Power dressing for the we don't give a damn generation.'

The other thing I loved about Virge, was that she never dressed *for* things. There are people who spend half their lives worried about being appropriate, about fitting in and looking right and wearing the uniform. Virge said tosh to all that, every opportunity she got, and it made me laugh now, as we picked up our bags and walked down to the train station, because it was May and warm and we were in the middle of Italy, and there she was looking as if she had just stepped off Fifth Avenue, by way of Old Compton Street. Sometimes I thought I was making too much of all this, that it was just a way of dressing, but for me it went right to the heart of Virge herself, the thing I loved about her, that she never did the usual thing.

'You know,' I said, as we got on the train. 'What it really is?'

'What?' said Virge, turning her long grey eyes on me.

'You look grown up,' I said. 'That's what it is.'

'Well,' said Virge. 'And about bloody time.'

This thing of growing up, of being a grown up, was something I thought of often, at that time. It was very confusing and not what I had expected. Sometimes I looked back on my teen years with a tugging nostalgia, because at least things were simple then. When you're a teenager you despise your parents because they don't understand a single word you say, and they were young themselves so long ago that they have forgotten what it's like, and you have a constant sense of astonishment that these people should have actually given birth to you, when you feel so divorced from them that they might be a different species. And the good thing about that is that you know most other people your age feel the same, so you know that this is only to be expected. It's later, when you start thinking about being grown up yourself that it starts getting confusing.

You know that once you're out in the world, with your job and your car and your own place and your life, that this means, somehow, that you have entered into the halls of adulthood. You stop staying in to watch *Top of the Pops*, you read a broadsheet, you understand about tax returns and pension plans: you understand the deep implications of all this. Someone, somewhere along the line, (who? Books, films, magazines? Society? The government?) has told you that this is right and proper. And also the progression of things is deeply ingrained in you. Here is how it happens: you are a child, sweet, cuddly, maybe a bit naughty, then you are a teen, difficult, moody, hormonal, and very naughty, then you cross the bridge into GROWNUPNESS, and suddenly you are responsible and mature and wise and capable. And then you get married and have children and they get married and have children, and you indulge your grandchildren shamelessly, and your teeth fall out, and probably your hair as well, and you get old and then you die.

But, here we were, across the great divide, three years on from university, and we didn't feel any different. At least, I didn't. I remember when I was twenty, thinking that twenty-five was old, and here I was, only a month away from this landmark, and I didn't feel as I had expected. I wanted my money back. I didn't *feel* grown up. I felt like I was faking it, as if any moment someone would come along and unmask me as a fraud, as if I was going into a nightclub with forged ID and the bouncer was about to give me one of those knowing looks and say, 'There's no way *that* one's over eighteen.'

I didn't know what else I could do. I had all the trappings. I had a job, a house, a newspaper; I had friends and a working wardrobe and a national insurance number. I even had, as of six months ago, a therapist. What more did you have to do?

Giovanni, Michael's lover, had a big old stone house hidden up in one of those curving wooded valleys that they have near Siena. It had been converted from an old barn, and it had thick stone walls and smooth flagged floors and small terraces looking out over the cypress trees and a sloping garden which ran as wild as artifice would allow.

Giovanni was a cultured gentle measured man of around forty-five, handsome in a clever thoughtful way, precise in his movements and courteous in his speech. He was an art critic, and was, when we first met him, in the middle of writing what Michael described as a definitive work on Braque.

'How splendid, how clever, how perfect,' said Virge. 'I always think it was unfair that Picasso got all the credit for inventing cubism when Braque had been at it for years.'

He was also, interestingly, when it was so much on my mind, absolutely grown up. We stayed in his house for a week, and he was a consummate host, charming and never intrusive and absolutely unpatronising. He discussed art with us and laughed at our jokes, and for much of the time left us alone, the three of us, separated by conflicting geography for so long, so that we could catch up.

18

That's what we did all week, catch up. We mounted one expedition to Siena, to sit in the curving medieval square and watch the evening crowds passing by, and one afternoon we drove into the hills so that Michael could show us a house he had found out towards Arezzo, which had extraordinary views, 360 degrees over the surrounding hills, which really did roll, the way hills are supposed to, and was derelict.

'My dream house,' he said, as we picked our way carefully up its crumbling staircases and across its treacherous floors. 'We must win the Lotto so I can buy it and restore it to its former glories.'

But for the rest of the time we just sat, on one or other of the terraces, and talked. There was one terrace which looked out over the wooded hillside and caught the sun all morning, and we sat there early in the day, and drank cups of heavily sugared black coffee. After lunch we moved downstairs where there was a pergola, and we would sit under it, watching the way that the shafts of sunlight came through the vines over our heads, the light green and gold and cool and dusty. Later, in the early evening, we went round to the other side of the house, up to the third floor where there was a small balcony covered in pots and shaded with a long awning, just room for the three of us to sit and have a glass of wine and watch the sun set, before Giovanni finished his work for the day, and came out to call us down for dinner.

'How happy you are, Michael,' said Virge, on one of these sunset evenings. There was a strange note in her voice, something jealous almost. I heard it, but I wasn't sure quite what it was, whether she was jealous, of Michael's happiness, or because that happiness had taken him away from her, that his heart belonged to someone else before her.

Michael gave her a look, and I think he heard it too, but he let it go.

'I am,' he said. 'Terribly terribly happy. Isn't it strange?'

I knew he meant it. I knew that he couldn't believe his luck, that he did really think it strange. I always wondered about that. He and Virge, after all, had been surrounded by happiness their whole lives. They had their parents to look to, absolute proof that happiness existed, was something attainable and even to be expected, and yet they both had the same astonishment that they should find it, a fear that it was something that would be taken away, or paid for, or destined not to last. I liked that in them. They could so easily have been smug or blasé or taken it for granted, but they never did.

'Oh,' said Virge, that same strange note in her voice. 'If only we could all stay here for ever and ever and be happy.'

Later that night, Virge and I sat up late, sitting outside looking out over the dark moonlit landscape. It was Virge's idea.

'Let's stay up,' she said, after Michael and Giovanni had gone to bed. 'Let's take a glass of brandy and all our cigarettes and just sit up all night.'

We sat quiet for a while, watching the stars and the dark and the moon sailing over the hills, which loomed around us, benign and mysterious. I liked that, that we could just sit and be still, that we had known each other so well for so long that we didn't always have to be talking.

'Do you feel different?' said Virge, after a while. I liked that too, that she knew she didn't have to explain what she meant, that she could trust me to understand absolutely.

'Yes,' I said slowly, thinking about it. 'But not in the ways I expected. I feel different and I feel the same, and I can't work out where the line is.'

'Isn't it curious,' said Virge, 'that here we are, with all this, and we are different and we look different and none of it is at all as we thought it would be. Where did all the fantasy start in the first place?'

'Perhaps,' I said, making it up as I went along, which was a way I had when I was with Virge, 'perhaps it's because we always looked at other people. That we thought we would be like them, and we aren't because we're us. Perhaps that's the unexpected thing.'

Virge shot me a look.

'You always could do that,' she said. 'Oh, Ash, I miss that. That way you have of suddenly coming up with these little flights of perception just when I least expect it. You did that the first night we met, do you remember?'

I remembered.

'Like it was yesterday,' I said. 'I still think it's when my life really started. Everything up until then seems like a dress rehearsal for the real thing.'

'In America,' said Virge, 'people are always telling me that life isn't a dress rehearsal, which is nonsense, because that's exactly what it feels like, half the time. Sometimes I feel like I'm walking around half the time, saying Is this it, is this it?'

'Yes,' I said. 'I know. I do too.'

'It's so strange,' said Virge. She stretched her neck back and looked up at the black sky and let out a long sigh. 'I sit in my office, and I go to meetings, and I have conference calls, and sometimes I feel like I'm playing a game. I want to stand up and say, Look, I'm only twenty-five, I know nothing, you've got the wrong person, there's been a mix-up. I feel as if any moment the real person, the one they really wanted, is going to walk into the room and say, You're sitting in my seat, like Goldilocks and the Three Bears.'

'Oh, Virge,' I said. 'Yes, I know that too.'

'And then,' said Virge, 'other times I feel old as the hills, as if this has all been going on forever, and I wonder how we will get through another twenty-five years, that it will take us to the end of time.' She stopped for a moment, and sat very still. There was no sound, not even the wind. There was a deep thick silence which seemed to cover us. I had never thought much about silence before, but you can hear it, if you listen hard enough. 'No one ever told me,' said Virge, with sudden violence, 'that it was this complicated. Why do they never tell you that?'

'Do you think that we think too much about it?' I said. I remembered what Albert had said, that first dinner Michael had given in Oxford, about won't it be lovely being old, when all this is behind us. I wondered if he meant that when we were old we could just stop thinking about everything quite so much, and learn to let things be.

'No,' said Virge. She shrugged, suddenly fatalistic. 'I think we must. I think it's right that we do.'

'Wouldn't it be restful,' I said, 'if we didn't. If we could let things slide past us, just accepted everything and said, Oh well, this is life, this is what happens, and not be always asking why or how and what is the sense in it all.'

'Oh yes,' said Virge. 'It would be restful. But it's not

possible. It's the way we are, that will never change. Whatever else changes, that never will.'

'Will you stay much longer in America?' I asked her the next evening.

I was changing for dinner, and Virge was lying on my bed while I dressed. I loved my bedroom, it was high and light, with whitewashed walls and a red stone floor and a wide wooden bed that creaked when I got into it at night.

'They want me there for another year,' said Virge. 'I'll stay. I hate it and I love it, you know.'

She paused for a minute and lay back on the bed and stared at the ceiling. I wondered if she would tell me some more about it. I wondered about the details of her life, but she didn't like to talk about that. She only ever described it in broad brushstrokes, jokes or teases. Perhaps it was just too far away, I don't know.

'It's this I miss most,' she said. 'Lying on your bed and chatting. They don't do chatting in Los Angeles. They do power lunches and business meetings and conference calls. They even have a fax at the gym, just in case. But they don't do chatting.'

'Will you do my zip?' I said, turning my back to her.

'There,' said Virge, doing me up. 'Don't you look lovely in your pretty print frock?'

'It's my new look,' I said. 'I have a feeling for the forties and bluebirds over the white cliffs of Dover, don't ask me why.'

There was a knock on the door.

'Come in, Michael,' said Virge. 'We're decent. We have clothes on, anyway.'

Michael came in and sat himself on the bed next to Virge.

'I couldn't resist,' he said. 'I knew you would be chatting and putting on your lipstick. Two of my favourite things.'

'What do you think of Ash's new dress,' said Virge.

'Perfect,' said Michael. 'I love that floating print thing. You should grow your hair, Ash,' he said seriously. 'I yearn to see you with a kind of Veronica Lake hair style.'

'Perhaps I will,' I said. 'Perhaps the peroxide look has gone on long enough.'

'So,' said Michael. 'I want to know about your life, Ash. Is there love?'

I shook my head. 'No love,' I said.

'She saw Hem again,' said Virge.

'Oh dear,' said Michael. 'I do see. Do you think we ever recover from our first love?'

'I recovered from Keane quick enough,' said Virge. 'Look how I got over that one. Just look at how I picked myself up and dusted myself off and got on to the next trick.'

'Ah,' said Michael. 'But that was because you made a mistake. Now, there was no mistake with Hem, because he never stopped being lovely, he just left. Will he wander forever, do you think Ash, or will it be just a phase?'

'I don't know if he'll ever stop,' I said. 'Not now. I dream of him coming back and saying he's had enough and that we should just go and live in a little white house by the sea, but see how dangerous that is, because I really do know it will never happen.'

'Oh, bugger it,' said Virge, sitting up. 'What is it with bloody old love? Why can't Ash just have Hem, because it is him she still loves? Why can't that happen?'

'Because, my darling,' said Michael, 'we aren't living in a lovely motion picture like the kind they make in your town. Personally, I think the movies have a lot to answer for, tempting us with the possibility of happy endings like they do.'

'It's not so much to ask, though,' said Virge, 'is it? A happy ending?'

'I think,' said Michael, with a sudden unexpected moment of gravity, 'that it's more to ask than we know.'

That week went by quickly, and soon it was Monday, and time for Virge and I to leave.

Michael, who was doing some work at the British Institute, had left early that morning for Florence, so Giovanni drove us to the station.

'Well,' said Virge, as he dropped us off. 'Thank you for everything. You are a very great and wonderful gentleman, if I may say so.'

Giovanni gave us his slow courteous smile and kissed us goodbye and waved us off, and as the train pulled out of the station and we leant out of our window, waving at his dwindling figure on the platform, Virge said, almost under her breath, 'Lucky lucky Michael. I hope he realises his luck.'

19

I saw Virge again at the end of December, when she and Gus and Stevie and I went to Naples for four days, to see in the New Year. It was a fine holiday, the sun shining strongly in that lovely clear way it has in the winter. It was cold enough for us to have to wear heavy coats, and bright enough for sunglasses, so we all wandered around looking like something out of a Norman Parkinson photograph, which of course was the idea.

We drove along the Neopolitan coast, and returned to Capri, very different now from the way we remembered it at the height of the summer season, and we spent New Year's Eve in Naples, and watched the fireworks over the bay and all the people out on their balconies banging saucepans and throwing firecrackers into the street, along with all their rubbish, a famous Neopolitan tradition, we were told, and not any old iron, but enormous articles, broken washing machines and defunct ovens.

'Goodness,' said Virge, 'now I see why the streets are so empty.'

We had stayed late at dinner, and when we asked our waiter for a taxi he had just laughed, and told us that it was impossible after eleven. *Molto pericoloso*, he kept saying, shaking his head sadly at our ignorance.

In the end, Virge had taken matters into her own hands

and bribed him to drive us himself, which he did, in a rickety old Fiat, speeding through the deserted streets at sixty miles an hour, ignoring red lights and stop signs, hunched over the wheel, muttering under his breath.

At our hotel, we got out quickly, and Virge gave him many thousands of lire and told him he was *molto, molto gentile*, the most *gentile* man in Italy. He barely stopped long enough to take the money, taking off with squealing tyres and crashing gears, as if the devil were at his back.

We still didn't understand until the clock struck midnight and the mayhem started: within moments the lights round the bay were obscured by a cloud of cordite from the fireworks roaring from every ship, and the streets were filled with the sounds of bangers and the crashing of heavy machinery being dropped from fifth-floor balconies. We watched it all in amazed delight, and drank champagne and waved sparklers which Virge had bought that afternoon.

'We'll remember this for the rest of our lives,' said Virge. 'It's the maddest most perfect thing I've ever seen.'

Soon after that, she moved to San Francisco. She said she couldn't bear the Hollywood Hills a moment longer, and so she managed to persuade her company to let her set up an office in San Francisco, which she loved on sight.

'Don't ask me how I did it,' she wrote. 'But it's heaven here, you must come at once.'

Gus and I went together, the following September, and stayed with Virge in her little apartment in Sauselito. It was lovely, that city of hills, living up to its publicity. We loved the Golden Gate bridge (although Virge seemed a little affronted that it was not golden at all), and the steep inclines and the cable cars and the Haight and North Beach. We went to the City Lights bookshop and Caffe Trieste and Vesuvio, an old beat hangout which seemed not to have changed at all since Jack Kerouac was a boy. We drove along the coast to Monterey and Big Sur, and into the interior to visit the Napa Valley, and spent a weekend among the astonishing mountains of Yosemite.

'Oh,' said Virge, gazing up at the great sheer walls of the valley. 'How like the Americans. Even their scenery is bigger than everyone else's.'

But for all the wonder of these trips, and they were very wonderful, I missed having Virge there day to day, not just for holidays. I missed being ordinary. I missed the inconsequential revealing conversation you can only have with someone who is there all the time. I missed, strangely for me, the mundane, the everyday, the routine. I found that occasional meetings and crackling telephone calls and air mailed letters weren't enough; that too many of the important things went unsaid, that that old feeling I'd always had with Virge, the one of always walking in step, was starting to fracture, and I missed it.

I learned from my shrink that this was perfectly normal and to be expected, considering my background. He said it wasn't at all strange that I missed Virge so badly, because it was the closest I had ever come to having a family. He said also, cryptically, that he was not surprised by Virge's staying away, moving on, although he didn't tell me why.

She didn't come back at the end of her two years. She moved to New York, where her film company had an office, and she met someone, a musician, and shared a loft with him in SoHo.

'I am in love,' she wrote to me. 'Isn't it unexpected? The musician is perfect, although I am convinced he has a dark secret. You must come to Manhattan and meet him.'

I hid my disappointment carefully. I was happy for her that she was in love. I thought it must be good, after Keane.

Coincidentally, I was in love myself, with a writer I

had met through my job. For three months, I played an agonising game of flirtation and courtship, a terrible grandmother's footsteps will he won't he. When finally, he did, it didn't make it much easier. Although we seemed to be established as a couple, in that he would take me to things, and come round for dinner at the house, and be friendly with Gus and Stretch and Denny and Etta and Stevie, although he behaved with perfect propriety, calling when he said he would, arriving punctually when we were to meet at a restaurant, listening carefully to everything I said, there was something missing.

For a long year, we wandered through this strange relationship, and when at the end of it, he told me that he didn't think it was working, I was desperate and hurt and wounded, but I wasn't surprised. Sometimes I wondered why we had bothered in the first place; I loved him, there was no doubt about that, but I never felt he was mine. It was as if it was just something for him to do, to pass the time, as if, quite literally, his heart wasn't in it. I never knew him, hard as I tried. I knew that he was clever: he had degrees and awards and letters after his name, and he wrote in a spare elliptical style, which I admired. I knew that he was ambitious and thoughtful and distrustful of authority. But he was also close and secretive and wary of giving away any part of himself, like those tribes who believe that if you take their photograph it steals their soul.

The shrink was sympathetic and sensible, a combination he had down to a fine art, and said that it was hardly surprising. He told me, in a matter-of-fact way, that I was only drawn to unavailable men. This was the kind of thing he said. I rather liked these technical shrink terms: dysfunctional family, gestalt, inner child, anima and animus, persona as a mask. It made me feel that I was learning something, that there perhaps was some nice tidy scientific explanation for the strange vagaries of life.

Unavailable men, it seemed, was my theme for the moment. I had thought it just coincidence, before I decided that there was no such thing, that both Hem and the writer had, finally, left me. I had thought it was something to do with me, that I wasn't good enough, lovable enough, sexy enough – *anything* enough. It seemed perversely natural that they should go, eventually. The shrink told me that, given everything, I would think that.

There is always a gap between hearing something and understanding it intellectually and really believing it, deep down in the gut. Until the gap closes, it seems impossible to act on this new knowledge. Whatever it was, I had some kind of masochistic bent in me that led me to go to great lengths to prove it. So in the months after the writer left, I threw myself into a series of unrequited love affairs. I developed violent and transient passions for the most impossible people, the most motley and hopeless cast of characters.

'What is it this time?' said Stevie, about once a week, as she came downstairs for breakfast and inspected my pale lovelorn face over her cornflakes. 'Don't tell me, let me guess. He's married? He's gay? He's ingesting large amounts of crack cocaine? Or is it all three at the same time?'

'Oh dear,' said Gus, who worried about it, when he wasn't painting another masterpiece. 'All the usual suspects, let's round them up.'

'Oh Ash,' said Stretch, when he and Denny came round to visit. 'You do know that they never leave their wives, however much they say they are misunderstood. You do know that that is one of the great laws of the universe?'

'Of men who leave their wives for their mistresses,' said Stevie, '75% split up within the first year.'

'Where do you get these statistics?' said Denny. 'How do you know this?'

'Some of us,' said Stevie with dignity, 'read a reputable newspaper, thank you very much.'

'Yeah yeah,' said Denny. 'Roll out the barrel. It's a long way to Tipperary. I do beg your pardon, my old sister.'

'Don't call me sister,' said Stevie, with her dangerous look. 'Have a little respect.'

It was a horrible panic-filled time. I had a true feeling of life on the edge, of walking a tightrope, almost as if I was willing myself to fall.

And then one morning, I woke up and realised that it was over. One thing I was learning as I grew older was the essential mystery of why and how things happen, that for all my new learning, my perusal of Jung and my visits to Hampstead, the secret veil that hangs over our lives can only be lifted a little corner at a time, that most of the time we really do only see through a glass darkly.

So it was a surprise when I woke up one morning in August, and found that the awful destructive yearning for the unattainable was no longer stirring in my stomach.

It was a Saturday, and the house was empty. The others had gone for a weekend in Dublin, having a sudden imperative desire for Guinness and chasing in the steps of Joyce, and instead of wandering aimlessly about the big empty rooms, gazing at the telephone and reading terrible romantic books with happy endings which only emphasised my own failure to find one, instead of finding myself sluggish and cross and only really wanting to lie about and have taunting day dreams, I found myself with a sense of calm, as if the storm had blown by, and I was surprised and relieved to find myself still standing.

I liked the quiet of the house for once, instead of finding it oppressive, and I got up and put on my dressing gown and made myself a pot of real Colombian coffee and put some crooning jazz on the record player and sat down with the paper. Just a nice civilised weekend breakfast, for one.

I wondered what I might do. I felt that I could do anything I chose, a walk in the park, or a trip to the seaside, or a double bill at the pictures. And then I heard the door open, and steps coming quickly up the stairs, and Virge walked into the room, and said, 'Breakfast, what a perfect idea.'

And because I didn't believe in coincidence, I felt utterly unsurprised that she should be here, back from America on the very day that I had fought my way out of the months of darkness and despair and self-doubt, because she was the one person in the whole wide world who always made me feel that I was lovable and desirable, and good enough. Virge made me feel as if I was good enough for anything.

She smiled at me, and looked at the coffee pot, and said: 'You are clever, Ash. You must have known I was coming, you've made enough for two.'

When we finished breakfast, we decided that since the sun was shining and it was a lovely day, we should go to the country.

'Ma and Pa don't know I'm back,' said Virge. 'Let's surprise them.'

So I got dressed and packed a bag and we got into my car and drove to Dorset.

'Are you back for good?' I asked Virge.

'For good,' she said. 'I don't want to be a wandering Jew any more. I think I've had it with all that.'

She didn't say why, just then. Later, she told me that the musician's dark secret turned out to be a wife and two children, which she thought was terribly mundane and pedestrian. She had held higher hopes of him than that, she said, but there we were.

Then, driving through the sleepy green English fields, all I knew was that I was happy to have her back again. It felt as if a chapter had ended, as if we were starting again, not with a backward-looking idea, not of going back to the way things had been before, but really starting again, with a brave new world, and us walking into it, arm in arm, our eyes wider open than they had once been.

Perhaps because of this, the familiar drive looked different, as if I was seeing it for the first time, while knowing that I had been there before, but in another life, another incarnation. It had a sheen and a freshness, something promising and old, a nice visual sense of paradox. And when we drew up at the house, I looked at that with new eyes as well: it was as charming and inviting as ever, but it looked changed to me in some small significant way, like when you go back to the house of your childhood and everything seems the same, only smaller, because you are grown now, and no longer looking up at everything. It's the angle that has changed, so old familiar things seem new and exciting.

I think Virge had the same feeling I did, and she summed it up, in that way she had.

'Funny,' she said, looking at the house, a secret smile on her face, 'what three years can do.'

She turned to me, and took my arm.

'Come along then,' she said. 'Let's go and see what the folks make of it all.'

As we walked through the arch which led to the main house, we could hear the tapping of Diana's chisel as she worked on a block of stone. I smiled. It was the distinctive noise that I always associated with that house, along with the low billing of the doves in the quiet of the early evening. You could always tell when the sculpture was taking on the form that Diana wanted, because then the tapping would be easy and rythmical, as if keeping time to some silent sonata. When she was blocked and unable to find the right way you would hear her starting over and over, a few hollow taps, followed by a pause, then beginning again, a little faster, then a break, until she found her tune.

'Sounds like Mozart today,' said Virge. 'Even Bach, perhaps, one of those formal minuet numbers. It will be a thing of beauty.'

As we entered the house and came into the high central living room, we heard its counterpoint: Jonathan rattling away at the typewriter keys, fast as machine-gun fire.

'Oh,' said Virge, smiling. 'What it is, being back in an artistic household.'

We decided not to disturb them, so we made lunch and ate it at the kitchen table, and started the long process of filling each other in on our lives. It was something that gave us pleasure, and we were in no rush, because we had that lovely feeling that you only get with old and true friends, that there is no need to hurry, because there will be so much time to talk, so much time to tell all the things that had to be told. And as well, there was an added piquancy to it, that we were sitting here in secret, like intruders or conspirators, while the real inhabitants of the house went about their daily work, quite unaware of our presence.

At five o'clock on the dot, they both appeared, through different doorways, coming in for their tea.

'Creatures of habit,' said Virge. 'So nice to see that nothing really changes.'

'Nothing really does,' said Jonathan, smiling with pleasure and kissing us both. 'When I'm ninety, the one thing I can rely on is that you two will arrive just when I least expect it.'

After tea, Virge and Diana went to look at the roses, and

talk about whatever it is that mothers and daughters do talk about. Jonathan and I settled down on the sofa, and lit up cigarettes.

'One of the great mysteries,' said Jonathan. 'How do you manage?'

'Without?' I said.

'Yes,' he said. 'I've always wondered that about you, whether you miss your mother.'

I thought about it for a moment.

'The strange thing,' I said slowly, 'is that I don't miss her, because there isn't really anything to miss. But I suppose I miss having one.'

'Yes,' said Jonathan. 'I see that. Do you know, Ash, that I didn't address a word to my father after the age of twenty-one?'

I hadn't known. I was surprised. I couldn't really imagine Jonathan having a disagreement with anyone, he always appeared so unruffled and logical.

'How strange,' I said. 'So you know exactly.'

'Not exactly, but it's within my imagination,' he said. 'Remember the old line, that children start off loving their parents, then they judge them, and rarely if ever do they forgive them?'

'Yes,' I said. 'That just about sums it up, except I always hated them, really, even when I was too small to know why.'

'It sometimes amazes me that we've got away so lightly, with Virge and Michael,' said Jonathan. 'I'm not sure if they have judged, but if they have, they have forgiven. I wonder what I did to deserve such magnanimous children.'

'Led by example,' I said. 'You are the envy of us all. You and Diana are our paragons.'

'Oh dear,' said Jonathan, making a comical face. 'I'm flattered, of course, vanity being what it is, but I can't help but wonder if it's altogether a good thing.'

'You can't get enough of a good thing,' I said, because that was what I believed just then. I didn't think much about what he had said at the time, but afterwards I sometimes looked back and remembered that conversation, and wondered.

'How is your life, Ash?' said Jonathan, changing the subject, which was something he did when the conversation veered too close to him. He would talk for hours about what he thought, what he believed, what excited him and intrigued him and frustrated him, but always in the abstract. The intimate and inescapable nature of the personal made him uncomfortable; he wanted always to know about our lives, in the most unflinching detail, but he didn't like to betray his own. I thought it was just because he was English, after all, or perhaps it had something to do with him being a writer, happier observing others rather than himself. I didn't mind it, or think it meant anything very much, and anyway, I was happy to talk, it was almost as good as the shrink, and I didn't even have to leave a cheque at the end.

'My life,' I said, 'is changing. I think it's growing up. I think that's what it is.'

'How old are you now?' he said.

'Twenty-seven,' I said.

'Oh yes,' he nodded. 'Let me see if I remember, is that the age when you feel suddenly old?'

'Yes,' I said. 'It's curious. Do you remember when I first came here, when I was nineteen?'

'Like it was yesterday,' he said. He started to laugh. 'Can it really be eight years ago? Have we really known each other for eight years?'

'Well, you see,' I said, 'that's it. When we were nineteen we felt not so much old as grown up, sophisticated, that kind of thing. Then there was the phase when we were about twenty-three and twenty-four, when we lost all those certainties, and felt rather young and scared and foolish and as if we had to fake it, and now . . .'

'And now?' he said, looking at me with the absolute attention that he always paid me, the best compliment he could ever offer.

'Now,' I said, 'there is eight years, you see? That's what makes me feel old. That me and Virge have been best friends for almost nine years – if you've had that long with someone, it must mean you're old. But then half the time, I feel as if we are still eighteen, and I can't figure it out.'

'Yes, I understand,' said Jonathan. 'Isn't it strange how it works?'

'More than strange,' I said. 'Mind you, I'm at the stage where I think everything is strange. I think the whole shooting match is the oddest and most bizarre thing I could ever have imagined. I thought it would be the other way round.'

'I still feel like that,' said Jonathan. 'And I'm almost sixty.'

I was shocked then. I looked up to him so, I couldn't imagine him being unsure about anything. It wasn't just his age, it was the way he saw life, as if it was something he could understand.

'You mean, you don't feel that there are certainties?' I said. 'I would have thought that you would feel different.'

'Oh, no,' he said. 'It never changes. I'm still not sure why everyone has the illusion that it's age that brings sureness. One does learn more with age, you have more experience, and perhaps a clearer perspective on things, although that doesn't always follow, but you still find the whole thing as strange and mysterious as you ever did, more possibly. It's only in youth that you think you know it all.'

'How annoying it is,' I said. 'I did so hope I might get to fifty and find I had all the answers.'

'I don't think,' said Jonathan, 'that we ever find all the answers. I think it's just that we learn to understand the questions better, if we're lucky.'

Virge and I did all the old things, that weekend. We had tea on the lawn, and walked through the woods, and drove up to look at the grave of T.E. Lawrence. We went to the beach at Studland, late in the evening, just before the light left it, the best time, when it was empty, all the families packed up for the day and gone home for tea, just a few people about, walking their dogs, and men on little dune tractors, trawling the sand. We went back to Lulworth, and sat on the white pebbles, and remembered the time we had gone there with Gus and teased him about his virginity.

It was looking back, retracing our steps. Virge and I shared a tacit interest in our mutual past; we liked to go over it, remembering. It was as if we needed to define ourselves in some way, as if this habit of looking back was our means to make sense of ourselves, as if by trying to see the whole picture we could discern some pattern in it, some clue as to who we were and what we might be. I don't know. Perhaps I'm making it sound too grand and highflown, perhaps it was just that we both had a streak of nostalgia in us, perhaps it was no more than that we liked to remember the good times, just like people do.

But whatever it really was, we both had the same feeling just then, moving in to the last third of our twenties, that it was time for our life to begin, that we needed now some coherence, some inchoate idea of meaning and significance, almost as if just living wasn't enough.

20

So, together again, we embarked on this new phase, and typically, we did it in quite different ways. Virge, with the grandiosity which had always characterised even her smallest actions, decided that the time had come for her to change the world. ('Of course you are, dear,' said Gus, who was, most uncharacteristically, going through a whimsical stage at the time. 'If you won't do it, who else is there?')

One of the great differences between us was that she really believed that such a thing was possible: the strong streak of the idealist that ran in her, which led her to believe the best in people and ideas and theories, gave her the conviction she needed for such a plan. She truly did believe in the old dictum: give me a lever, and I can move the world. She had always had heroes, and she aspired to them. I, with a severe sense of my own limitations, watched them only, from afar, in admiration and awe and a sense that they were on another plane. So while Virge believed that the world was ripe for changing, I only wanted to put my small mark on it, to carve out my own tiny corner of the universe, and live in it.

I had no aspirations to immortality, because I never really saw the point of it. However much your name lives on, the body is gone, dust to dust, and the soul off too, to another plane, or another life, or wherever it was it went. I had a strong belief that it went somewhere, I could never quite accept that while the mortal body will corrupt and rot and be eaten by worms, which seemed logical, that the same could happen to the human spirit. I thought of it like one of those lighters that sailors use, the kind where the flame never goes out, however much of a gale is blowing.

So, Virge persuaded her film company to give her a separate department, a small production company under the wing of the main corporation, which would be devoted to making films by women for women. She said that the world needed the female voice, that it had been marginalised for too long.

'We won't leave men out of it altogether,' she said. 'Poor old things. It's just that they will have to get in touch with their female side before they're allowed to buy a ticket.'

So she set up her new office, and recruited Stevie to come and work with her, and settled down to her crusade.

I was sometimes jealous of Virge, that she could just do this kind of thing. I was sometimes envious of that great conviction she had, as if the broad sweep of her vision was somehow more valid than my small view. She knew this, without me ever having to say it. She told me once that I reminded her of Jane Austen, who had described herself as a painter of miniatures, sketching in the details of one tiny corner of life. I felt reassured by that, a sense that we all have our place, big and small.

'And don't forget,' said Virge. 'We are like Jack and Mrs Sprat. Someone has to eat the fat, and someone the lean.'

Although I knew that in the great scheme of things, working in a bookshop wasn't the end of the world – if I was gone, would anyone miss me?—it wasn't as if I was curing cancer or reinventing the wheel, but for all that, it was satisfying in its small way.

It was one of those little neighbourhood shops, one of the few that remain. I liked the pride we took in personal service. A great part of my day was spent dealing with orders: the morning post brought letters from all over the world, asking for a particular book, and it always gave me a thrill when I saw a postmark from Hong Kong or California, and found that one of our old customers would be writing from so far away, requesting that I find some book or another. I took equal pleasure in writing back on our thick white lettered paper, telling them that the book had been located, offering a well chosen list of other titles which might be of interest.

I loved sending off the packages, imagining the pleasure of the recipient, feeling perhaps a pang for England, so far away, wondering if there was honey still for tea, as they undid the string and opened the smooth brown paper to find their books, and our letter, a little reminder of one corner of London.

I liked it that we got to know the regulars, that we knew their likes and dislikes, their interests and curiosities. Some didn't even ask for a particular book but just requested that I choose them a selection of titles that they might like, so they could open the package like a Christmas present, and be surprised.

So I loved my job, although sometimes I felt I had to defend it. There were so many people from our year in Oxford who were earning fat salaries, playing with millions of pounds of other people's money, who were writing critically acclaimed novels or producing documentaries for Channel Four, people who walked the streets of Soho or the Square Mile with a sure tread, knowing that they were Somebody. They were the people who were going to have their picture taken for the papers, their opinions recorded in print, their biographies listed in *Who's Who*; the kind, when we looked back on the class of '85, who would make the list – the known, the famous.

I didn't mind it so much. I didn't want to be famous. I recognised absolutely that I was not made for it. Virge, now, she was one who cried out for fame, I felt she was built for it, deserved it, was wasted on anything less than notoriety. I don't want it to sound as if I was the little mouse in the shadow of her lion, it wasn't like that at all. It was just that we were different, wanted different things. It was our difference that we liked after all, enjoying the fact that we were complementary, never in competition, we never had to fight over the same goal. It was part of what made our friendship so perfect.

But all the same, I had the same need that she did, just then, a desire to go out and start my life, to make something happen. And in my smaller way, I did. I was established in the shop. We were naturally egalitarian, there was no hierarchy, we all pitched in and did all the same jobs, whoever was on hand taking the most recent task, whether it was talking to reps, or calling authors in for signings, or ringing up the cash register, but I, on account of having been there longest, was about as near to the top of the pile as you could get in the nice little collective which we thought ourselves.

I had once had a dream of setting up on my own, one of those real old-fashioned bookshops, like in Soho in the fifties, where there is a coffee bar attached, and people can come in and drink a cup of espresso and have a cigarette and read, using the shop like a library, a small club. I had a romantic fantasy of it as a place where people could meet and talk, a sort of bohemian salon, Madame de Staël crossed with Francis Bacon. But the hard fiscal reality, the same kind of reality that intrudes when you finally realise that a credit-card bill actually has to be paid, that the fantasy of playing with pretend money has to be met by a real cheque every month, made me see that this was no more than a pipe dream. So I cast about for something else, nothing so very grand or clever or world changing, but just another *thing*, something that would give me another aspect to my life.

A publisher I knew, from one of the smaller houses, had been talking to me about getting someone to edit a collection of letters from a little known female artist from the thirties, one of those ones who get overlooked, cast in the shadow of her brighter more self-advertising contemporaries. I thought that this would be the perfect project for me. I felt an instant connection with this forgotten woman, talented and interested but not stellar, someone whose voice was so quiet that she needed a third party to place the microphone in the right place. So I suggested that I should do it, hesitantly, over lunch, and I was surprised and pleased when the publisher seemed delighted by the idea, said that he would have asked me, but thought that I was too busy, too taken up with the shop.

And so, surreptitiously, tentatively, and by the side door, I entered the world of letters.

'Isn't it perfect?' said Virge, when I told her. 'Now you really are Bloomsbury after all.'

With Virge back, the rest of us drew back together again. It was as if she was the pivot, the one whom we needed so that we could all spin around her.

Although Gus and Stevie still lived with me, we had been leading separate lives. Stretch and Denny had been busy writing a series for the BBC, and had moved into a different world, out in drinking clubs in Dean Street every night, playing complicated South American dice games with stand-up comics, living up to their own publicity. Etta was in love with an older man, who lived in a leafy street in Hampstead, and we lost her to North London. And I had moved on too, I had new friends, from work, and I didn't see the old people so much, the ones who had been there from the beginning.

There is always a stage, in your twenties, when it seems you have a lot of new people to see. I remember that. 'Oh yes,' you say, 'she's my new best friend, he's my new best friend, isn't it grand?' It's a little like falling in love; the new person comes along, and you think them absolutely perfect in every particular, and you want to spend all your time with them. I'm not sure if it's a reaction, a fear of getting stuck in a rut, of living in the past. For sure, whenever I did see Gus, or Denny or Stretch, or Stevie or Etta, we did always talk about the past, one way or another. We were each other's past, after all, and while that had some comfort in it, there was a feeling, just then, for the new. It was almost as if we needed to assert ourselves in some way, or perhaps not even that, more a feeling for definition, as if by seeing ourselves reflected off these new people, who didn't know us from way back, we could find out who we really were.

And again, for me certainly, there was a fear of taking the easy option. It seemed suddenly too easy just to stick with the old people, the old ways, it was time to strike out, do different things, with a different crowd. I felt there were whole new worlds out there and I wanted to find them. It was easy to take the old friends for granted, because we had so many years together, to know that they would always be there.

Of course, the great realisation, after a while, was that the new ones weren't so very different. These radical new circles were only other versions of the old ones, with a different spin on them. Virge had told me once, early in her career, that the films which were most successful were the ones which followed the pattern of the most ancient myths, that really we hadn't moved on so much from the Greeks, we were just putting a different slant on things. *Star Wars*, she said, that great futuristic odyssey, had been such a grand success because it was another version of the Grail myth.

I hadn't thought about it much at the time, but as the dust settled, and I looked at all these great new best friends I had made, I realised that there is a reason that universal truth is universal. People aren't so very different, after all. Under it all, under all that great craving for individuality that we guard so jealously, are all the same hopes and fears and dreams.

It was this that I was starting to see, when Virge came back. And as she gathered us together again, and we reformed about her, just as we had when we were eighteen, I felt a sense of relief in it, as if I had come home.

We had a year. It was a perfect year, a strange throwback to those times in Oxford when it had seemed that we were invulnerable. It was like a pause in real life, as if the world, which had been encroaching on us from all directions, was held off for a while, allowing us the fantasy that we had made it through, that we had come through the tunnel into the light, as if it could stay that way always.

Gus, who had moved on from agnosticism into a pantheistic view of the world, a belief that there were in fact many warring powers out there in the universe, making fools of us poor mortals, said afterwards that this kind of thing happened throughout life. He said that there are these teasing periods, where you are allowed for a while to think that you have struggled through to some kind of solution, as if the secret of life is some kind of scientific formula, that once you have worked out that E really does equal MC^2, you can apply it to everything.

He said, with the thoughtful sureness that he had always

had, that this was the great cosmic joke, the joke that we all really believed that there was a secret to life, and that if we worked hard enough at it we could discover it, and then everything would be lovely in the garden, roses everywhere you looked. The real joke, said Gus, was that the only secret of life is that there is no secret.

That was later. Just then, it felt as if there was. For that short time, it felt as if we had found it.

21

With Virge back, the big old house came alive again. For a time, I had neglected it. For months, I hadn't used the wide sitting room, and it had taken on a faded dusty unused air, like something out of a gothic novel. It had started to feel too big and old and cumbersome; I had wished for a small modern apartment, I had a yearning for chrome and tiles and clean lines. I had even thought about selling it, although I couldn't quite bring myself to do it. I felt that it would somehow be disloyal to my dead godfather, to let some stranger come and live in his house.

With Virge back in her room, it shrunk again. People started to drop by, just as they used to, the old people from Oxford, the ones I hadn't seen for years. Michael would suddenly appear for the weekend, strange men would once again issue forth from Stevie's bedroom and stay for breakfast.

And on Friday nights, the seven of us, the originals, would gather in the kitchen for dinner. Friday nights became sacred, for that year. Whoever else we were seeing, or whatever else we were doing, Fridays became just us. We took it in turns to cook. Stretch and Denny made fashionably exotic eastern dishes with lemon grass and coriander, showing off; Gus, who could only cook one thing, gave us sausage and mash; Stevie, who couldn't cook at all, got in take away and hid the boxes and we pretended not to notice. Etta, surprisingly, made comforting home cooking things, like Irish stew and cassoulet, and Virge, being Virge, made extravagant and elegant dishes that you only usually saw in restaurants, beef Wellington and salmon en croute and terrines and mousselines and all kinds. I made spaghetti with clams, because I liked clams.

They made me realise how much I had missed those evenings. I had forgotten about the comfort of old friends, the ones who know you best. I had forgotten how easy it is to be with people where you have nothing to prove. And if we did sometimes talk about the past, I thought that wasn't such a bad thing. Sometimes it's good to look back, to see how far you have come. The present makes no sense without the past, after all.

'Aren't we all grown up?' said Stevie, one Friday night. 'I mean look at us, with our jobs and our lives.'

'It is strange,' said Etta. 'I sometimes wondered if we would ever get this far.'

'You're a step ahead,' said Gus. 'You even have a committed relationship.'

'It's very adult,' said Etta. 'I have to admit it. We never even fight, you know, if things are going wrong we sit down and discuss it like real grown ups.'

'You don't?' said Virge. 'Now I really am impressed.'

'Do you still have sex?' said Stevie.

'Certainly,' said Etta, with dignity.

'I thought all that stopped when you'd been together more than six months,' said Stevie.

'Is that why you're still surfing the net?' said Denny. 'We did wonder.'

'You're a fine one to talk,' said Stevie. 'I don't see you settling down, thank you so much.' She paused, and lit a cigarette with a small defiant deliberation, and sucked in the smoke and blew it out in long blue plumes from her nostrils, which was a trick she had. She always said that she had watched Marlene Deitrich in the *Blue Angel* one too many times. 'But that is part of it, since you're asking. I'm a godsend to the rubber industry, me.'

'You two should settle down together and have done with it,' said Stretch. 'You could sit up nights and discuss your fear of commitment.'

'That's an idea,' said Stevie. 'How about it, Den?'

Denny grinned. 'I'll have to check if I've got a window in my Filofax,' he said.

Virge started laughing.

'Look what happens,' she said. 'I turn my back on you for ten minutes, and you turn into Media the Wonder Love.'

'It's a dirty job, my dear old duck,' said Denny. 'But I'm so good at it.'

'You should see him networking in the Groucho,' said Stretch. 'It's something.'

'Something is right,' said Stevie. 'I'm not saying what.'

'What about you, Ash?' said Denny. 'We haven't heard the patter of tiny feet coming from your bedroom, just lately.'

'I'm taking a sabbatical,' I said.

'Kinky,' said Stevie. 'Listen to her, talking dirty.'

'Ash and me both,' said Stretch. 'Our hearts are broken, our lives are over, and we're going into the garden to eat worms.'

'Is this what happens when you go into therapy?' said Stevie.

Stretch, who had had his heart good and smashed by a very beautiful and very cruel girl the summer before, had rung me up soon after and asked for the number of my shrink. He now went twice a week and said it was the best thing he'd ever done.

'Yes,' he said.

'There's a time,' I said, 'when you just need a rest.'

'Do you get lonely?' said Etta.

I looked at her for a moment.

'Yes,' I said. 'There are those times when it's three in the morning and the bed is cold and empty, and you long and long for there to be a warm body beside you. But what's much worse is when you do have a body there, and you're still lonely. You know those times when there's a foot between you in the bed and it might as well be the Grand Canyon?'

Everyone let out their breath in a little collective sigh.

'Oh, yes,' said Stevie. 'I know that.'

'That's the worst one there is,' said Virge. 'The very worst.'

'Why is that?' said Denny. 'You never expect it. No one ever tells you about that part.'

'It's the great fantasy,' said Stretch. 'That two is better than one. But it's more complicated than that.'

'It's much better to feel lonely by yourself,' said Gus, 'than with someone else.'

'That's why we have each other,' said Virge. 'Because whatever happens, we'll always be together.'

'It's all very well,' said Stevie, 'but it makes things difficult. I mean,' she said, 'because I have such absolutely superior friends, no lover can live up to that. I blame you very much,' she said to the boys. 'I do.'

Denny laughed and put his arm round her.

'But my old love,' he said, 'you know us so well that you've seen all our fatal flaws.'

'I know,' said Stevie. 'And still I love you best. What's a girl to do? If only I could be lesbian and be done with it. Then there wouldn't be all the communication problem.'

'No, no,' said Gus. 'That's the big fantasy. It's just as complicated.'

'Oh, excuse me,' said Virge. 'Stop the clock. Subtitles

for the hard of hearing. Does this mean that you have decided?'

'Not as such,' said Gus. 'I'm not actually having sex with men or women, just at the moment, if you must know. But I'm definitely looking at boys.'

'Look but don't touch?' said Stevie.

'I would bloody touch,' said Gus, 'if I could find someone suitable.'

'Me too,' said Virge. 'I wouldn't mind a bit of touching, to while away the long summer nights.'

The subject of love was much on our minds, just then, although more in an academic way than with any sense of real urgency. Since we had each other, and we were all busy with our work, that didn't leave time for much else. There was no great yearning for our other half, no great need for someone to come along and make us whole. But because of our age, we all seemed to be wondering about it, wondering if there was such a thing as true love, if there really was one person out there, waiting for us, whether we were really meant to find one soulmate and stay with them for ever and ever, till death do us part.

It was the time for it. The weddings were starting, for one thing. Suddenly, all the people we had known at university were getting hitched. Every day, great stiff envelopes fell fatly through the letter box, asking us to come and celebrate another little waltz up the aisle.

Virge loved weddings. 'Free champagne and men in tail coats,' she said. 'What more could a girl possibly ask for?'

She enjoyed dressing for them too. Throughout that summer, every weekend was a wedding, and Virge spent much of her time making eccentric hats out of old feather boas and hunting down old fifties print dresses in second-hand shops.

And off we would go, every Saturday, our little band, to churches in the city and halls in the west end and hotel ballrooms and inns of court and, for the more funky, working men's clubs in Kensal Rise.

'Isn't it strange?' said Virge, at one of these. 'I mean, you've got a two in one chance of it working, if you look at the statistics, and there's nothing now to say that you can't live in sin, and still everyone is doing it.'

'Hope over experience,' said Gus. 'The great human failing.'

'Oh, listen to our philosopher, would you please?' said Stevie. She loved these weddings, mostly because she said that you could always guarantee on getting laid. 'Thing about weddings,' she always said, 'is that they put people in a romantic holiday mood. It's like shooting fish in a barrel.'

She had a special bag that she carried for weddings, a dainty little thing in patent leather, just enough room for a pack of cigarettes, her keys, a lipstick and a box of condoms.

'He's right,' said Stretch. 'But then, without it, we'd still be sitting in our caves, waiting for the storm to pass.'

'Oh, you two,' said Stevie. 'It's like going out with bloody Kierkegaard. You should get out and have sex a bit more.'

'I had sex with the groom,' said Gus.

'You did not,' said Stevie. It took a bit for her to reach incredulity, but Gus could always manage it.

'Oh, Gus,' said Virge, giving him a kiss on the ear. 'And here you are, having to watch him get married to someone else.'

'Well,' said Gus, 'it was a while ago, you know.'

'Doesn't make much difference,' I said. 'I couldn't bear it if Hem got married, even now.'

'Actually,' said Etta, in her grave thoughtful way, 'I slept with him too.'

'Oh dear, oh dear,' said Virge, starting to laugh.

'Not at the same time, I hope,' said Denny.

'Sergeant Pepper's Lonely Hearts Club band, we are,' said Virge. 'I hope you all enjoy the show.'

I did enjoy the show, all the time I was in it. I felt a growing sense of sureness, of belonging, of being in the right place. I thought also that this was real, that it was the real world, that this was the way life worked. But I didn't really think about it that much. I was coasting along, just then, without a care in the world. I wasn't thinking about anything very much, just taking each day as it came.

Denny who picked up odd expressions and turns of phrase like a magpie, was using one often at that time – Getting away with it, that's what he said.

'We're still getting away with it,' he would say, with a nicely ironic little nod of his head, and half a smile.

I wasn't sure entirely what he meant, I wasn't certain what it was that we were getting away with, and I didn't think of it that much until one night something happened which brought me up short.

I had gone to a party given by the publisher I was working for. It was nothing special, about fifty people and a glass of wine and that kind of English cocktail party food which has a great deal to do with small mysterious pieces of toast. I rather enjoyed these evenings, I liked talking to agents and editors and people who worked for the trade papers, I liked the endless publishing gossip and rumour. It always made me feel slightly more important than I really was, which I never minded.

About halfway through, I was talking to my publisher when a tall man with a thin brooding slightly sinister face walked over.

'Oh Ash,' said the publisher, in his easy-going way. 'You should meet this one. He's a feature writer.' He waved at the stranger, beckoning him over. 'Johnny,' he said. 'Come and talk to Ash. I must go and flirt with the host.' And he walked away, leaving us alone.

It just goes to show how you never see these things coming. I smiled at Johnny the feature writer, and I thought that he was quite attractive, more Virge's type than mine, but you never knew. I wondered slightly if he was single. That was all I thought. So I held out my hand, and said, 'How do you do, I'm Ash Franklin,' and to my absolute astonishment he didn't take my hand, he just stood and looked down at me, and said, 'I know exactly who you are.'

He said it in an accusing way, as if there was some great secret I had been keeping for years and he was about to unmask me. I wondered what he could mean. I felt as if I'd walked into a foreign film without any subtitles.

'Oh,' I said, because I couldn't think of anything else to say.

'You're friends with that dreadful Virge Hudson,' he said.

I was still about twenty-seven steps behind. I had a sudden thought that perhaps he had slept with Virge and been hurt by her, that there had been some kind of misunderstanding, something. I couldn't conceive that anyone could think Virge dreadful for any other reason.

'Oh dear,' I said, laughing weakly. 'She's my best friend.'

'Best friend,' he said, in absolute derision. He was at least six and a half foot, and he drew himself up, and raised his eyebrows and looked down on me from a great height. 'That about sums it up. It sounds like you're eight years old.'

I thought perhaps he was drunk, or on medication. This was a party, after all, a nice genteel literary gathering. This wasn't the kind of thing people normally said. I felt faintly mesmerised, and rather ill.

'I've seen you all,' he said. 'Your little gang, all following Virge around like so many sheep, as if she was Little Bo sodding Peep.'

I suddenly started to laugh, it was so absurd. I discovered that I felt brave and not so weak, after all.

'What is this?' I said. 'Too much John Osborne? The return of the Angry Young Man?'

'God,' he said. He made a strange convulsion with his face, as if he suffered from indigestion or gallstones. 'Isn't that just like you lot? Did Virge teach you to talk like that?'

'Curiously enough,' I said, 'I learnt it all by myself.'

'Oh ha, ha,' he said. 'Isn't that just razor sharp?'

'What is it,' I said, conversationally, 'that you so dislike about Virge?'

'Oh please,' he said. He frowned impatiently at me. 'She's so affected and fey and smug, surrounding herself with all those fags and toadies, swanning around like Lady Muck. It's not the thirties any more, it's not a bloody Scott Fitzgerald novel. Jesus. She's the most shallow woman I've ever met in my life, that's all. You can't just wander through life treating it like one long cocktail party any more. We're not living in a bloody play by J.M. Barrie. Every time I see her I expect her to tell me to clap my hands if I believe in fairies.'

'You really mind,' I said. I felt curiously fascinated. It was like watching someone in the grip of road rage. 'Why does it bother you so much?'

He lit up a cigarette and started smoking on it in angry jerking puffs.

'It makes me sick,' he said. 'You lot,' he said again, 'you lot, with your cushy lives and your cushy jobs and your stupid in jokes and your absolute sense of your own superiority, as if you're all on the inside and the rest of us are on the outside looking in. It's like bloody feeding time at the zoo. Didn't any of you notice that the world has changed?'

I was suddenly tired of this conversation. I didn't see any point in arguing, so I didn't.

'Oh well,' I said. 'You must think what you want. I expect I'll just let you get on with it.'

I left him to his cigarette and his bile, and went to get my coat, and left. I was cross and shaken, and I felt restless and uncertain. I decided to walk across the park.

It was early, and the sky was still light, and I crossed Park Lane and headed across to Kensington Gardens. I loved the park. Virge and I often spent weekends wandering round the Serpentine, watching the families out for the day, and the roller bladers showing off, and those strange nutty old men who haunt park benches the world over.

Tonight, it was almost empty. The children had been taken home, for their tea and their baths and their bedtime stories. There were a few foreign students, seeing the sights, and strolling couples, arm in arm, and men in suits, walking home to make a change from the bus.

I walked up to the round pond and, tired suddenly, sat down on a bench. I watched the ducks for a bit. I wondered about what the man at the party had said. I remembered suddenly a scene from *The Big Chill*, which had been a big favourite with Hem and me in Oxford. We always used to go and see it, any time it was showing. I thought of the part when one character says to another, of the people they had known in college, 'I thought because they looked like us and dressed like us that they would think like us.'

I thought perhaps it was the same with me. Perhaps the man at the party was right, perhaps I had grown soft and complacent, in my nice safe house and my nice safe job and my nice safe group of friends. Perhaps I had just come to believe in the illusion that everyone saw life the same way I did.

I thought suddenly, childishly, that it was like the old way we had divided the world when we were younger, when all that mattered was which brand of cigarettes you smoked and which music you listened to. We used to believe the line that there were two kinds of people only – Beatles or Stones. That was what we had thought at university. Around that, there might be diversions, minor arguments about whether you preferred Lou Reed to Jimi Hendrix, or whether Bob Dylan had really sold out when he went electric, but it always came back to that central division, the absolute crux of the matter, whether you listened to Mick and Keith or Paul and John. We were Stones, no question about it. Virge and I just took it as read, not something to make a song and dance about, although Stretch and Denny went through a radical purist stage when they refused to even speak to anyone who didn't possess a copy of *Exile on Main Street*.

That was when we were younger, when that was the way the world worked. But now I thought, things hadn't really changed that much. We laid a more sophisticated veneer on it now, because we were older and we knew more about the way things worked, but perhaps, underneath all that, we still saw the world in black and white. Or at least, I thought that perhaps I did. I had fallen for the *Big Chill* fantasy that because people looked like me and talked like me they would think like me. It gave me a shock that I was so wrong.

I felt all at once confused and naïve, that perhaps it was I who had got it all wrong. I had always thought that my love and admiration for Virge was not so much a matter of opinion, but a matter of fact. I knew absolutely that the man at the party had made a mistake, I knew that Virge, of all people, was not shallow and fey and smug. What shocked me was that someone might think she was, could see her through such different eyes from mine.

It was growing cold. The summer was over. The leaves were starting to turn, and there was a faint smell of woodsmoke and coolness in the air, the smell of autumn. I got up and headed down towards Kensington Gore, pulling my coat around me. I wished suddenly, crossly, that I didn't have to do all this thinking. I wished that I could just have been the kind of person who would have turned round to that angry disaffected man and told him he was wrong and offensive and given him a good sharp set down and thought no more about it.

But as Virge had once told me, we weren't like that. Strangely, for all her romantic theatrical nature, she had a belief that she should accept what she was born with and get on with it. I, on the other hand, felt that I should be constantly struggling to change myself, to try and make sense of things and learn from them. But then, I think this had to do with my absolute abiding fear that if I just left myself be I might turn into my parents. I knew that if that wasn't to happen, I should have to work at it.

Virge was in when I got home, eating couscous and, for reasons of her own, reading a three-year-old copy of *Private Eye*. I laughed suddenly, thinking how this would infuriate the man at the party.

'I am glad you're here,' I said. 'Can we do something extravagant, like open a bottle of claret and eat cake?'

'Oh dear,' said Virge, getting it at once, as she always did. 'Was it horrible?'

'Horrible,' I said.

'Come on then,' said Virge, getting up. 'Let's go and look in the cellar.'

We found a nice old bottle of wine, and settled down on the sofa.

'What, then?' said Virge.

I told her.

'Oh dear,' she said, laughing, and not taking it the wrong way, as I had known she wouldn't. 'He would say that, wouldn't he?'

'Do you know him?' I said.

'Oh yes,' said Virge. 'We were at school together. There were two kinds of people at school. There were the hearty sporting types, who were considered the top dogs, the ones to know. To start with, I was part of that gang, because I didn't know any better. And then there were the drop outs, who didn't play rugger and had long hair and didn't wear the right clothes and didn't fit in. So, of course, I soon found out that they were far more interesting, and had much better taste in music, apart from anything else. The top dogs liked,' she said with delicately telling irony, 'Billy Joel.'

'Oh dear,' I said.

'They knew,' she said gravely, 'all the words to 'The Stranger'. So you do see. I defected, and it was always held against me. That wasn't playing the game at all. Isn't it strange,' she added slowly, 'how people never forget?'

'Funny old thing,' I said. I felt comforted and reassured, as if someone had told me that there still were fairies at the bottom of the garden after all.

'I don't mind fey and affected,' said Virge. 'Although I won't take smug. Maybe I am those things, but it doesn't matter so very much. Fuck 'em if they can't take a joke. You know,' she said, 'what the problem with some people is?'

'What?' I said.

'Some people just won't allow anyone to have any fun,' she said.

And then we stopped talking about it and turned on *Newsnight*, because Virge said that if she wasn't to turn into a complete idiot she had better catch up on some current affairs, and I didn't think much more about it.

22 ∫

It was that autumn, just over a year after Virge had come back to London, that things started to shift. Perhaps it was because of all that talking we had been doing, it felt as if now the time had come for action. I'm not sure.

Stevie started it off. One Sunday morning, she came downstairs from her bedroom, grinning all over her face. Gus looked up from his cornflakes.

'Oh, yes,' he said. 'Anyone we know?'

Virge, who was pretending to do the crossword, filled in another clue. She never actually did the crossword, she just filled in the blank boxes with any letters that came into her head.

'Sex, sex, sex,' she said. 'Can't we all have some?'

'So,' I said. 'Is he coming down? Shall I make some more toast?'

Stevie just sat there, grinning all over her face, and then Denny walked in and sat down, and said, 'Toast would be just ducky, Ash, if you can bear it.'

Gus and I sat and stared with our mouths wide open.

'Well,' said Virge calmly. 'Twenty-one letters, ending in T.'

Everyone turned to look at her.

'Who,' she said, 'would have guessed it.'

*   *   *

Once Stevie and Denny were together, it seemed so obvious, none of us could work out why we hadn't figured it out before. They really were in love too, you could see it written all over them, in shining great letters of fire. Stevie came over all dreamy and vague, forgetting things and losing her keys all the time and smiling at babies in the street.

'I'm such a cliché,' she said. 'Can you believe what a cliché I am?'

'I think it's reassuring,' I said. 'You know, that it really does happen like this.'

'I do love him, Ash,' she said. 'I love him with every little bit of me, right down to my fingertips. I want to live with him until we're old and grey.'

'Well,' I said. 'I should, then.'

Virge thought the whole thing perfectly splendid, so much so that she went off and did the same thing.

'Who is he?' I said. 'Where did you find him?'

I would have just gone and fallen in love myself, but I never seemed to meet anyone I wanted to fall in love with. 'All I want,' I said, most days, 'is regular sex and a hand to hold, it's not much to ask. I'm not asking for marriage and children and fast cars and houses in Spain.' Gus said I should get out more, and I did, but I still didn't meet anyone I wanted, or at least, anyone who came within a million miles of Hem. All these years, and it was still him I dreamed of, although I pretended I didn't. He was in the South Seas, somewhere lost in the South Pacific archipelago, and he sent me cards and said it was just like Somerset Maugham, and I pretended very hard that I could bear it.

'Oh, you know,' said Virge, which was what she always said when she wanted to be evasive. 'Around. He's the cat's whiskers. He's a gangster.'

'Fancy,' said Gus, walking in. 'I've always thought you would make such a good gangster's moll.'

'Just watch me,' said Virge.

I never met the gangster, when he was with Virge. She told me a little about him, when I asked. She was absolutely entranced by him.

'Oh,' she said. 'He's so perfect, with his cigars and his shiny suits and the dangerous glint in his eye.'

I asked her what kind of gangster he was. I had a faint feeling that I should disapprove, but I couldn't. I had the same fascination with the underworld that Virge did, and perhaps it was an English thing as well, just look at the Krays. I still got a little shiver up the back of my neck every time I drove past the Blind Beggar and thought of Mad Dog Cornell getting his.

Virge was a little vague on the details.

'Gambling, I think,' she said. 'Bootlegging, I don't know, whatever it is that gangsters do. Boxing, and things.'

He took her to expensive restaurants and after-hours clubs, hidden in foreign corners of the East End, where he was never allowed to pick up the tab.

'It's always champagne on the house,' said Virge. 'He thinks I'm a real lady,' she said. 'He treats me like a duchess.'

'If only he knew,' I said.

'I know,' said Virge, laughing gently. 'I know. Isn't it unexpected?'

Virge always said that. I think she really saw life as a pageant of curious events, none of which we could ever foresee, as if we were endlessly coming round corners, surprised by what we found on the other side. There was a part of her that truly did expect the unexpected, but when it really happened, she turned out to be the least prepared of all of us.

*   *   *

It was a dark day at the end of November when Michael arrived in the house, one Saturday morning. Gus and Stevie and Denny had gone out early, to see an exhibition on the South Bank. 'Just look at us,' said Stevie, as they left. 'Aren't we a happy little trio of cultural attachés?' Virge had spent the night with the gangster and wasn't home yet, so it was just me.

'Michael,' I said, with delight, when I opened the door to find him standing on the doorstep. 'The best surprise.'

He smiled at me, and kissed my cheek, and we went into the kitchen and I made some coffee. He didn't say much, which was strange, because normally he was as voluble as Virge, but I thought it was just that he was tired or had been late the night before. I didn't read anything into it, not at first.

'When did you get in?' I said.

'Tuesday,' he said.

I looked at him. 'Tuesday?' I said. 'And only now you're here?'

'I had things to do,' he said. And then I did look at him properly and I knew there was something terribly wrong. I knew also, immediately, what it was.

I sat down rather suddenly.

'Oh, Michael,' I said.

He looked at me, and saw that I knew.

'Doctors,' he said. 'Second and third opinions. What's the point? They're all the same.'

'Oh God,' I said. 'Oh, God.' I heard myself say the words; I heard them echo in my head. I felt as if I were divorced from myself, watching myself, apart. I felt my world shift off its axis, something dislocate. I felt absolutely unreal.

'Has Giovanni . . . ?' I said.

Michael shook his head. 'Thank God,' he said. 'It wasn't really sexual, you know,' he said. 'That was the problem.

I went elsewhere for that. He can't forgive me. He can't forgive me for that.'

'It's shock, I expect,' I said. 'He'll come round. After a while.'

'I don't think so,' said Michael. 'It's funny how it takes people. It's not like other diseases, like that.'

I nodded, trying to look like I understood. I didn't understand. I was still trying to take it in. I felt that I should want to cry, but I didn't. The desperate unreality I felt was holding me in a kind of limbo, as if we were just sitting at the pictures, as if at any moment the credits would roll and we'd all go out into the street, back into real life, where things like this didn't happen.

'What will you do?' I said.

'I'll come home,' he said. He shook his head slightly. 'I am home. He's sending my stuff.'

'Do you want to stay here?' I said. 'There's room.'

Michael took my hand and held it. I had a sudden flash of the early days, in Oxford, when we used to walk round the botanical gardens, arm in arm, so young and golden and assured, so sure that we would live forever.

'No,' he said. 'Thank you. I've rented a place. I need to be alone for a time.'

'Oh, Michael,' I said.

He smiled at me again, a little ghostly. I think he knew what I meant. I didn't have to tell him that I didn't know what to say, because we had known each other too long for that.

'You never know,' he said. 'It could be years, you know, before it's fullblown. And they're making advances every day. It's not the end, not yet.'

I don't think he believed that. I wanted to believe it, but I don't think he did.

'Of course it isn't,' I said bravely. 'Of course not.' I smiled at him, feeling my face stretch with the effort. I thought that if he could bear it, I could too.

The door slammed and Virge came in and took off her coat and threw her bag down on the table.

'Michael,' she said, kissing him. 'Darling Michael, what a perfect thing.'

Then she stopped and looked at us for a moment.

'What are you two doing, sitting so solemn?' she said gaily. 'Did someone die?'

It was then that I felt a sudden rise of nausea. That Michael was truly not going to live forever was still too distant and shocking for me to take in, but knowing that Virge's world was about to be shattered was instantly unbearable.

'I'll go,' I said.

'Don't,' said Michael. 'Please stay, Ash.'

Virge looked at us again, her face curious.

'What is going on?' she said. I couldn't believe that she couldn't see. I was angry suddenly, that she couldn't.

Virge and Michael stared at each other for a moment. It seemed like a lifetime. It seemed like hours and days and weeks, the longest time. Then Michael said, in a quiet voice, 'I'm HIV.'

'You're what?' said Virge. Her voice came unnaturally loud into the room.

'HIV positive,' said Michael.

'No,' said Virge. 'No.'

Michael nodded.

'Just no,' said Virge. She was almost shouting. She stood in the middle of the room, looking at him.

'This doesn't happen,' she said, very clearly. 'You're in a steady relationship.'

Michael took a deep breath and let it out again.

'We didn't really have sex,' he said. 'It wasn't about that.'

'So,' said Virge. 'I don't understand. How can you be ill?'

She couldn't say it. I saw that. She couldn't say the letters, those three little letters. She could talk longer and better than anyone I'd never met, but she had finally found one thing she couldn't say.

'I had sex with other people,' said Michael. 'I don't know when it happened. It could have been ten years ago, for all I know. It could have been last month.'

'What do you mean?' said Virge. 'What do you mean, you don't know?'

'Virge,' said Michael. His voice was low and strained and patient. 'I just don't know. What does it matter who or where or when? I got tested, and I'm positive, and that's all there is.'

'That's all?' said Virge. 'That's all?'

I felt frightened suddenly, because I saw what she was going to do, and I wanted to stop her before it was too late. I sat there, impotent, knowing there was nothing I could do.

'You bloody bastard,' said Virge. 'You bastard. Why couldn't you just go to bed with women? Why couldn't you use a condom? Why did you have to be a fucking homosexual?'

'Virge,' I said.

She turned her fierce stare on me. Her eyes were like marbles, blank and clouded.

'Shut up,' she said loudly. 'It's not your bloody brother. It's not your brother that has been having sordid cheap one night stands with men who don't know his name. What was it?' she said to Michael. 'What? Cottaging in some back street bar, getting it from some boy you'll never meet again? Was that how you got your kicks? You really got your kicks, didn't you? It's going to be a great fucking kick, this.'

'Virge,' said Michael. 'Don't do this.'

'No,' she said. She started to cry, fat heavy tears, running down her face, streaking it with mascara. 'No. *You* don't fucking do this. You did this. Why did you have to do this? Why? Why did you have to be a fucking *queer*?'

She turned then, and picked up her coat, and ran from the room, and I heard the front door slam shut after her, and there was a small silence, the ugly words hanging in it like a dark cloud on a sunny day.

Michael let out a sigh. I couldn't look at him. I felt ashamed for Virge, even though I understood what she meant, and why she had done it. I felt absolutely drained, as if there was no more blood in me.

'Oh, Michael,' I said again, entirely inadequate.

I heard his voice coming from a great distance.

'It's all right, Ash,' he said.

He left soon after that. I was left alone in the house. I carried on with my day, just as if it were all normal. I didn't feel a single thing.

It was only a day later that it hit me. I was in the newsagent, buying the Sunday papers, and suddenly it came, right out of the blue. I ran home, and when I got there, I went and sat on the side of my bed, and I cried and cried, as if it were the end of the world.

Virge came home on Monday. As happened so often, we had done the same thing, called in sick from work, so when she came back, she found me sitting in the wide upstairs room, staring at the wall.

It was so big, that room, I suddenly thought, as I turned and saw Virge standing at the far end. It was the kind of room which should be filled with beautiful women with satin dresses and powdered hair. It was an eighteenth century room, redolent of lost grandeur. I wondered what we were doing in it, just me and Virge.

She didn't say anything at first, just came and sat down opposite me, and watched me for a while.

'I don't know why I said that,' she said, at last. Her voice had lost all the shades of colour and meaning that it usually held, leaving it flat and bare. 'What did you say?'

I looked back at her.

'I didn't say anything much,' I said. I shook my head slightly. 'I didn't know what there was to say.'

'You see,' said Virge. 'You see? That's the difference between us. You just accepted it, didn't you? You didn't say anything because you know that there isn't very much you can say when someone tells you that they're going to die. How did you know that? Did your shrink teach you that? How come you know that, and I don't?'

'Virge,' I said.

'Don't try and make it better,' she said, fiercely, cutting me off. 'Don't excuse me and smooth it over and tell me that it wasn't so very bad, not really. Please don't tell me it's all right.'

That is what I was going to do. I always wanted to make things better, it was one of the things I did. I was glad, in a way, that she asked me not to, because this one was over my head, too tall an order even for me, whatever panaceas I had at my disposal.

'All right,' I said. 'I won't try and make it better.'

'Thanks,' said Virge. 'Do you want to get drunk?' she said.

'No,' I said. I shook my head. I had thought about it, all weekend. That's what you're supposed to do, isn't it, when you get bad news, when tragedy strikes. That's what they always do in the movies, all those scenes with the desperate man and the bottle of bourbon.

'I don't either,' said Virge. 'I wish I did. At least it would be something to do.'

I knew what she meant. I felt like that too. I wanted

something to *do*, something, anything. Anything so that I didn't have to sit and think about what had happened. I think that almost the worst thing is when you know that there is absolutely nothing that you can do, nothing that you can do to change things, to make them go back to the way they were before, the way you want them to be. It's that thing of suddenly being confronted with your own absolute impotence, your puny plan in the great scheme of things: however clever you think you are, and however hard you work, and however much wisdom you gather, and however hard you try, you are just one tiny little speck in the vast unimagined universe, and you don't count for very much after all. It's times like that that you think it doesn't matter how many levers you have, you still won't be able to shift the world, because it's just too big, and you are too small, and that's all there is to it.

'Come on,' said Virge. 'We can't sit here. Let's go for a walk.'

We drove up to Hyde Park and went and sat in the Italian garden. There was something neglected and melancholy about it, on that dark thin winter day. The flagstones and the fountains which shone so gay and golden in the summer sun were grey and dull, and the benches, normally filled with people, were empty and forlorn.

We sat on one of the benches, staring straight ahead, like two old ladies in a formal portrait. Beyond the fountains, the park was bare and almost deserted, the steely paths broken only by a lone runner, pounding away towards the horizon.

'Of course,' said Virge, 'I do know why I said what I said.'

'Yes,' I said. I knew too.

'I'm so angry,' said Virge. 'I'm so angry I don't know what to do. I mean, why? Why Michael? Why couldn't it happen to someone else? Why does it have to be him?

He's the most perfect person I know, apart from you. He's the best and brightest and the bravest. It's so unfair. Why is it always the good ones? Why can't it be someone horrible and stupid and cruel? Why?'

She looked at me suddenly, as if I should be able to tell her. I felt again that utter sense of helplessness. I so wanted to give her an answer, but I had none to give. Like her, I had only questions.

'I don't know, Virge,' I said heavily. 'I really don't. It doesn't make any sense. None of it makes any sense. It's strange, isn't it? I mean,' I said, and I was just talking now, for myself as much as for her, just talking, as if words somehow could make it better, 'why do we all think that it should make sense? That there should be some pattern to it all, some rhyme and reason, when there never is? Where did that fantasy come from? Who is it who first says that there is a plan, that there is something logical and rational about the whole thing, that if we are good girls and eat up our greens and go to bed early then everything will be all right? Who tells us that in the first place? Why do we all think that we should have a happy ending, that we deserve a happy ending, that life should be something that we can predict and understand? Because it just isn't like that.'

'Shit happens,' said Virge. She started to laugh, with a sharp jagged edge of hysteria to it. 'All this shit just happens. It just happens.'

She started to cry then, painful, rasping sobs, shaking her body, those terrible racking tears that come right from your gut, until you think you will be sick from them. I wanted, urgently, to hold her and soothe her and tell her it would all be fine, it could all be fine, but I knew it wasn't, and it couldn't, so I let her cry.

It was one of the hardest things I ever had to do, sitting in those strange empty Italianate terraces, on that hard cold bench, feeling her in all her despair, and knowing that there was not one single thing I could do to take it away.

After a while, she stopped. I put my arm round her shoulders, and she leaned against me, and we sat like that for a while, drawing some faint comfort from each other, as little comfort as there was.

'I can't bear it,' she said.

23

We did bear it, of course we did, because you just do. I sometimes think you never know how much you can bear until you have to, until you are faced with it. You surprise yourself, amazed that confronted with the unbearable you just carry on, putting one foot in front of another, with a lingering sense of astonishment that you still know how.

For a while, things went back to normal, as normal as they could get. After Virge and I left the park, she went round to see Michael. I never knew what they said to each other, but whatever it was, they repaired the damage, forgave the unforgivable, and they drew closer than they ever had. I was grateful for that. I really don't think I could have stood it if it had driven them apart.

The original little band, Stevie and Etta, Denny and Stretch, Gus, Virge, and I, gathered closer than ever before, like survivors of a storm, huddling together for warmth and shelter. We spent a lot of time in my house. Michael came often for dinner, and we did things together, trips to the theatre, and walks in the park, and skating at Queensway, things we hadn't done since we were in our teens. We went down to Dorset for weekends, and made excursions to Richmond and Greenwich, and on one freezing December day, took the train down to Brighton and walked along the beach.

Virge wanted grander plans, talking of flying off to West Indian islands, or cruising down the Nile or through the Dardanelles, but Michael didn't want to do those things.

'I just want to be normal,' he said. 'Whatever that means. I just want to stay in London and live from day to day.'

It still gave me a shiver when he used words like live, because I was so constantly aware of what it meant, now, now that he didn't know how much longer he would be able to use it. It's one of those things that you take for granted, like the old adage about you never know what you've got till it's gone. Perhaps you never really appreciate something until you know you are going to lose it.

Some of the time, I could forget. Some of the time, it seemed as if we were just having fun, like we always used to. Michael didn't look ill. He was a little pale, was all, and sometimes he got tired, and he took a lot of pills and vitamins and green drinks for his immune system, but it was one of those things, that you wouldn't necessarily know, if you hadn't been told. I kept thinking about what he had said, that it could be years, and as the winter gave way to spring, and the sun came out again, and the blossom started on the trees, and people had that relieved and surprised look because the winter finally seemed over, I thought that perhaps he was right after all, that perhaps he would just go on and on, and there would be a breakthrough in medical science, and it wouldn't have to end after all.

But it didn't happen like that. He fell ill at the end of April, a fierce and lingering bronchitis first and then pneumonia, and he lost weight and couldn't put it back on, and he grew strange purple marks on his face and his back, and we couldn't pretend any more.

After the first time in hospital, Virge brought him home with her, and we moved him into the study on the ground floor, because he couldn't manage the stairs.

Michael said, over and over, that he would pay to get someone in to look after him, but Virge wouldn't allow it. She left Stevie in charge of the office, and she stayed home, so she could take care of Michael.

Faced with the dramatic and unexpected slide in his health, she seemed to grow stronger. There were days, when I got home from work, when I found it hard to go into his room. We had brought all his things, all the beautiful objects he had found over the years, all the pictures and the rugs and the artefacts that he had collected with his unerring eye, and arranged them around him, and although there was something lovely in it, I found it distressing too. It was so clear that he was never going to leave that room, that this really was his final resting place.

The days when he couldn't get out of bed were the worst; it was a great big old bed, planted in the centre of the room, and I found it hard to walk in, and see him there, sunken and reduced, propped up on his pillows, and talk and laugh as if everything was normal.

That was what we did, what we all did, as if by mutual consent. Now that it was upon us, we never talked about it. Michael would sometimes make jokes about the thirty-seven pills he had to take each evening at six, but that was as near as we came to referring to what was happening to him. Sometimes it made me want to scream, because it was all so English and stiff upper lip, but I suppose it was one way of dealing with it, and anyway, it was what he seemed to want. I think even then he couldn't bear to think that he was being a burden, that he might be dull.

Through all this, Virge was magnificent. I remembered those times that we used to go and sit with my old godfather, and how she had always seemed completely at ease with his madness and gibberish and decline, and how I had marvelled at it. It was the same thing now. I felt as if I were putting on a façade, which didn't quite cover over the cracks, but Virge just carried on. She bossed Michael mildly, and teased him, but she never fussed over him or pitied him or showed that terrible compassion which would have been almost the hardest thing for him to bear.

He had a remission in June, when he could walk again, and he got up from his bed, and we took him out, and he seemed almost like his old self, and I allowed myself again that false, taunting hope.

And then in August, he relapsed very quickly, and grew weaker and thinner than before, and his mind started wandering, which was almost the worst thing, he who had always prided himself on his wit and his words and his jokes and his repartee.

On the morning of August 28th, Virge came into my room at six o'clock and stood at the end of my bed and looked down at me. I was awake, lying on my back, staring at the ceiling. None of us could sleep, that summer.

'What?' I said. But I knew what. I knew absolutely.

She looked at me, almost unimaginable pain in her eyes.

'He's dead,' she said.

It's extraordinary how much there is to do when someone dies. I had no idea. There are death certificates to get, and undertakers to see, and people to call. Virge, who was Michael's executor, did it all. I went with her to the undertaker, Mr Scott, a deeply humourless man, younger than we expected, who took his business very seriously.

Virge had to fill in many forms. I think we were both still in shock, and I was startled and slightly ashamed that we seemed to be making jokes. No one tells you about that part, at least no one I'd ever met. I'd always assumed that death meant sorrow, that it was as simple as that, that you cried all the time. That is what I had felt before, after my godfather, those are the pictures and images we are shown: the grieving widows, the weeping children, the bowed heads and reddened eyes. But no one tells you about all the other stuff.

No one tells you about the sudden bouts of hysterical laughter or losing your memory or not knowing what to do with your hands. No one tells you about the sudden inability to perform all the usual acts that made up your life before, that small insignificant granted things like cleaning your teeth suddenly become forgotten and have to be relearnt.

No one tells you that the threads that make up the fabric of your existence start to unravel, that all the things you did so unthinkingly before become redundant, that you can't watch the television or read a newspaper because they have lost all their meaning. I kept remembering, over and over, that line about the past being a foreign country, they do things differently there. Well, I felt as if I were in a foreign country, and in this other country, for the moment, in this strange alien undertaker's room, we were making jokes.

'Look at this one, Ash,' said Virge, staring at one form. ' "To your knowledge, did the deceased die of, A: violence, or B: poison." What do we think?'

Mr Scott tried to restrain his absolute disapproval, but it was a battle doomed from the start. Virge, who for reasons of her own, was dressed from head to foot in deep Catholic purple, and had dyed her hair the same colour the night before in the bath, gave him a look.

'Does everyone have to do this?' she said. 'Isn't it straight out of Agatha Christie?'

Mr Scott clearly didn't know what to say to that, and fell back on undertaker speak, which we were discovering was a whole other language.

'It's a requirement,' he said, his voice trailing off into a repressed mutter. 'Executor,' he managed, rallying for a moment. 'Duty . . . Home Office regulations . . . death act.'

'It's all right,' said Virge, taking pity on him. 'We'll sign.'

Then we had to choose the urn.

'Is this all?' said Virge, staring dubiously at the meagre collection of boxes.

'We usually find,' said Mr Scott. He was starting to develop a tic under his right eye, a nerve jumping edgily just under the skin. I stared at it in sudden urgent fascination.

'Serves our purposes,' said Mr Scott, having another go at it. 'This one has a screw top,' he added, with an effort to be helpful.

'Oh dear,' said Virge. 'Oh, dear.'

Her eyes suddenly filled with tears.

'I can't look,' she said. 'I can't bear to think of Michael ending up with a screw top. You choose, Ash. Oh, God,' she said, starting to laugh. 'Ash, oh dear, it wasn't meant to be a pun. Isn't it awful and morbid and tasteless, death?'

I started to laugh then too, and we both stood there, in that tiny impersonal neon-lit office, and we laughed and laughed and laughed, and Mr Scott stood by and watched, in complete astonishment.

'Choose, Ash, go on, do,' said Virge. 'It doesn't matter. Just not the one with the screw top.'

We had to go and see the vicar at the church we had

chosen. We had to request the hymns and decide on the order of service and choose which music we wanted for the sung mass. Michael had been brought up in the Church of England, but left at an early age, mostly because, as he always said, it was all too dreary. But for all that, he had left written instructions that he wanted a high church funeral, sung mass and incense and all.

'I know that I don't believe,' he wrote, 'but I might as well go the religious way, just in case there is something in it after all. Look at it as insurance. Obviously, for the aesthetic value, what I'd really like most is a lovely R.C. party, since they do the ceremony so much better than anyone else, except possibly the Greeks. However, since this is out of the question, can we go as high church Anglican as possible. I should like Fauré's Requiem, and incense, and pretty altar boys, if the silly old Prots run to such a thing.'

'So typical,' said Virge, when she read it to me. 'Where on earth are we to find a high church? What is a high church, anyway? I thought high churches were something on a hill. I don't know any.'

In the end, we called Etta's boyfriend, because he had a certain expertise in organ music, and we felt that this might qualify as knowledge of the church. It turned out that he did know, and he gave us a list of six, and we went and looked at them all, and chose the one we thought Michael would have liked best.

The vicar started off gently mournful and gravely sympathetic, and was extremely helpful until Virge told him that Michael didn't really believe in God, but wanted the service just in case He did really exist. After that, the padre became rather brusque, and we were relieved to get out of the dark serious church into the light.

'Let's go and have a drink and a cigarette,' said Virge. 'It's awfully tiring, all this death thing.'

*　　*　　*

We had to see the florist, and go to the hotel where Michael had asked for his wake to be held. We had to talk to catering managers and sommeliers. We had to go to the printers to see about the service sheets. We had to call the papers to ask them to put in the announcement for the funeral. We had to call friends and relatives.

There was something preposterous about all this, and we moved through it with a faintly hysterical feeling of unreality, acting and talking as if we were in a novel by P.G. Wodehouse. But for all that, it gets you through, in some strange way. It makes the first few days bearable.

This unnatural party mood persisted right up to the morning of the funeral. Diana and Jonathan arrived early. I hadn't seen them for a while, Michael had told them not to come and see him in the last weeks of his illness. 'I couldn't bear it, Ash,' he said to me, in one of his rare moments of gravity, 'for them to see me like this. It's bad enough that I let them down by not being a lovely happy hetero, married to the perfect wife and bringing up the perfect children, without them having to see this.'

I wanted to tell him that he was talking nonsense, that he hadn't let them down, that they wouldn't mind what he looked like, but I didn't. He minded, and that was enough. I wasn't going to tell him what he should be feeling, not now. It was too late for that.

So it was curious to see them on that sunny Friday morning, as if we were meeting at a cocktail party. I kissed them both, and said Hello how lovely to see you, because it was, it always was, and I wanted to say that I was sorry, but I didn't know how, so we left out that part.

Virge came down, still all in purple. She wouldn't say much about it, but I think she had a horror of black, as if that really would be too much, on top of everything else. Jonathan and Diana hugged her, and told her how lovely she looked, how well she had done to organise everything, that she should have let them come up and help, and Virge said it was fine, she preferred to do it alone, and anyway she had me.

I watched them, doing the right thing, with that instinctive delicacy and tact and ease that they all had, and I thought how curious it was, that even in this situation, even now, they still all seemed to remember how to behave. If it was my parents, they would both have been drunk already, for a start, and one of them would have made a scene, and they would probably have ended up fighting and sniping and crying tears of self-pity, tears not for the dead person, but for themselves.

It was only when we got to the church, and it was packed with mourners, and the priest and all those other strange people in their robes came up the aisle, and the music started with a great sonorous swell of the organ, and I looked to my left and saw the coffin, covered in high waxy white lilies, that I suddenly realised that it was Michael in there.

It was only in that very moment that I fully realised why we were all there, what we were all doing, what the past days had been about. It was only then that for the first time since it had happened I really absolutely finally knew and understood that he was gone, and I felt my heart break in me.

I wish they wouldn't do things like play Fauré at funerals, because what chance have you got then? The English are so strange. You have to gather together, all smart and dressed up and with your shoes polished and your face painted, and then they play the saddest pieces of music and read the most moving pieces of verse, and you're not supposed to cry in case your eye black runs.

I did cry, because I couldn't help it. I sat there, and I couldn't stop thinking about Michael in that box, just not alive, just not existing any more, just gone, and I listened to that terrible aching music, and I tried as hard as I could, I really tried, but it was no good. Next to me, Virge held on very tight to my hand, her back ramrod straight, her face absolutely motionless, tears pouring down her cheeks.

Afterwards, they took Michael away, to be burned. Virge and I stood a little apart from the rest, watching him go. He had asked that no one go with him, that the undertakers take him away and deliver the ashes back. He wrote that he had been to a cremation once and it was the worst thing he'd ever seen in his life, and he didn't want any of us to have to go through that. So the hearse took him away, and Virge and I stood together and watched, and that was the last we ever saw of him.

The hearse indicated, the amber light flashing slowly, and drew away round the corner, and was lost from sight, and Virge and I looked at each other.

'Don't,' said Virge urgently. 'We have the party. We must be gay and suitable.'

And we were. Everyone was. We talked about the old times and made jokes and remembered.

'Oh, he would have loved this,' everyone said, looking around the wonderful gilded hotel room, at the banks of flowers and the shiny green bottles of champagne. 'How he would have loved this.'

Virge, in her purple, stood in the centre of the room, tall and bright and merry. I was suddenly sharply reminded of those first days in Oxford, those times I used to see her across a crowded room, surrounded by all those people who aspired to her. I remembered how I used to catch glimpses of Michael at those same parties, in his cuban boots and his velvet suits.

I wondered how we could ever have been so young and unscarred, so absolutely untouched by life. I wondered how it could be that now we were so marked by it, and yet we looked, from the outside, so much the same. We had perhaps lost the absolute clear bloom of youth, that faintly unformed aspect to our faces. Our features had sharpened and grown defined, there were a few faint lines about our eyes, but from a distance, there was no difference. We carried our scars on the inside, and I thought suddenly it was strange, how it worked, that if you didn't tell anyone, they would never ever have known.

When it was over, Virge and I walked home together, through Green Park, thick with early evening sun, past the lawns and the trees and the deck chairs and the neat little paths. We crossed over Hyde Park Corner and wandered down Knightsbridge, looking at the shops and the buses and the taxi cabs, through South Kensington with its nice white houses and garden squares and neat black railings.

We didn't say much, on that walk. It seemed as if it had been the longest day, as if it had gone on forever, half our lives. So we walked slowly and silently, as if reassured by the simple mechanical action of moving. It was as if we were looking at the city in the same way, simply observing the absolute fact of it, in its relevant detail, almost as if we were surprised it was still there.

When we got home, we took a bottle of champagne and went and lay in the garden, watching the light fade, and we smoked cigarettes, and let the feeling of unreality which we had carried with us for so long settle and start to fall away.

'Where do you think we go?' said Virge.

I thought about it for a moment. It was one of the

questions that I would have known the answer to instantly, a few years ago. Now I wasn't sure, but then we weren't sure of anything any more.

'Somewhere,' I said. 'There's too much of us for it not to go anywhere. I think maybe we come round again.'

'It was you that first made me believe in reincarnation,' said Virge.

That surprised me. It wasn't often that Virge surprised me, but she surprised me now.

'Did I?' I said. 'Why?'

'Because,' said Virge, 'when we met I thought that we must already have known each other. It was like turning on a light switch and seeing a familiar room. It was like walking into a house that you've never visited before but knowing that in the left-hand drawer of the desk you will find a letter with your name on it.'

I sat for a moment, thinking this over. It had been the same exact thing for me too.

'Yes,' I said. 'It was. That's just what it was like.'

'So, you see,' said Virge. Her voice was steady and sure, strong as it always was, and I heard it, and I thought how extraordinary it was, that we were sitting here and talking, as we had always done, that it was almost as if none of it had happened, that we were just together, because we'd always been together, and nothing had changed.

'You see,' said Virge. 'I got to thinking. I thought that it must have been that we'd already been here before. I don't see why that should be strange. Who are we to judge? Religion is only made up by men after all, gods are only invented to try and explain the inexplicable, because we all want some kind of plan and logic and order to a thing which has no logic or order . . .' Her voice shook for a moment, the merest tremor, and I knew that she was thinking of Michael, of the absolute lack of logic and order in his death.

'To make us feel safe and comfortable,' she said, 'as if just because we can account for things they must make sense. I don't understand why the English, with their Anglican church, scoff at the idea of other lives, when they believe in the holy ghost and the flames of hell, which are just as strange.'

'The devil you know?' I said.

'I prefer the angel you don't,' said Virge. 'Michael could be back already, you never know. We might meet someone tomorrow, and have that same feeling, and it could be Michael, already come round again.'

'Yes,' I said. 'I think that must be it. I think that we go on. Because heaven is silly.'

Virge started to laugh.

'Oh, Ash,' she said. 'Oh, Ash. Here we are, at the end of the twentieth century, and ever since we came out of the caves and started thinking, sages and philosophers and sceptics and seers and holy men have been talking about the nature of heaven and earth, about the mystery of being, about the possibility of other worlds and other lives, and you've just summed it up.'

'Thank you,' I said.

'You're right, anyway,' she said. 'It's what Chaucer said about heaven being an impossible concept, because it's supposed to be perfect, but perfection would be the dullest thing you could ever imagine in your whole wide life, and so it would just be boring, and boring isn't perfect. So we know that heaven is the silliest idea anyone ever came up with.'

'Me and Chaucer both,' I said. 'Good old Geoff.'

Virge started to laugh again.

'Oh, dear,' she said. 'I think we must be tight.'

'I think we must,' I said. 'I think that it's right and proper that we should be, a little. Isn't it strange that champagne is always what people drink at weddings and funerals and births.'

'Life and death,' said Virge, 'and a bottle of bubbly. There must be something symbolic in it, but I can't think what it is, just now.'

'Perhaps we shouldn't think too much, just now,' I said. 'Perhaps this is one of those times when we really shouldn't.'

'Perhaps,' said Virge. 'Perhaps you're right.'

She stared up at the sky for a moment. It had taken on that transparent gleaming aspect that it sometimes did on summer evenings, that high arched infinite blue, absolutely clear and unmarked, except for the evening star, just starting to shine in the distance.

'It's a perfect evening,' said Virge. 'It's the most perfect evening I ever saw.'

We sat there until late, until the light was gone and the dark came in, the sky turned indigo then black, and the stars came out, and we could see the plough and Orion and Sirius and the thick white stream of the milky way, and we talked and talked, until it was morning and we were too tired to talk any more.

24

I was misled by that night, the last night we spent together for many weeks. Because of it, I thought that we would just carry on, the two of us together, as we always had, that we would help each other come to terms with what had happened.

But it wasn't like that at all. The unreality and strange feeling of distance, of removal, from the actual fact of Michael's death, that strange hysterical mood which had taken us through the days after, up to the funeral itself, disappeared immediately the next day.

I woke up feeling as if I had been hit by a truck, the odd lightness that I had felt for the last week replaced by a feeling of heaviness so tangible and physical that I had difficulty getting out of bed. I felt drained and tired and sluggish and empty. I suddenly realised that life had to go on, but there was no Michael in it any more.

I dressed sadly, and went down to breakfast, and I found Virge drinking coffee.

'Oh, Virge,' I said, sitting down stiffly, like an old lady whose bones are seizing up from rheumatism and arthritis and age. 'What are we to do?'

Virge looked at her watch, and said that she was late and she had to run and she would see me later, and she got up and left the room and I watched her go in absolute surprise, the second time in two days that she had surprised me.

I had the exact feeling that you get when you've first gone to bed with someone, and the night has been dark and close and full of secret laughter and easy intimacy, and you go to sleep happy and dreamy and thinking what may come of all this, and you wake up the next morning, and it's harsh and light and bright and the person is dressing at the end of the bed, and their voice is changed, no longer full of sex and intimation, but brusque and businesslike and embarrassed, and they say that they've got to go and they'll call you, and you know absolutely that they won't, and you lie there and watch as they can't quite meet your eyes, and you see them go, and you hear the door slam, and you lie back and wonder how in the world you could have got it so wrong, how it is that something can change so radically in such a very short passage of time.

That was what it felt like. I had felt like that with men in the past, when I had made the mistakes which we all have to, however clever and modern we think we are, but I never ever expected I should have that feeling with Virge.

I drank my coffee, and I got up slowly and walked into work, and I thought it must be just a reaction, that she was having the same feeling that I was, the shock of the shift in our lives which Michael's death had brought, the sure knowledge which we could no longer avoid that nothing would ever be the same again. I thought it would be all right, that she would come back, that she at least would not have changed, that we would still be the friends we had always been.

But it didn't happen like that. Everything changed after that, more than I could have imagined. I believed in change, it was one of the things I hoped for, looked for, expected. I hadn't when I was younger; for years I had believed, even

hoped, that everything stayed the same. I had been searching, in those days, for permanence, certainty. If Michael
dying had taught me anything, it was a confirmation of my
growing belief that nothing is permanent, even the things
that you most hope might be.

I found myself often not believing that he was gone, for
all that I had watched him being taken away in his box,
for all that his ashes had been delivered the next day in
their little cask, where they still sat on the mantelpiece,
because Virge wouldn't look at them or talk about where
they should be scattered. For all that, I found it hard to
believe that someone so vital, so essentially alive, no longer
existed.

Sometimes I really did believe that he was away, abroad,
that someday soon I should open the front door and find
him standing there, in one of his gaudy coloured suits, his
face brown and lean from a foreign sun, full of the laughter
and stories that he always carried with him. Sometimes,
when the telephone rang, I would pick it up, wondering
vaguely if it were Michael, calling from the airport, and
found myself puzzled and disappointed and resentful that
it never was.

I missed him terribly, more than I could have imagined;
there was a tangible emptiness left where he had been.
At first, I tried to fight it, to fill it, with other things,
but gradually, almost imperceptibly, I learnt to let it be,
to accept that there was this gap in me, this space, this
melancholy. I felt, in some strange way, a comfort and
rightness in the simple appropriateness of my grief –
that this is as it should be, this is how I should feel.
I think it would have been worse if I had felt nothing.
So, in some unexpected way, I learnt to carry my sadness
lightly. I learnt that it is possible to be happy and sad at
the same time, that there is room for both, space for
gladness and regret.

So I didn't fight it, but Virge did, with every weapon she had. I hardly saw her in the weeks after the funeral: she was so busy always, spending long hours at the office and nights with the gangster, that all we ever did was pass on the stairs or in the hall, and she never seemed to have time to stop and talk. She wore a set expression of purpose, her face closed and tight in strict defence, and she was always going somewhere, as if the one thing she could not do was to stand still, as if the devil were at her heels, and if she stopped for a single moment he might catch her by the throat.

I could see what she was doing, because I had done it myself, after the writer, that trick of not letting yourself stop for a solitary moment, just in case you might have to feel something. Lucky for me, I had the shrink to help me through, and if you're lying on a couch once a week, you have to allow all those things to catch up with you in the end, and once they're out there's a tremendous relief in it, because it's the fighting and the running that are the worst pain, the real paralysis, the things that bring that terrible leaden feeling that there is no reason to anything, no meaning or rhyme or point, that you might as well just stay in bed all day because there is nothing to get up for.

But Virge didn't have that. In the early days of my visits to Hampstead, she used to say that she envied me, that she wished she had a nice wise gent who could help her with the mysteries of life. I said that she should go, that everyone should, that we all needed a little help, but she said she had no excuse.

'I have perfect parents, Ash,' she said. 'I have had a perfect life. What excuse do I have? I have no pill-popping mother and gin-soaked father, I have no childhood traumas and teenage scars. How on earth could I go and get help when I have it all?'

But now she was lost. I could see it in her eyes, in the

way she couldn't look at me, or exchange more than four words of conversation. I could hear it in the tight, brittle timbre of her voice. It was as if she was holding it all inside, all the things that had been unleashed by Michael's death, as if she was too frightened to let go in case it should all come up and overwhelm her.

I spent a lot of time with Gus, in those weeks. Missing Virge, we took to going up to the old places in Soho in the evenings, those close dark bars that we used to frequent when we were nineteen, like the place where I first went with Virge, that very first night.

There was some comfort in it, as if by going back to those old places we could recapture something of the feeling that we had back then, that idea that we could be anything and do anything, that the world was ours, infinite possibilities stretching out before us, dreams and hopes and belief in that tomorrow which would never come; that old lost forgotten feeling that we were all going to live forever.

'Did we really believe all those things that we think we believed?' I said to Gus, on one of those nights. 'Sometimes I can't remember. Or is it just that we like to think that we were certain then because we are so uncertain now?'

Gus looked at me with his thoughtful eyes. One of the things I loved in him was the way he had of giving gravity to the real questions, the ones which needed an answer. He could be as inconsequential and foolish as any of us, when the mood took him, but he knew that sometimes there was a time for more than that, that we can't just laugh and tell jokes and give out lines all the time, however tempting it might be, that sometimes we need to feel that there is something more to say, even if it all has been said before.

'It's perspective,' he said. 'That's what changed. We could see so little then, so it seemed that the world was very small and we were very big. Now it's the other way round: we can see too clearly the great size of the world, and it makes us feel small.'

'And logic,' I said, nodding slowly. 'That's what went, that belief that there was a logic to it, a grand plan, something rational and ordered. Perhaps it's the random thing that's hardest to take.'

Gus looked at me again, and lit up a cigarette and smoked at it for a moment. I could see that he knew exactly what I was really talking about, what I really meant, because he always had. I thought then that he always would, that perhaps here was one small thing that might not change, whatever else happened.

'Do you think about him all the time?' he said.

'All the time,' I said. 'It's strange, I think about him more now he's dead than I ever did when he was alive.'

Gus nodded.

'Yes,' he said. 'I think that's how it works. I do too. It's some comfort, almost as if he's still here, because we carry him in our heads.'

'I think that too,' I said. 'I do. But then there are times when all that is all very well, but I want him here, in person, in his suit, not just in my head, as if that sometimes isn't enough.'

'Oh yes,' said Gus. 'I expect we'll always want that, always and forever and till the end of it, until we are almost too old to remember.'

I heard something in his voice, and I turned sharply and looked right at him.

'Did you . . . ?' I said.

'No,' said Gus, quickly. There was a small pause. 'No,' he said again, in a hard fast fierce voice that was unlike him, that I'd never heard him use before. 'But I wish I had.'

I knew that he was in love with Michael and Virge, just as I was. I had always known that, it was one of the things about Gus, his great love for them both, but I had never thought of the difference between us. For me it was just love, the kind you have with friends, clear and easy and simple, but I suddenly saw that for Gus it was not the same, and I wondered if it were more complicated than that, whether through all these years he had loved them in some other way, that tension of possibility always just below the surface.

We talked about Michael for a long time that night, remembering. I think, although we didn't say it, that we were both afraid of forgetting, that by going back over and over those memories we held so closely we could keep some part of him alive.

'Has Virge said anything to you?' I said, later.

'No,' said Gus. 'Nothing. I never see her.'

'Who is this gangster?' I said suddenly, angry. 'Who is he?'

Gus sat for a moment, very still, looking away across the room.

'Probably,' he said at last, 'the only person in the world who doesn't make her think of Michael.'

'It's hardest for her,' he said, another time, another night, another of those times it was just us, because Virge still couldn't come back from wherever it was she had gone. 'It's hard, now it's just her.'

'She has us,' I said. 'There's us.'

'No,' said Gus. 'I mean the burden, of that family. We can't help her with that. Before, it was her and Michael together, they could share it, spread the load. You see, Ash,' he said, looking at me very seriously, 'in a sense, we're the lucky ones, you and me. We just left our families. They were no good, so we just walked away. That's easier, in some ways.'

'Yes,' I said, thinking about it. I hadn't seen either of

my parents for over two years. I had seen finally, that there was no point: they had become meaningless to me, no more than a shadowy intimation of what might have been. There were times that I missed the idea of having a family, but as I had said to Jonathan that time, I didn't miss them, because there was nothing to miss. I felt, more than anything, freedom rather than loss.

'Yes,' I said.

'It's a net, family,' said Gus. 'A web. You can get caught in it, enmeshed in expectation. So it can be harder to live your own life, to be yourself, for yourself, because you are always someone's child, or someone's brother or sister. There's something rather wonderful in being able to shake that off. But Virge can't do that, because there's no excuse for it, and now she has the unattainable perfection of those parents to live up to all on her own, because Michael let them down. Children aren't supposed to die before their parents, that's not part of the deal. Michael didn't play the game, so now Virge is playing for two, and that's hard.'

I knew what he said was true. I could see it, but I was baffled and angry still, because I wanted to help her and she wouldn't allow it.

'I see that,' I said. 'I do. But why won't she talk? If only she would talk.'

Virge had always talked. We had an expression, when we were younger, about people. What we always wanted to know was what was their point. So, someone's point might be that they were bitchy or sexy or an expert on the Byzantine Empire, witty or fey or lawless or a cross dresser. For many years the worst we could say about someone was that they had no point.

Virge, being Virge, had more points than I could count, but one of the main ones, the one that was perhaps most obvious, was that she could talk. She had a sureness in talk, without buts or ifs, no you knows or I means or sort ofs. Sometimes, when she was really travelling, she spoke almost in prose, almost as the words might appear on the page, which is a rare and wonderful thing to hear. Gus could do it sometimes, but not at such length or with such fluency, not quite in that way Virge had, of really using language, carrying a fluid facility for running words into glittering sentences, as a child will artlessly thread beads onto a string.

I sometimes thought that it was a waste, that she should have been a writer, with the talent she had for lateral connection and swerves of thought and sudden precision of meaning. But then, I liked it that there were many times when the talk was just for me, a private edition, not available for public consumption.

I was used to hearing writers talk, and sometimes I couldn't help the suspicion that in those conversations I was acting as a sounding board as they tested out ideas and passages and small streams of consciousness, holding them up to the light, turning them this way and that to see the effect, before going home and writing them down, so that very talk would be found the following spring in all good bookshops, there for anyone willing to pay their money and take their chances. But Virge wasn't practising or posturing or polishing, and so, in some small sense, I felt her talk to be less cheap.

I missed it. I missed her. I was living with someone who wasn't there and it made me lonely, more lonely than the simple fact of solitude. When you have another person there and yet absent that's the worst loneliness there is. I wanted to ask where she had gone, what private hidden part of her mind she had retreated into, but my facility for language had never been as bravura as hers and now I truly didn't have the words. I was, in the real deep sense, lost for words.

This pain of separation was almost harder to bear than Michael dying. I felt that Virge was dying somewhere inside, a living death, and that was a truly terrible thing to watch. I stood by, helpless, in the dark cold months of that winter, losing her a little more day by day, watching her drift further and further away from me, out onto some wide sunless sea of her own, and knowing that there was nothing I could do.

25

She came back, suddenly, one day at the beginning of December. It was a Saturday morning, and I was lying in bed, half awake, watching the early winter sun come in through the slats of my blinds, when the door was abruptly pushed open, and I looked up to see Virge standing at the end of my bed.

She pointed at her belly, and said,

'What the hell am I going to do about this?'

I looked at her. Even though I could see it, I didn't get it for a moment.

'What?' I said, stupidly.

'I'm pregnant,' she said, and I looked again, and I could see that she really was, that her stomach was full and heavy and distended, and really pregnant.

'Virge,' I said, because I didn't know what else to say. 'You are.'

'Oh fuck,' she said, sitting down on the bed, as if the mere effort of standing upright was suddenly too much for her. 'I can't have a baby. I didn't think I would actually *have* a baby. I thought if I didn't think about it it would go away. Why would it want to stay inside me? I thought it would just go away, all on its own. What does it want to be doing in my stomach anyway? What does it want with me?'

I shook my head. I remembered what Hem had said to me once, that there are questions to which there are no answers, that sometimes there is no point in trying to answer them. Sometimes, he used to say, there are just questions. I wished, suddenly, urgently, that he was here, now, to remind me of some of the things that I had forgotten.

'I don't know,' I said. 'But it is there, for all that. That's all there is.'

'Ash,' said Virge, fiercely. 'For God's sake. Could you just for once not do this fatalistic Buddhist thing? Couldn't you just for once be as confused as I am? Couldn't you just not act like there is some great cosmic plan which we must learn to accept, just for one moment. Couldn't you just accept that sometimes in life there are accidents and contingency and that they aren't always meant to be and they aren't always good things that we can learn from, and sometimes whoever there is up there making these great cosmic plans takes a day off or goes out for coffee and then everything goes haywire and things like *this* happen.'

She pointed again at her stomach, jabbing a furious finger at her swollen belly, and stared at me with angry questioning eyes. I don't know what she wanted me to say, whether she did want me to try and answer all her questions. I don't know why she had suddenly come to me, after all this time, brought this new strange side of her nature into my room, a side I had never seen before, and I don't know how she expected me to react to it. I felt tired, suddenly.

'I don't know,' I said again. 'I don't know any of it. All I know is that you are having a child, and however much you argue about it, that is the one fact in all of this, and it doesn't matter how or why or what it all means, but you are going to give birth to another person, whatever you think about it, so you might as well accept it, and start thinking about what you are going to do.'

Virge looked at me in amazement, as if this was the last answer that she had expected. But I had been growing up while she had been away, and if I had learnt one thing since Michael died, it was that life is too short not to talk straight.

'Oh,' she said, her voice carrying a rising wail, like a child who won't admit that it's bedtime. 'I can't have a baby.'

But she did have a baby, in May. She fought it and complained about it and snarled and sniped and dragged her body about the house like a strange alien thing that didn't belong to her. And when the baby did arrive, a little girl, she came out into the world bawling and howling as if bringing all Virge's fury and frustration with her.

'Good pair of lungs,' said the doctor in efficient satisfaction. 'Nothing wrong with her lungs.'

Virge turned her face away, crying long racked tired tears.

'There's nothing wrong with it,' she said, bitterly. 'But there's something wrong with *me*.'

The doctor smiled, in that mildly patronising way that medical men sometimes have, as if they know more than we do, us poor lay saps.

'Come along, Mamma,' he said. 'Here's your daughter.'

Virge kept her face to the wall.

'Take her away,' she said. 'Please. Take her away.'

They told us that postnatal depression is experienced by thirty per cent of mothers. They told us many facts and figures and nice technical terms. They told us that there was nothing to worry about, that it would pass, that Virge would come round. I think it was meant to be comforting, but for all their talk, the fact remained that Virge would not touch her child.

The gangster sent flowers and envelopes full of cash and details of a trust fund. I arranged the flowers and used the cash to get a monthly nurse. She was middle-aged and comfortable, maintaining a stalwart calm in the face of Virge's indifference. Between us, she and I looked after the baby, the poor little thing who didn't even have a name. I kept thinking of those children who are left in dustbins or carrier bags, found by some kindly member of the public, taken to hospital, and named by nurses, because there is no mother there to do it.

'You must give her a name,' I said to Virge. 'You must.'

'Why?' said Virge. She lay in bed all day, sunk into a distant suspended state of her own, carrying with her some distorted irrefutable logic.

'Everyone needs a name,' I said. 'We can't just go on calling her the baby.'

'You think of something,' said Virge. 'I don't care.'

Gus said we should do it.

'I think she needs a name,' he said. 'It doesn't matter so much who chooses it, not now.'

So we called her Viola, because Gus was in a strangely sentimental mood, and he said it was appropriate, since she was all the brothers and the sisters of her father's house, and anyway it was a pretty name.

'Your baby is called Viola,' I told Virge.

'Is it?' she said. 'Well.'

I knew I shouldn't be angry. I knew that Virge was suffering from some kind of serious mental disturbance, that she couldn't help herself, that it wasn't cruel or malicious, what she was doing, it was sickness. But I was angry, all the same.

'She's not an It,' I said. 'You could at least say she. You could at least try and do that.'

Virge didn't say anything. She just stared at me with her blank eyes, as if I were a stranger she didn't know, as if she were a stranger I didn't know.

I left her. There was nothing more to say.

There was a desperate air of unreality about the house in the first months after Viola was born. Stevie and Etta came round to visit the baby, we had teas and suppers. Denny and Stretch spent a lot of time there as well, and there were times when we all sat down to eat with each other, and it almost seemed like the old times, except there was the empty place where Virge should have been, and as we talked and laughed and acted normal, we were all aware that she was lying upstairs, in that world of her own into which she had withdrawn, and none of us were sure where it was and whether she would come back.

Diana and Jonathan came to visit, to see their grandchild. As always, they made all the right noises, did all the right things, but even they had an air of strain, as if they were barely keeping their heads above water, baffled and saddened by what had happened to their children, those lovely shining children whom they had raised so well. I didn't know what to say to them. I was glad when they left.

So there we all were, none of us really knowing what to do, and amazingly, through it all, the baby grew and prospered. She was a darling child, happy and smiling and responsive. I had never thought about wanting a child myself, and I was surprised by the absolute love I felt when I held her live solid little body, and I marvelled at her complete trust, how she would allow herself to go to sleep in my arms, knowing, in that strange instinctive way that very small children have, that no harm would come to her. I wished, more than anything, that Virge would just once pick her up, because I couldn't believe that once she felt that small person she could go on in this state of indifference.

Virge lay in bed for six months, sunk into a distant suspended state of lethargy. The doctors and psychiatrists tried talking cures and medications and nothing made any difference. We were in despair. And then suddenly, one day, she came downstairs.

I hardly recognised her. She had brushed her hair and put on lipstick, and she had a bright, knowing air on her, as if the last six months were an aberration, something that had hardly happened.

I was feeding the baby, and I looked up in astonishment and delight as the door opened and Virge came in.

'Hello,' she said. 'I'm up.'

'Virge,' I said, with pleasure. 'Look. Here's your baby.'

'Oh yes,' she said, but her eyes skated away too quickly, and I saw then that it was not really Virge, it was someone who looked almost like she used to. It was as if some vital part of her were still missing, something was still lost. But, I thought, at least this must be a step in the right direction – she is up and talking, and even if there is something brittle and changed about her, at least she is walking and talking. It must be a start. We can't hope for miracles, not all at once, not any more.

'Oh,' said Virge, and her voice rattled a little as she spoke, as if rusty from lack of use. 'Have I been the most terrible bore? You are good, Ash, looking after . . .' She nodded at Viola, and I saw that she still could not say her name, but I let it go, because if there was one thing I was learning it was patience. 'You are good and true. What did I ever do to deserve such a good and true friend as you?'

'You did plenty,' I said. 'It's no trouble.'

Virge sat down and lit a cigarette. Her hand was solid as a rock. I watched it, expecting tremors, but there were none. She sat and smoked, perfectly composed, for all the world as if she were at a nightclub in the thirties, waiting for some dashing playboy to come and ask her to dance.

'What we've been through together,' she said, in a slightly more normal voice. 'You and I, Ash. Always together. Do you remember how we used to talk about always?'

'Yes,' I said. 'You said it the very first night we met. Here's to always, you said.'

'Did I?' said Virge. She looked distracted. 'Yes. I did,' she said. 'I did, didn't I? Goodness, always is a long time. And how we were going to be friends even when we were eighty and sit in the Ritz in eccentric hats and scandalise people?'

'I remember,' I said.

'Yes,' said Virge. 'It was perfect, wasn't it? What perfect friends we were.'

'We are,' I said. 'It hasn't changed so very much. It can't be perfect all the time.'

'No,' said Virge. 'Not all the time. There was perfect, though, wasn't there? There was a lot of perfect. Do you remember that first holiday in the summer from Oxford, when we went abroad? Do you remember those long days in Hem's house, when we wandered about those high empty rooms and took tea at four o'clock?'

'Yes,' I said. I remembered also what she had said about that time, about how it would never be so perfect again.

'You do know, Ash, don't you,' said Virge, 'you do know that you are the one I love best. I never loved anyone so much as you. You were always there. I never had anyone like you.'

'I know,' I said. 'It's the same for me.'

'Yes,' she said. 'Yes.' She put out her cigarette and got up suddenly.

'Now I'm back in the world,' she said, 'now I'm back,

I must go out. I need a new pair of shoes. I need a bag. What a mess I've become. I'm going shopping.'

'Shopping?' I said. I was taken aback. I had expected many things, but I had not expected shopping.

'Yes,' she said. 'Do you mind? Can you manage? I won't be long. I must have a new bag.'

And she left, before I could think of anything else to say. I heard the front door slam, and I looked down at the baby, sucking contentedly at her bottle, happy in her own small universe, still young enough to stay untouched.

Virge did go shopping. She went and bought a new bag, and a new pair of shoes, but she didn't come home. She drove down the M4 to Bristol, and she walked along the Clifton Suspension Bridge, and she took off her new shoes and arranged them carefully beside her shiny new handbag, and then she jumped.

The police called, later that night. Gus drove me down to Bristol, and I identified the body. It looked amazingly untouched, just a little pale. I had thought it would be twisted and broken, but it wasn't. It was Virge, there, and not.

We drove slowly back to London, through the night. There was no traffic. It seemed we were the only people on the road.

We didn't say a single word on that long drive back. We drove and drove, through the darkness, until finally the light of London started, the familiar welcome landmarks that greet you when you come in from the west, the illuminated Lucozade sign and the big white clock and the Hammersmith flyover, and then the big arched windows of the studios in Talgarth Road.

We were waiting for the lights to change at the junction

with the North End Road, when I suddenly looked at my watch and saw the date.

'Oh God,' I said.

I heard my voice come tinny and unnatural into the car. Gus turned and looked across at me.

'It's her birthday,' I said.

26

It was anger got me through this time. With Michael, it had been a cocoon of unreality, but with Virge, it was fury. I don't know if I've ever been so angry. I didn't know who I was angry with; her, or fate, or that cosmic plan that she had once spoken of, but whatever it was, it served some kind of purpose.

It got me through the formalities, all those ones I remembered from Michael. Gus came with me, and we went through the exact same things all over again. I could hardly believe that I should have to do it all again so soon.

They came from all over for the funeral, all the old faces, all the people I remembered from the careless days of our youth. Albert came, and Chas and Dimitri and Con and Ruby and Clover, and all the Oxford people. Keane came, looking older and less sinister. Stevie and Etta and Stretch and Denny came together, in a little band, just like the old days, just like, except for their faces, set and white and stiff with lingering disbelief. Diana and Jonathan sat with me and Gus. Hem arrived late, straight from the airport, with his suitcase and his camera bag, and sat at the back.

At the wake, after the coffin had been taken away, the

crowd gathered and swelled. We went to the same hotel as we had for Michael, that same gilded room, with its chandeliers and its belle epoque, because I hadn't had the energy to think of anywhere else to go.

It was the same place, and many of the same people, but it was absolutely different. There weren't the same jokes there had been at Michael's, the same brave air of remembering the good times. Perhaps it was something to do with it being a suicide, I don't know. Killing yourself is a very different business from letting something else do it for you. There is something specially horrible about going to the funeral of someone who does it themselves, rather than waiting for some outside agency, like you're supposed to. I felt weary and angry and displaced, and I didn't want to remember the old days and think how much she would have loved this, as I had with Michael. It was just different, that was all.

There were strange faces in the crowd, people I didn't know. I wondered a little about that, as I sat and watched, but then I remembered something that had always struck me, all the years Virge had been away. I had always wondered that while we talked and wrote and saw each other, she had never actually told me very much about the details of her life, the one she lived when we were apart.

One of the strangers, an old West Indian man in a perfect pressed blue suit and shined co-respondent shoes, came over to where I was sitting and asked if he could sit with me.

'Of course,' I said. I was glad, in a way. It was the old faces I could bear least, the ones I knew from way back, because they reminded me of all our youthful hopes and dreams, the ones that Virge and I had held together, the ones which didn't seem to count for anything any more.

'You're Ash,' he said. 'I can see that you are Ash.'

I felt a faint surprise, but only faint. I had the feeling that nothing would ever surprise me very much again.

'Yes,' I said. 'I am Ash.'

'I recognise you from Virge's description,' he said. 'My name is Jules,' he said. 'I knew Virge in New York. I am a musician, you see. We met in a jazz club she liked. I play the trumpet. I play the horn.'

I was surprised, then.

'You're the musician?' I said. 'The one with the loft? The one Virge was in love with?'

He laughed gently. He had some easy way with him, an air of having seen enough of the world to accept it, however strange it became. I wondered if it was his age, or whether it was a musician thing. Perhaps you got philosophical from playing the horn, who knew?

'She told you that?' he asked. 'That she was in love?'

'Yes,' I said. 'She said that she wasn't coming home because she had met a musician and she was in love.'

'She stayed with me for a while,' he said. 'But not in that way. My family were in Saint Vincent, my wife has relations there. Virge was living in a hotel, looking for a place to rent, and I asked her to stay until they came back. I suppose,' he said, taking out some papers and rolling himself a neat little cigarette, 'that it was almost like being in love, in a way. That was something Virge had, don't you think?'

I wasn't sure that I wanted to think about what Virge had now that she had taken it away so precipitately. I wasn't sure that I wanted to think about her and those gifts that she brought us when it was all dead and gone and wasted.

I think the musician saw it. He nodded slowly and lit up his cigarette and drew on it with concentration, the way you have to when you roll your own. I remembered when Gus went through a stage of rolling his own, and how we had teased him about it. I remembered him saying that you really had to smoke them, not like the ready-made ones.

'She said that she wished we could be in love,' the musician said. 'She said that she wished she was twenty years older and I was twenty years younger. And then my family came back to New York, and she moved out. I didn't see her so much after that. I think she didn't like having to give up her fantasy.'

I remembered also what Hem had once said about Virge not having much to do with the real world, preferring to make up her own version, and I wondered suddenly how well I had known her, my dearest and oldest and best friend. I would never have guessed at the musician. I wondered how many other secret lives she had had, how many other lives she had kept from me, the one person whom she professed to tell everything.

'You should forgive her,' said the musician. 'Will you forgive her?'

I sighed. I ran a hand over my eyes. I didn't know who this man was, this strange old man. I wasn't sure I wanted him telling me what I should do. But then, he had loved Virge too, and I supposed in a way he had as much right as anyone.

'I don't know yet,' I said. 'I don't know if I can.'

'There are,' he said, very slowly and with a low gravity in his voice, 'some people for whom living is just too much.'

'But she was so good at it,' I said. I could hear the anger rising in my voice. I felt it straining at my throat, the furious straining that had been there since I first got that late night telephone call. I swallowed, trying to push it down. 'That was always the point,' I said, 'about Virge. She was so good at living. She brought life to everything she did.'

The musician looked at me again, with absolute compassion.

'But don't you think,' he said, 'that it is sometimes the ones who seem best at it, the ones who seem to have the most to give, who crack, suddenly, like a china plate, like an old cracked china plate . . .'

'It's Fitzgerald,' I said automatically. 'That's F. Scott Fitzgerald. That's what happened to him, in *The Crack Up*, that's what he said.'

'So,' said the musician, 'it is sometimes those who burn brightest who burn out. It is too much for them, you see? They are using up their life quicker than the rest of us, going at twice the speed . . .'

'I who had no more dreams of my own,' I said.

The musician watched me for a moment, seeming not to resent the interruption. He seemed to be one of those people who don't run against the tide, but swim with it, clever enough not to fight the current. He seemed to be wondering whether I wanted to continue, happy to wait for me to make up my mind.

'That's what he said,' I said abruptly. I was speaking fast now, not sure what I was saying; there was something in me suddenly that wanted words, like the words that Virge had always used with such felicity.

'That there was a time when he could find himself back in the mind of his younger self,' I said. 'The young man with cardboard soles who had walked the streets of New York, that for a moment he could share that young man's dreams. And then he said: I, who had no more dreams of my own. Perhaps that was what it was with Virge. She always had dreams. Perhaps she ran out of dreams.'

It was nonsense. I knew it was. It was the kind of sentimental inconsequential rambling you get when you haven't had enough sleep and you're tired and worn out and filled with sorrow and hurt and confusion because your best friend goes and throws themself off a bridge for no reason that you can see.

'I used to think Fitzgerald was romantic,' I said. 'A great romantic figure. All that early death and unfulfilled promise and wasted talent. But there's nothing romantic about it, there's nothing romantic about death. It's just . . .'

I wasn't sure what it was, what it just was.

'It's just death,' I said, at last. 'That's all.'

Keane came and talked to me after that. I had a sudden sense that they were queueing up, waiting their turn to come and tell me things, say their piece. I had a sudden absurd notion that there was someone behind a door somewhere giving out tickets: Come in, number seven, your time is up.

'Hello, Keane,' I said.

'Hello,' he said. He sat down beside me, carefully, and I saw then that he was quite different. He had filled out and grown rather ordinary. He had a pleased comfortable look, as if his life wasn't so very hard to figure.

'Well,' I said. 'Here you are. After all these years.'

'I got married,' he said. 'I have two children. I work in the city.'

'Oh, Keane,' I said. 'How strange. You were always so strange, but this is the strangest thing of all.'

'It was an act,' he said, shrugging his shoulders a little. 'I was afraid of my own dullness, so I made up that sinister façade. I just invented it, because I thought it would cover up my own mediocrity. That was what Virge couldn't forgive me for.'

'What did happen in Mexico?' I said, because I had always wanted to know, and I didn't know what else to say to him.

'Exactly that,' he said. 'I'd told her all these stories about my sinister made-up life, and when we were in Mexico I admitted that they were make believe, fairy tales, and she couldn't forgive me for that. I suppose that was the worst thing I could have done to her, take all her fantasies away.'

'Yes,' I said. I felt heavy and fatalistic and as if all the birds were coming home to roost. 'I see. She said it was very terrible, but she never told me what it was.'

'I live in the Home Counties,' said Keane. 'People call me Maurice now. You see.'

I saw. I absolutely saw.

'Yes,' I said. I nodded. 'Yes.'

It was a strange wake. No one seemed to know what to do or how to act. We all seemed to be standing around waiting for someone to tell us how we should be.

I just sat, on my chair, letting people come to me. I watched everyone moving and talking and drinking, cautiously, as if afraid of doing or saying the wrong thing, and I felt like that too, as if I was not sure what I should say or how I should act or where I should go.

After a while, Jonathan came and sat down next to me.

'Ash,' he said. 'Dear Ash.'

His voice was worn and faint, that voice which had always carried such certainty and life in it. I thought of all the years I had known him, of all the times we had spent in his lovely house in Dorset. He looked old, suddenly. Perhaps that is what death does; perhaps it is death that makes you grow old, not life.

'Oh, Jonathan,' I said.

He took my hand.

'I wish I could tell you something,' he said. 'I wish I had something I could say which might bring you comfort. But I don't.'

I nodded. I felt the same. I knew, finally, that there was no comfort here. Time, perhaps, would heal, as everyone always promised it would, but words were no good, just now. Even if Virge had been here, with her great capacity for talk, even she would have had nothing to say, because there are times when there is nothing to say.

'Perhaps,' said Jonathan, 'we will find some sense in all this, in time. Perhaps. There is no sense in it, just now. Not that I can see.'

'I can't see any, either,' I said. 'Maybe there just isn't any. Maybe that's why I feel so angry, because it is all truly nonsense.'

'Yes,' said Jonathan. 'Yes, perhaps that's what it is.'

'You mustn't blame yourself, Ash,' said Diana, later.

I remembered her telling me that, exactly that, years before, the first time I had met her, when we sat in her perfect garden and watched the early roses.

'I do,' I said. 'I go over it, over and over, and I wonder if there was something I could have done. I never expected this. I always thought Virge would live forever. I feel that I didn't see it because I didn't let myself, that I wasn't brave enough to see what was happening, because I didn't want to see it. The signs were there, but I didn't have the courage to read them right.'

Diana shook her head. Her eyes were dark and bare with sorrow.

'We all feel like that,' she said. 'We all do. But it's not right. If people are going to do something, they will go and do it, whatever we try to do about it. I wish it weren't true, but it is.'

I looked at her, at her open, serene face, marked and lined now with loss, and all of a sudden, I felt that I really could not bear it. I couldn't bear it for her, and I couldn't bear it for me, and I didn't know what to do.

'I just want her back,' I said.

I sat it out, until the end, until everyone had gone home. I sat and smiled and nodded as people came to say goodbye, made all the expected noises, thanked me for organising the whole thing, as if I were a society hostess at some tony soirée. It felt twisted and skewed. I wanted to scream and shout and curse, but I didn't.

Finally, I was left alone in the empty room. They had all tried to take me home, offer me a ride, do something, but I refused. I wanted to sit for a moment, just me and my ghosts. I don't know what I thought would happen. I think I hoped that if I could just sit there, in that great room, the same room where we had said goodbye to Michael, that I might find some insight, some instinctive solution to the absolute emptiness inside.

I didn't. I just felt tired and old and alone. I looked round the room, at the tables with their empty glasses and full ashtrays and half eaten sandwiches, at the flowers already started to wilt, and I felt at an absolute loss, as if finally I had come up against some impasse, that for the first time in my life I really could not see a way round. I wondered what people did. I wondered. I didn't know.

Hem came to find me, in the end. I sat in that room for an hour or more, watching the light grow dim, until I was sitting in the shadows, in the twilight, staring into nothing.

'Here you are,' he said. I hadn't spoken to him that day, there had been too many people. I had seen him in the church, with the shock of recognition and memory I always felt with him. I had given him a small wave in greeting, and he had smiled back at me, but that was all.

I was unsurprised to see him now, standing in front of me, in his black suit. It seemed right that it should be him, now, I don't know why. Perhaps because he was the person I had always loved most, along with Virge, although it wasn't love I felt now, as I looked up at him. I didn't feel anything much, except a flat inevitability. My anger had gone, and left nothing behind, just a big old nothing, as if my insides were stuffed with cotton wool.

He took my hand and led me out of that room, away from the grand hotel, into the open city streets. I let him. I had no direction or decision any more. I didn't know where we were going and I didn't care.

We walked for a long time, through the evening streets, where people were going about their business, just as if everything in the world was right and proper and as it should be. I felt absolutely unconnected with them, these strangers, with their lives and their hopes and their dreams and their places to go.

In the end, we reached the river. I had always loved the river. The last of the light was catching on the water, and the bridges ran away into the distance, and I stared at it as if it was something I had never seen before.

'Oh, Hem,' I said. 'What are we to do?'

He didn't say anything. He had always known that, that sometimes there is nothing to say. He just held my hand. I thought of the day I had first met him, that summer in Oxford, when we had walked back to my room, hand in hand, just like this. I wondered how it could be possible that we were standing here together, all over again, when so much had changed.

'I wish,' I said, 'at least I could cry. I haven't cried. I wish I could cry.'

He took me home, after a while. The house was dark and empty. Stevie and Gus were out. It reminded me of the first time Virge and I had come here, and found the kitchen drab and bare with its cupboards full of soup and dry biscuits, and how we had made each other promise that we would never end up like that, old and alone with only soup to eat.

Hem turned on the lights, and I saw a pot on the table.

'Oh, God,' I said. 'Oh God.'

I sat down heavily. 'It's Virge,' I said. 'Gus must have brought them back.'

I looked at the mantelpiece, where the casket with Michael's ashes still stood, and I've never felt so strange in my life, sitting there, in that big old room, with the remains of my friends in their little boxes.

I cried then. Hem sat next to me, his arm about my shoulders, and I cried and cried for all those tomorrows that now would truly never come.

He stayed with me that night, all that long night. We didn't sleep, we just sat up and he let me cry, until it was morning and I had no tears left.

'I'm back for a while,' he said, the next day. I had slept until tea time, and when I came down, I found him in the drawing room, looking through old photographs.

'I think,' he said, 'that with everything that's happened, it's time to stand still for a moment.'

'Did you ever find what it was you were looking for?' I said. I had always wondered, but I had never asked, until now.

He shook his head. It gave me a sudden shock, looking at him, to see how little he had changed, to see that although we had been apart for almost ten years, with nothing but occasional brief meetings and scribbled postcards, he was still so dear and familiar to me, that nothing between us was really so very different, that he was still one of the people I knew and loved best.

'I don't think,' he said, 'that I was so much looking for as running from.'

'Yes,' I said. 'I see.'

'I'm thirty, Ash,' he said. 'Isn't it strange? It seems ten

minutes ago we were all eighteen, and now I'm thirty. I think I've travelled enough, just for the time.'

I remembered Virge saying almost the exact same thing, when she came back from America, that Sunday morning when she had walked into this very room and found me sitting, having breakfast. I remembered thinking that she was back for good, that we would never be parted again. I thought suddenly of that old saying, the one about the way to make the gods really laugh is to tell them your plans. I couldn't remember who said it. I thought perhaps it was the Chinese.

Hem looked away for a while, out of the window, into the day. We sat quiet and still in that high wide room, the room that we used to fill, where we used to have parties and evenings full of people and talk and laughter, when we really were young.

'I always wondered,' he said, at last, 'when I finally came back, if you would still be here. It's probably not the right time to ask, but I always wondered.'

'I was never going anywhere,' I said. 'I only ever wanted to stay still.'

Hem nodded. 'I used to envy you that,' he said. 'I used to wonder what it might be like to have that ability. It's strange, isn't it, how you have changed, but you're still the same, still here.'

'I wonder myself,' I said. 'I do.'

'I'm glad you are,' he said.

A week later, we took Virge and Michael back to Oxford. The same little band, all of us still together, after all these years, got into two cars and drove down that familiar drive, Stretch and Denny and Etta and Stevie and Gus and Hem and me.

We took the urns down to the meadows behind Christ Church, and we scattered the ashes in the long grass. We didn't say much, but I think we all felt that it was right, because although we were all out in the world, had been in the world for longer than we ever spent among those dreaming spires, it was here that our most precious and enduring memories lay, because it was those careless days when we held the answers to all the questions that we never knew we would have to ask.

'That's it, then,' said Gus, watching the wind blow the ashes away until there was nothing left.

I put my hand through his arm and held on to him.

'Yes,' I said. 'That's it.'

We drove back to London, and we went out to some bar that we'd never been to before, and we drank vodka and tried to get drunk, because that's what Gus said we should do.

We didn't really know what else to do, but we felt that we should do something. There was some terrible restlessness in us which wouldn't allow us to sit still. We had done the final thing we had to do, there were no more decisions to be made or formalities to go through, and it had left us with only the bare fact of Virge's death, and the ordinariness of our lives, waiting for us. It was as if we didn't know how to go back to the day to day, which so strangely seemed to have remained intact through this great disruption.

So, that night, we went from bar to bar, one after another.

With each one, our mood changed. In one we found a kind of gallows humour, which got us through the first round of drinks, the first half hour. Later, we grew nostalgic, and told stories about the old days, as if we were pulling together all the fragments of memory, to try and make some whole of it. We remembered things we thought we had forgotten, all the good times, all the best parts of Virge, and the parts of us that she brought out. We managed that for a while, but then we went to a small dark empty place, and suddenly it was all too much, and Stevie, of all people, clever modern brave Stevie, was the one to break, and shockingly and without warning, she started to cry.

'I'm sorry,' she said. 'I can't . . . I don't . . .' Denny put his arm round her and gave her a handkerchief, and we all sat and watched her in silence, because we were all feeling the same, but none of us knew what to say.

It was a long night. I think we were all afraid to go home, to stop, but eventually we had to. One by one, we dropped away, until it was after three in the morning, and there was just me and Gus and Hem left.

We went home and sat in the big upstairs room, and Gus went downstairs and found a bottle of wine. We weren't drunk, hard as we'd tried.

Gus came back, and opened the bottle, and I sat back in the sofa, and I heard him and Hem talking, as if from a distance, and I suddenly thought how strange it was that we had all spent that long night together, and we had talked and talked and talked, but nobody, not one of us, had asked *why*.

I wondered, sitting there in my house with my two old friends. I wondered what it was that led someone to go and jump, like that. I wondered what had been going through her head as she went to the shops and bought her shoes and her new bag. I wondered what she had thought as she took that long drive west.

It must have taken her two hours at least. I wondered what she had felt during those hours. I wondered why Clifton, of all places. We had never been to Bristol. Why did she go all the way to Bristol? If she was really so determined to do it, why didn't she just get some pills, or if it was a bridge she wanted, why didn't she do it in London. What did she want to go all the way to the west for?

'I suddenly realised what it was that shocked me most, part of it. I had always looked to Virge as my example. I had thought of her as way ahead of me, as far as life went. I had envied her what she had, that perfect family, that seamless life. I felt that part of the reason I went to the shrink every week was to try to catch up with her. I felt that I had to learn some of the things that she instinctively knew. I thought that one day I too might be able to carry some of her confidence and brightness, that brightness that always shone so light on her.

That she, of everyone, was the one to crack, destroyed my entire world order. If she couldn't make it, then which of us could? I didn't understand. I felt as if I had been struggling with some oblique mathematical formula, and finally thought that I had found the answer, the exact equation, only to find that it was the wrong one, after all that. I was lost without her, not just because she had been my friend, my absolute companion, but she had also been the one I looked to for how life should be, and how we should be in it.

'Don't, Ash,' said Hem. He and Gus had stopped talking, and I looked up to see them both staring at me, and I suppose that they could see something in my face, see what it was I was doing. Hem could, anyway.

'I can't help it,' I said.

'It's no good,' said Hem. 'Whatever we do, we'll never know. We'll never ever know.'

27

If there's one thing that teaches you the old line about life going on, it's a child. It was having Viola that really got me through those first dark months after Virge died.

I had legal custody, and the gangster had set up a fund for her, so there was money coming through every month, although I never heard from him, and he professed no desire to come and see his daughter. So I looked after her, and did my best to bring her up as Virge might have wanted, and concentrated all my energy on her.

Stevie moved out soon after the funeral. She and Denny got a place together and set up house and even talked about marriage. We all saw each other, just as we used to, although we didn't talk much about Virge, after that long night when we had talked of nothing else. I suppose we all knew we were avoiding the subject, but it was as if there was nothing more to say, not just now. Perhaps there never would be.

Gus stayed in the house with me and the baby, and quite soon we got another lodger, a quiet thoughtful man called Philip, someone Gus found. I didn't think much of it at the time, but after a while I noticed that he wasn't just a lodger.

'You're in love,' I said to Gus one morning.

He nodded. 'Yes,' he said. 'I finally decided. I finally

decided that both isn't really so very much good, when you get to our age.'

'He's lovely,' I said. 'I'm pleased.'

He was lovely, Philip. He was enchanted by the child, and spent long hours playing with her, so between the three of us, we managed to give her some kind of family. It wasn't perfect, but then I thought about Virge and Michael, with their perfect family, and what had happened to them, and I thought that perhaps Viola might have a better chance, with her strange set up.

Hem, against his will, had been sent to Paris for six months. Strangely, he seemed almost more bereft by the loss of Virge and Michael than anyone. I thought perhaps it was because he had seen them so little in the years he had been away – that he had expected them to be here, always, waiting for him, the same way he did with me, and now he had come back and they were gone, and it was too late, because you can't ever go back, make up those years you've missed, they're just gone. He didn't say as much, but I knew him well enough to read between the lines, and I think he felt it.

He called me most days, for no reason, just to talk. Sometimes he would ring in the middle of the night, at three or four in the morning. 'I just wanted to hear your voice,' he always said. 'Do you mind?'

I didn't mind. I didn't mind at all.

I was walking through the days, putting, as I had after Michael, one foot in front of the other, carefully, in case I might miss the mark. There were too many things I could think about, and I didn't want to think of any of them. I thought I was doing well, that my façade was in place, but Gus, of course Gus, saw through it, right through into all the spaces that lay underneath.

One Saturday, he sent Philip and Viola to the park, and took me out to lunch at a little neighbourhood Italian place we knew, round the corner from the house.

'We're going to lunch,' he said, 'just you and me.'

We walked down the nice leafy avenues, the nice ordered civilised London streets, where everything was in its place.

We got to the restaurant, and sat down, and ordered some food, and one of the waiters, who we knew from way back, brought us glasses of prosecco on the house, which was his way of telling us he was sorry for what had happened.

I made an automatic gesture, half raising my glass in a toast, which is what we always used to do – 'Here's to it,' we used to say, in those days when there was something to celebrate, but suddenly I couldn't think of anything to drink to, so I put the glass down and looked at it. I felt tired and foolish.

'So,' said Gus. 'Are you going to go to Paris?'

I pretended I didn't know what he meant.

'Paris?' I said. 'Why would I go to Paris?'

He looked at me, in that same straight way he had the first night we met, when he had told me I had almost symmetrical features. I thought, suddenly, it was all very well, but look where it had got me.

'You should do something about this, Ash,' he said. 'You know you should.'

'About what?' I said, obtusely. I didn't want to do anything, not one single thing.

Gus kept right on looking at me.

'You know,' he said.

I shook my head.

'Oh, Gus,' I said. 'I don't know. I'm not sure I want to think about it.'

'Just because not everything worked out the way you

planned,' he said, slowly, 'doesn't mean that some things can't.'

'We're old friends,' I said. 'It's nice that he's not six thousand miles away any more. I don't know if I can think about it any further than that.'

Gus stubbed out his cigarette fiercely.

'You should,' he said. 'You, of all people, know about life being too short. Do you think Virge would want you to cut yourself off, like you are? When did you last go out?'

'I am out,' I said. 'I'm here with you.'

'You know what I mean,' said Gus. 'You could be happy, Ash. You could get what you want. I did. I have. I have Philip, and you know what? It's better. It's better than being alone.'

He stopped for a moment. I had a sudden sense that he had rehearsed this, set the stage, polished the script. I felt that he had reached the denouement, and was wondering whether to see it through, to the end.

'You know,' he said, going on, 'it's not your fault that Virge did what she did. You don't have to punish yourself. You don't have to feel guilty that you might be happy, because she's dead.'

There it was, the one thing we didn't say, not in our house.

'I'm afraid,' I said.

I suddenly realised that I was. Talking on the telephone was one thing, but going to Paris was another. I was truly frightened.

I looked at Gus, almost pleading.

'I had two great fantasies,' I said, slowly. 'Two great dreams in my life. That me and Virge would sit in the Ritz when we were eighty, and that one day Hem would come back. But look what happened. That's all they were, fantasies.'

Gus looked at me, very straight, and took my hand.

'You don't,' he said, 'have to give up your dreams just because she gave up hers.'

I thought of what Gus said, over the next couple of weeks. I thought of it as I went through the motions. I had never thought much about that expression before, but I saw its truth now. When someone comes along and kicks the props away from the fragile structure which you think of as your world, it's all you can do. You go through the motions, the sheer physical actions of making it through the day.

It was three months on. Three months is a curious time, after a death. It is the time that people seem to think you need. They treat you with kid gloves, gentle as porcelain, at the beginning. Then they seem to get bored, as if the sad part has gone on long enough and it's time to pick yourself up and dust yourself off and get on. I found it with people at work, and even with the closer ones, even Gus. I felt it with myself. There was some small voice in my head saying that it was time to start again. But I was frightened. I felt like a patient who has undergone a major surgery, who has been given the all clear by the doctors, but still doesn't want to walk, in case all the stitches holding the wound together just burst open.

It was just at that time that two very strange things happened. I'm still not sure why I thought them strange – after all, the strangest thing I could ever have imagined had happened, the most unexpected, the most unforeseeable. Perhaps my capacity for wonder was still there, after all.

It was two weeks to the day after I had sat with Gus in that little restaurant and talked about Virge. I had gone up to the West End, which was not something I had done since I could remember. I had made one of those inexplicable imperative decisions which didn't seem to have any particular sense to them, and which I didn't, these days, have the energy to question. It was a Saturday, and I had woken up early and thought that I should go to Hamleys to buy Viola a toy. Perhaps it was something to do with my own childhood. I remembered one of the few things I ever did with my father, when he was doing his bogus I'm really a Dad number, was to go to Hamleys and look at the train set which ran round the whole of the first floor. Perhaps I was just in a nostalgic frame of mind. I'm not sure.

Anway, whatever it was, I left the baby with Gus and Philip, and took the bus up to Piccadilly Circus, and started to walk up Regent Street. I had forgotten about London, the wide part of the city which lay beyond my own front door. The pavements were full with shoppers and tourists and all those unidentifiable people who walk the streets of big cities with such purpose. Lines of gleaming black cabs were parked in ranks outside the big hotels, and backpackers were sitting around the base of Eros, watching the electric signs flash their urgent messages.

I felt at home and out of place at the same time. It was familiar and known: it felt as if this was something I used to do in another life, as if I had spent years abroad and come back to find everything only half remembered.

I looked at all the strange faces in the crowd that moved toward me, and suddenly I saw one I knew. It took me a moment, it was so out of context, and then the tumblers fell into place, and I smiled, and said:

'Hugo?'

It was Hugo, from that party, the first party where I met Virge. He stopped and narrowed his eyes in surprised recognition, and then he smiled.

'Ashley,' he said. 'Well I never.'

'Ash,' I said.

'You changed your hair,' he said. 'It's the hair that's different.'

'You,' I said, 'haven't changed at all.'

He hadn't. He had the same precise military short back

and sides, and the same fresh expectant well-scrubbed look, and the exact same hopeful innocence shining out of his untroubled blue eyes.

'Did you ever get your horses?' I said. I said it in a joking way, because I quite expected him to tell me that he was an army major or a stockbroker. I knew all about youthful dreams and what happened to them.

'Yes,' he said. 'Oh yes. I did.'

I was absolutely surprised. I didn't know what to say.

'You did?' I said.

He looked proud and made a small polite effort to hide it. He stuck his hands in his pockets and cleared his throat, just as he had the very first time we met, when we were eighteen. I laughed, remembering.

'I have a stud,' he said. 'We're doing very well.' And then he smiled, a wicked conspiratorial smile.

'Do you remember,' he said, 'what you told me? That you hoped that I married a very rich woman and bred the winner of the Grand National?'

'What a memory you have,' I said. 'Yes, I did say that.'

'Well,' he said, smiling wider than ever, 'I haven't bred the winner of the Grand National, not yet, but I did marry a very rich woman.'

'You could knock me down with a feather,' I said. 'That's the best thing I ever heard.'

'It's not bad,' said Hugo. He nodded his head up and down, and laughed gently through his nose. I could just see him with horses. 'Not bad at all.'

We stood for a minute, as all the Saturday people streamed round us. Then Hugo smiled kindly at me, and kissed my cheek, and looked at his watch.

'I must,' he said, 'get on. It was lovely to see you again.'

'Yes,' I said. 'Yes, it was.'

He gave me a small formal wave and walked away, and I watched him go, shaking my head in disbelief.

I went shopping, and took a cab home, still thinking of how strange it was, the way things worked out, and when I got into the house and walked down into the kitchen, I found my mother sitting at my kitchen table.

I didn't know much about the laws of coincidence and synchronicity, but I thought they were outdoing themselves this weekend.

'Hello,' I said.

My mother looked up at me. I hadn't seen her for over three years. Her skin was lined and dusty and shallow, and her eyes had grown watery and bloodshot. She had dyed her hair a roguish hopeful shade of orange, which didn't altogether help matters.

'I was passing,' she said.

We both knew this wasn't true.

'Your father's gone to live abroad,' she said. 'Did you know?'

'No,' I said. 'I didn't.'

'He's got a girlfriend,' she said. 'He got a job in the middle east somewhere, one of those places they cut your hand off if they find you drinking.'

She mulled over this for a moment. It appeared to give her vast satisfaction.

'Well,' I said. I watched her. I had no feeling in me for her at all: not love or hate or anything, just indifference, as if she was someone I had met once, in the past, and hardly remembered. I had more feeling for Hugo with his dreams and his horses and his rich wife than I had for my own mother. I felt no more than a vague sorrow for her, with her old face and her cherished bitterness and her orange hair. I didn't know what to say to her.

'I'm going abroad myself,' said my mother. 'I have a friend who has a house. I'm going to take a break.'

I wondered what she wanted. I couldn't tell. I thought it was perhaps curiosity, that like people who automatically slow down to rubber neck at a car crash, she had come to have a look at me, to see what I looked like, if I looked different.

'I saw your friend died,' she said.

'Yes,' I said.

'A jumper,' she said. 'That's what they call them, isn't it? Funny,' she said, 'about those people who have everything and then go and jump.'

There was a pause. There truly was nothing to say to that.

My mother stood up.

'Well,' she said. 'I can't stay.'

'No,' I said.

I followed her up the stairs to the front door. She was starting to move a little awkwardly, as if age was creeping into her bones, slowing her down. She had always moved with a furious, ragged energy, but that was gone now, leaving nothing behind it.

I held open the door and she walked through it, out into the street, and then she stopped and turned and delivered her parting shot.

'It's illegal, you know,' she said. 'If you don't do it properly, they arrest you afterwards.' And then she walked away.

I heard steps coming down the stairs above, and Gus put his head over the balustrade, and said,

'Has she gone?'

'Yes,' I said. 'She's gone.'

'I didn't know what to do,' he said. 'She just came and knocked on the door. I couldn't tell her to go away. I didn't know what to do with her.'

'It's all right,' I said. 'I never knew what to do with her either.'

'Do you want to go out for lunch?' said Gus. 'Philip

and I are going to take the baby to the park and have a sandwich.'

It struck me, how strange that sounded. It was such a normal thing to do, go to the park, take a walk, look at the ducks. That was what people did, with their children, on a Saturday. I thought suddenly that it was curious how the axis of life can shift and twist and break, and yet the small conventions of the usual still remain intact. I thought it was strange that, despite it all, there was still lunch in the park.

'No,' I said. 'You go.'

So they went out for lunch, and I was left alone in the house. I don't know what it was, something to do with the unexpected events of that day, seeing Hugo and my mother perhaps, but I didn't go to the park, because there was something else I suddenly had to do.

I put it off for a while. I made myself a salad, and I sat in the kitchen and ate it. Then I took a cup of coffee and a cigarette and went up to the drawing room, and sat for a while in the sun that came through the wide windows. And then I went up to Virge's room.

I stood outside the door for a moment, wondering if I could do it, if I should do it. I hadn't been in there since she had died.

I pushed open the door and walked in. It was so familiar and remembered, that it gave me a shock – all her things, sitting there. The bed was unmade, the sheets thrown back, as if she had just got out of it in a hurry. I had a powerful feeling that she would walk in at any moment, that she had just run down the street to get a paper or a pint of milk. It had no neglected tomblike air to it, it was a room of someone living, who has just stepped out for a moment, and will be back.

There it all was, all her stuff, all the small objects which told the story of her life, each of them heavy with memories and associations. There was the ashtray that she had stolen from the Hotel Hassler in Rome, the delicate perfume bottles that we had bought together in Siena when we went to visit Michael, the worn copies of *On the Road* and *The Naked Lunch* which we found in a second hand bookstore in the theatre district in San Francisco. On the chest of drawers against one wall there was a tray with all her pieces of jewellery, earrings and necklaces and heavy silver rings, and her collection of sunglasses – the Jackie O shades, the purple hippie glasses, the tortoishell granny ones, with green smoked lenses which she could never see out of very well. There was a box full of photographs and mementoes. She kept everything, and she always said she was going to do a scrapbook, 'I must do my books, Ash,' she always said, but she never got round to it.

I sat down on the unmade bed, the box on my knee, and started to go through it. There were snapshots of the two of us in Oxford, and the group photograph we had taken before our pink party, all of us, Stretch, Denny, Gus, Stevie, Michael, Hem, Etta, Virge and me, in all our finery, trying not to laugh. We looked younger than I remembered. I never remembered thinking we looked that young. There was a bundle of scraps of paper – ticket stubs from museums and jazz clubs and exhibitions, from the funicular in Capri, the train from Pisa, the tram in San Francisco, the subway in New York; a hotel bill from a place in Mexico, I supposed the one she had stayed in after she left Keane, her Bodleian library pass, a roulette chip from the casino at San Remo. There were all the letters I had sent her while she had been abroad, and postcards from Stevie and Gus. There was twelve years, in a box.

I can't say how I felt, while I sat, and looked at all those pieces of the past. I felt as if it was something which they didn't have a name for yet. I thought suddenly of 'The Love

Song of J. Alfred Prufrock', which was Virge's favourite poem. I thought of the women, in the room, coming and going, talking of Michelangelo; of a life measured out in coffee spoons; of those voices, with their dying fall; of dusk, and narrow streets, and yellow fog, and lonely men in shirt sleeves; of wearing trousers rolled; of human voices, and the mermaids singing.

And then I got up, and I put everything back into its box, and I packed up that room into three suitcases, and I took it all down to the cellar, and I changed the sheets on the bed, and I polished the windows, and wiped the dust from the shelves, and I left it empty and bare and clean.

28

I did go to Paris. I didn't want to, but I did go, all the same. I called up Hem, and said I was coming, and I packed a bag, and caught the train from Waterloo, and when I got off it at the Gare du Nord, hardly able to believe that I was right here, in the centre of Paris, I saw Hem waiting for me on the platform, holding a bunch of freesias, and suddenly I was glad I'd come.

'Here,' he said, laughing, handing me the flowers, 'I brought you flowers.'

I shook my head and I started to laugh too, because it was so strange, standing in that foreign station, with all the noise and bustle around us, and me holding that preposterous bunch of flowers, like something out of an old film. We stood there, letting people move past us, looking at each other, and we laughed and laughed. I suddenly realised that I hadn't laughed since I could remember. It seemed something I used to do, before.

'Oh Ash,' said Hem. 'Why is this funny? I don't know why it's funny.'

'I don't know either,' I said. 'I don't.'

He took my arm.

'Come on,' he said. 'Let's go and have some lunch.'

We went to one of those dark little intimate restaurants that they have in Paris, hidden away in a twisting back street, with white tablecloths and pannelled walls and surly waiters. It reminded me a little of the place that we had gone to with the monkey man, all those years ago.

We sat for hours, after the food had been cleared away, and drank cups of coffee and smoked cigarettes, and talked. The waiters, resigned, withdrew into a corner to play poker and left us to it. The light drew in, and people started to arrive for early dinner, and still we sat. I think it was as if we needed to do this on neutral turf, that here, in this dark anonymous restaurant, we could say all the things that needed to be said.

We spoke about ourselves for a while. Hem told me something about his work and his travels; I told him about London. We spoke about the past. We talked about Gus and Philip and Viola. And finally, we talked about Virge.

And all the time we talked, I watched Hem, trying to see if everything was still the same, to remember him as he really was, rather than the dream I had carried in my head for so long.

He was the same. He was changed, in the way that we all were, but he was the same too. He still knew what I meant without me having to explain it. I felt a passionate gratitude that there was still that, that that understanding we had always had was still there, miraculously intact, despite everything.

Eventually, we walked back to his apartment. It was bare and empty, most of his things in packing cases, ready to be shipped out.

'You're ready to leave,' I said, looking around.

'Yes,' said Hem. He stood very still in the middle of his empty room, watching me.

'Will you come back to London now?' I said.

He looked away for a moment, and then walked over to the window and stood like that, his back to me, silhouetted against the last of the light. He didn't say

anything for a while. I remembered that. It was a way
he had.

I let the silence grow and deepen. I thought of the first
day in Oxford, when Gus and I had sat in Virge's room,
and we had watched the sun go down, and he had talked
about reaching for the moon, about how we should aim
high. I remembered visiting Michael in Italy, and how he
had talked about asking for a happy ending, that perhaps
it was more to ask than we knew. I wondered about that.
I wondered how we ever got what we wanted in life,
how we even knew what we wanted. I wondered if we
could make ourselves a happy ending, if we were brave
enough to try.

'I would,' I said then, 'like it very much if you did.'

Hem didn't move.

'Would you?' he said.

'Yes,' I said. 'I would.'

He turned then, and he smiled at me, and he looked
exactly like he used to when we would sit in my room
in Oxford and have breakfast, on those sunny Sunday
mornings.

'I will, then,' he said.

It was soon after Viola's first birthday that I noticed something
startling about her. It was quite shocking and unexpected and
I wondered why I hadn't seen it before, but then when
babies are young they just look like babies, with their big
eyes and unformed features, they don't really look like
anyone, they just look like themselves. When Viola was
one, she started to look like someone, and it wasn't who
I expected.

I wasn't sure what to do about it, but after a while I
realised that something would have to be done, so I called
up the gangster and went to see him. I suddenly realised
that I was curious to see him. He hadn't come to Virge's

funeral, just sent a vast arrangement of out-of-season flowers, with a card. I had no idea what he looked like.

We met in a small restaurant in the East End, near the docks, a small, old-fashioned restaurant with checked table-cloths and wooden floors. It wasn't what I had expected. I don't know what I had expected, but from Virge's description of him, I had perhaps had a vague notion of plush carpets and linen tablecloths and champagne in buckets.

The gangster himself wasn't at all what I had imagined, either. I had a picture of a big bruising thug, with a camel coat and a cigar, a real gangster gangster, a proper collector's item. He didn't look anything like that. He was a small neat dark man, with good tailoring and a precise air about him. He looked like an accountant, a man with a desk job and a pension plan and no surprises.

He was very polite. We talked for a while about innocuous things like the weather and the state of the government, and I suddenly wanted to laugh, because it was all so strange.

'Are you really a gangster?' I said.

He laughed then, but not in surprise.

'Did Virge tell you that?' he said.

'Yes,' I said. 'She never even told me your name. She always called you the gangster.'

'I'm a businessman,' he said. 'My family come from Southwark, Irish originally. I used to be a boxing promoter, so she got ideas, I suppose. Perhaps I was just too ordinary for her, she felt she had to make up something more interesting.'

'Yes,' I said, nodding slowly. 'That was something she did. She did that.'

At the end of lunch, I told him why I had come. It was a hard thing to say, and I had put it off, because I wasn't sure how to tell him. In the end I told him straight. He, of all people, had a right to know.

'Viola,' I said, 'is not your child.'

He nodded, again with that absolute lack of surprise.

'I know,' he said.

I looked at him in complete astonishment. I remembered sitting at Virge's wake, thinking that nothing would ever surprise me again. I thought it was just another thing I was wrong about.

'You do?' I said.

'I can't have children,' he said. 'When Virge got pregnant, I knew it must have been someone else. But she always said it was mine, she said it would be a little gangster baby, and I thought I would let her. I thought that way I could make sure she was looked after, give her money for the child. I knew she wouldn't let me if she knew it wasn't mine, so I just went along with it.'

'Is that why you never came to see her?' I said.

He nodded.

'There are limits,' he said. 'Even for me.'

'I should give you the money back,' I said. 'It's not fair.'

'Keep it,' he said. He took out a cigar, and cut the end off it, and lit it up, and as he spoke he waved his hand in a faintly grandiose gesture, and I saw for the first time that perhaps he was more than a man with a desk job, that Virge hadn't been so very fantastic after all.

'I can afford it,' he said. 'I'd like to think of Viola having it. It's all I can do for Virge now.'

I tried to refuse, because there was something in me that felt that this whole situation was wrong, but then it was all so strange and unusual that I wasn't sure where to start applying the normal rules. I felt perhaps that in this curious mess which Virge had left me, there wasn't much point looking for the rights and wrongs. I felt, as I had once told Virge, that sometimes there is no point searching for all the whys and hows and whats, that in this case I should just accept the facts, and get on with it.

'All right,' I said finally. 'You are a remarkable man,' I said, as we parted. 'Thank you.'

He put me in a taxi and waved me off, and I thought, as I watched him standing on the pavement, his hand lifted in a small, final salute, how things never work out the way we expect, that truth really is stranger than fiction, half the time.

Gus was in the kitchen drinking coffee when I got back. He was working furiously, just then, always covered in paint, all over his clothes, on his hands, in his hair.

'Philip took Vi for a walk,' he said.

'I had lunch with the gangster,' I said.

Gus looked at me, long and level. He had a streak of red paint down one side of his face. It made him look like an Indian brave in an old western, riding out to war.

'Yes,' he said.

'He's not a gangster at all,' I said. 'He's a very nice very ordinary man.'

'Figures,' said Gus. 'What did you talk about?'

'I told him that Viola isn't his child,' I said. I looked at Gus, straight, to see if he knew, if he could see what I could so clearly.

He nodded.

'She's mine,' he said. 'Isn't she?'

'Yes,' I said. 'She's yours.'

Gus gave a long sigh.

'I wondered,' he said. 'I only saw it recently, but I did wonder. It was just before Michael died. I suppose I had always wanted to sleep with Virge. I always wanted to sleep with Michael. I was in love with them both. So finally, after all those years of wondering, we did it. It was only one night. It was as if, finally, I was having them both. So, there, Ash,' he said. 'Now you know. Now you know. And there is a child.'

'The gangster knew too,' I said. 'But he still wants her to have the money. He says he wants to do something for Virge.'

'That's nice,' said Gus.

'He's a nice man,' I said. 'What will we do?' I said.

'Well,' said Gus. 'She has you, for her mother. And she has me, and she has Philip. And she has the gangster, as her sugar daddy. I think it will be all right. If you are still happy having all of us living here together.'

'I'm not angry,' I said. 'Did you think I was?'

'No,' said Gus. 'But it must have been a shock, all the same.'

'Oh, Gus,' I said. 'After everything that has happened, I don't think I'll ever be shocked again.'

'And,' he said, 'we still have a little piece of Virge, a whole new life, something left behind. That must be worth something. And maybe it will work better the second time round.'

I started to laugh. 'Oh,' I said. 'It won't be perfect, will it? But maybe it's better that way.'

'I think,' said Gus, 'that it will be better this way. Look where perfect got us.'

I nodded. I heard the door slam, and Philip came down with the baby, her face all pink and glowing from the fresh air, and I put on the kettle, because it was time for tea.